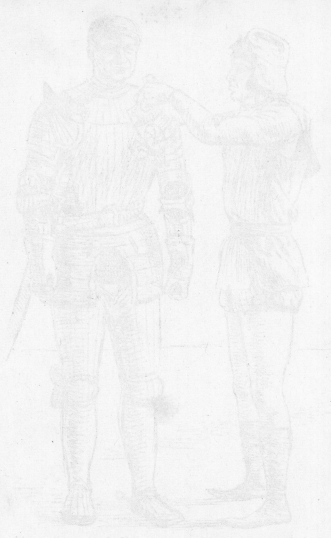

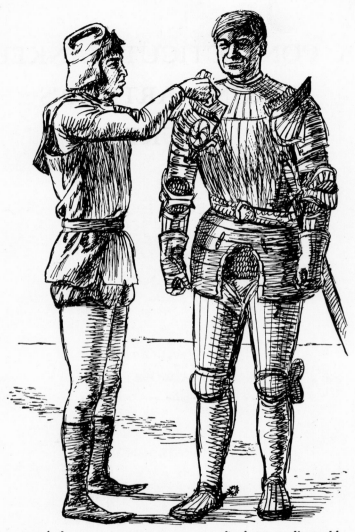

—and there you are, snug as a candle in a candle-mold.
This is no time to dance. (Page 71)

A CONNECTICUT YANKEE IN KING ARTHUR'S COURT

By

Samuel Clemens

Adapted by

RUTH T. KING

Counselor and Teacher of English
Farragut High School, Chicago

In Collaboration with

ELSA WOLF

Teacher of English and Journalism
Bowen High School, Chicago

and

HILTON D. KING

Formerly with the
University of Chicago Press

GLOBE BOOK COMPANY, NEW YORK 10, N. Y.

Copyright, 1948
by
Globe Book Company, Inc.
All rights reserved

Illustrations by
Thomas Fraumeni

EDITOR'S PREFACE

In adapting the text of *A Connecticut Yankee,* every attempt has been made to keep the style and the spirit of the original. The changes have for the most part consisted in substituting words to meet the understanding of the reader with a limited vocabulary, and omitting or abstracting descriptive and philosophical passages which seem too detailed or difficult for such readers.

A Connecticut Yankee meets a real need for secondary schools because of its imaginative qualities and its humor on a level easily understood. The twentieth century youngster can with the "Boss" comprehend the mechanical gadgets and feel his superiority. More important, he can comprehend also the democratic ideals of the "Boss"—ideals of tolerance, humanity, and opportunity for all. The thesis of the destruction of a civilization through the introduction of new weapons is of vital interest to modern youth.

The questions on the text have been made with two purposes in mind. Those for the pupil should help him to carry forward the story independently through his own reading. They have been made as simple and objective as possible and a key will be furnished so that they may be corrected with student help. The questions for discussion should help to develop group thinking and understanding of the ideas back of the story. The emphasis on silent reading is thus given due weight, but group discussion and exchange of ideas are also provided for. Included in the key is the correlation of chapters with the original, making it possible to use the original text with superior students if desired.

R. T. K.

TABLE OF CONTENTS

CHAPTER I

A WORD OF EXPLANATION

It was in Warwick Castle that I came across the curious stranger whom I am going to talk about. He attracted me by three things: his simplicity, his familiarity with ancient armor, and the restfulness of his company—for he did all the talking. We fell together at the end of the group that was being shown through the museum and he at once began to say things which interested me. As he talked along, softly, pleasantly, he seemed to drift away out of this world and time, and into some remote age and old forgotten country; and so he gradually wove such a spell about me that I seemed to move among ghosts and shadows of ancient times. Exactly as I would speak of my nearest personal friends or enemies, or my most familiar neighbors, he spoke of Sir Bedivere, Sir Bors de Ganis, Sir Launcelot of the Lake, Sir Galahad, and all the other great names of the Round Table—and how old, unspeakably old and faded and dry and ancient he came to look as he went on! Presently he turned to me and said, just as one might speak of the weather, or any other common matter—

"You know about souls passing from one body into another; do you know about bodies passing into other ages or times?"

1

I said I had not heard of it. He was so little interested that he did not notice whether I made him any answer or not. There was a moment of silence, immediately interrupted by the sing-song voice of the guide.

"Ancient hauberk, date of the sixth century, time of King Arthur and the Round Table; said to have belonged to the knight Sir Sagramor le Desirous; observe the round hole through the chain-mail in the left breast; can't be accounted for; supposed to have been done with a bullet since invention of firearms—perhaps purposely by Cromwell's soldiers."

My acquaintance smiled and muttered apparently to himself:

"I saw it done; as a matter of fact, I did it myself."

By the time I had recovered from the surprise of this remark, he was gone.

All that evening I sat by my fire at the Warwick Arms, deep in a dream of the olden time, while the rain beat upon the windows and the wind roared about the corners. From time to time I dipped into old Sir Thomas Malory's enchanting book of King Arthur.

I lost myself in its adventures and dreamed. At midnight I reached the tale of how Sir Launcelot killed two giants and then overcame three knights who were attacking Sir Kay; and of how he ordered the knights to appear in the court of King Arthur and yield to Queen Guenever as prisoners of Sir Kay.

As I laid the book down there was a knock at the

door, and my stranger came in. I gave him a pipe and a chair, and made him welcome. I also comforted him with a hot drink; gave him another one; then still another—hoping always for his story. After a fourth drink, he drifted into it himself, in a quite simple and natural way:

The Stranger's History

I am an American. I was born and reared in Hartford, in the state of Connecticut. So I am a Yankee of the Yankees—and practical. My father was a blacksmith, my uncle was a horse-doctor, and I was both, along at first. Then I went over to the great arms factory and learned my real trade; learned all there was to it; learned to make everything: guns, revolvers, cannon, boilers, engines, all sorts of labor-saving machinery. Why, I could make anything a body wanted—anything in the world, it didn't make any difference what; and if there wasn't any quick new-fangled way to make a thing, I could invent one—and do it as easy as rolling off a log. I became head superintendent; had a couple of thousand men under me.

Well, a man like that is a man that is full of fight—that goes without saying. With a couple of thousand rough men under one, one has plenty of that sort of amusement. I had, **anyway.** At last I met my match, and I got my dose. It was during a misunderstanding conducted with crowbars with a fellow we used to call Hercules. He laid me out with a blow on the head that made everything crack, and seemed to spring every joint in my skull. Then the world went out in darkness, and I didn't feel anything more, and didn't know anything at all, at least for a while.

When I came to again, I was sitting under an oak tree on the grass, with a whole beautiful and broad country landscape all to myself—nearly. Not entirely, for there was a fellow on a horse, looking down at me —a fellow fresh out of a picture-book. He was in old-time iron armor from head to heel, with a helmet on his head the shape of a nail-keg with slits in it; and he had a shield, and a sword, and a huge spear; and his horse had armor on too, and gorgeous red and green silk trappings that hung down all around him like a bedquilt, nearly to the ground.

"Fair sir, will ye joust?" said this fellow.

"Will I which?"

"Will ye battle with me for land or lady or for—"

"What are you giving me?" I said. "Get along back to your circus, or I'll report you."

Now what does this man do but fall back a couple of hundred yards and then come rushing at me as hard as he could tear, with his helmet bent down nearly to his horse's neck and his long spear pointed straight ahead. I saw he meant business, so I was up the tree when he arrived.

He allowed that I was his property, the captive of his spear. There was argument on his side—and all the advantage—so I judged it best to humor him. We fixed up an agreement whereby I was to go with him and he was not to hurt me. I came down and we started away, I walking by the side of his horse. We marched comfortably along, through woods and over brooks which I could not remember to have seen before—which puzzled me and made me wonder—and yet we did not come to any circus or sign of a circus. So I gave up the idea of a circus, and concluded he was from an asylum. But we never came to an asylum, so I was up a stump, as you may say. I asked him how far we were from Hartford. He said he had never heard of the place, which I took to be a lie, but allowed it to go at that. At the end of an hour we saw a far-away town by a winding river; and beyond it on a hill, a vast gray fortress with towers, the first I had ever seen out of a picture.

"Bridgeport?" said I, pointing.

"Camelot," said he.

My stranger had been showing signs of sleepiness. He caught himself nodding now, and smiled one of those sad smiles of his, and said:

"I find I can't go on; but come with me; I've got it all written out, and you can read it if you like."

In his room, he said: "First, I kept a journal; then by and by, after years, I took the journal and turned it into a book. How long ago that was!"

He handed me his manuscript, and pointed out the place where I should begin:

"Begin here—I've already told you what goes before." He was almost asleep by this time. As I went out at his door I heard him murmur. "Good day, fair sir."

I sat down by my fire and examined my treasure. Most of it was yellow with age. I turned to the place indicated by my stranger and began to read—as follows:

CHAPTER II

CAMELOT AND KING ARTHUR'S COURT

"Camelot—Camelot," said I to myself. "I don't seem to remember hearing of it before. Name of the asylum, likely."

It was a soft, restful summer landscape, as lovely as a dream, and as lonesome as Sunday. There were no people, no wagons, there was no stir of life, nothing going on. The road was mainly a winding path with hoof-prints in it, and now and then a faint trace of wheels on either side in the grass—wheels that apparently had a tire as broad as one's hand.

Presently a fair slip of a girl, about ten years old, with golden hair streaming down over her shoulders, came along. Around her head she wore a hoop of flame-red poppies. It was as sweet an outfit as ever I saw, what there was of it. She walked lazily along, a peaceful look on her face. The circus man paid no attention to her, didn't even seem to see her. And she was no more startled at his queer make-up than if she was used to his like every day of her life. She was going by as indifferently as she might have gone by a couple of cows; but when she happened to notice me, *then* there was a change! Up went her hands, and she stood as if turned to stone; her mouth dropped open, her eyes stared wide and timidly; she was the picture of astonished curiosity touched with fear. And there she stood gazing, fascinated, till we turned a corner of the wood and were lost to her view. That she should be startled at me instead of at the other man was too much for me; I couldn't make head or tail of it. And that she could seem to consider me a funny sight, and totally overlook her own queer costume, was another puzzling thing. There was food for thought here. I moved along as one in a dream.

As we approached the town, signs of life began to appear. At intervals we passed a wretched cabin with a thatched roof, and about it small fields and garden patches poorly kept. There were people, too; husky men, with long, coarse, uncombed hair that hung down over their faces and made them look like animals. They and the women, as a rule, wore a coarse linen robe that came well below the knee, and a rude sort of sandal, and many wore an iron collar. The small boys and girls were always naked, but nobody seemed to know it. All of these people stared at me, talked about me, ran into the huts and brought out their families to stare at me; but nobody ever noticed that other fellow, except to make him humble greetings and get no response for their pains.

In the town were some sturdy windowless houses of stone scattered among a wilderness of thatched cabins; the streets were mere crooked alleys, and unpaved; troops of dogs and nude children played in the sun and made life and noise; hogs roamed and rooted contentedly about, and one of them lay in the middle of the road and suckled her family. Presently there was a distant sound of military music; it came nearer, still nearer, and soon a noble cavalcade wound into view, glorious with plumed helmets and flashing mail and flaunting banners and gilded spearheads; and through the mud and swine, and naked brats, and joyous dogs, and shabby huts, it took its gallant way, and we followed; followed through one winding alley and then another—and climbing, always climbing—till at last we gained the breezy height where the huge castle stood. There were bugle-blasts; then an exchange of words from the walls, where men-at-arms marched back and forth under flapping banners with the rude figure of a dragon displayed upon them; and then the great gates were flung open, the drawbridge was lowered, and the head of the parade swept forward under the arches; and we, following, soon found ourselves in a great paved court, with towers and turrets stretching up into the blue air on all the four sides; and all about us men were dismounting and there was much greeting and ceremony, and running to and fro, and a gay display of colors, and an altogether pleasant stir and noise and confusion.

The moment I got a chance I slipped aside and touched an ancient common-looking man on the shoulder and said, in a confidential way:

"Friend, do me a kindness. Do you belong to the asylum, or are you just here on a visit or something like that?"

He looked me over stupidly, and said:

"Marry, fair sir, me seemeth—"

"That will do," I said; "I reckon you are a patient."

I moved away, at the same time keeping an eye out for any chance passer-by in his right mind that might come along and give me some light. I judged I had found one, presently; so I drew him aside and said in his ear:

"If I could see the head keeper a minute—only just a minute—"

"Pray do not hinder me."

Then he went on to say he was an under-cook and could not stop to gossip, though he would like it another time; for it would comfort his very liver to know where I got my clothes. As he started away he pointed and said yonder was one who was idle enough for my purpose. This was a slim boy in shrimp-colored tights that made him look like a forked carrot; the rest of his clothes were of blue silk and dainty laces and ruffles; and he had long yellow curls, and wore a plumed pink satin cap tilted over his ear. By his look, he was good-natured; by his walk, he was satisfied with himself. He arrived, looked me over with a smiling and impudent curiosity, said he had come for me, and informed me that he was a page.

"Go 'long," I said; "you ain't more than a paragraph."

It never bothered him. He began to talk and laugh in happy, thoughtless, boyish fashion, as we walked along, and made himself old friends with me at once; asked me all sorts of questions about myself and about my clothes, but never waited for an answer— always chattered straight ahead, as if he didn't know he had asked a question and wasn't expecting any reply, until at last he happened to mention that he was born in the beginning of the year 513.

It made the cold chills creep over me! I stopped and said, a little faintly:

"Maybe I didn't hear you just right. Say it again— and say it slow. What year was it?"

"513."

"513! You don't look it! Come, my boy, I am a stranger and friendless; be honest and honorable with me. Are you in your right mind?"

He said he was.

"Are these other people in their right minds?"

He said they were.

"And this isn't an asylum? I mean, it isn't a place where they cure crazy people?"

He said it wasn't.

"Well, then," I said, "either I am crazy or something just as awful has happened. Now tell me, honest and true, where am I?"

"IN KING ARTHUR'S COURT."

I waited a minute, to let that idea sink in, and then said:

"And according to your notions, what year is it now?"

"528—nineteenth of June."

I felt a mournful sinking at the heart, and muttered, "I shall never see my friends again—never, never again. They will not be born for more than thirteen hundred years yet."

I seemed to believe the boy, I didn't know why. *Something* in me seemed to believe him though my reason wasn't satisfied. I didn't know how to go about satisfying it, because I knew that the words of men wouldn't do it—my reason would say they were crazy. But all of a sudden I stumbled on the very thing, just by luck. I knew that the only total eclipse of the sun in the first half of the sixth century occurred on the twenty-first of June, 528 A.D., and began at three minutes after twelve noon. I also knew that no total eclipse of the sun was due in what to *me* was the present year—*i.e.*, 1879. So, if I could keep my anxiety and curiosity from eating the heart out of me for forty-eight hours, I should then find out for certain whether this boy was telling me the truth or not.

Wherefore, being a practical Connecticut man, I now shoved this whole problem clear out of mind till its appointed day and hour should come, in order that

I might turn all my attention to the present moment, and be alert and ready to make the most out of it that could be made. One thing at a time is my motto, and just play that thing for all it is worth, even if it's only two pair and a jack. I made up my mind to two things: if it was still the nineteenth century and I was among lunatics and couldn't get away, I would presently boss that asylum or know the reason why; and if, on the other hand, it was really the sixth century, all right, I didn't want any softer thing: I would boss the whole country inside of three months, for I judged I would have the start of the best-educated man in the kingdom by a matter of thirteen hundred years and upward. I'm not a man to waste time after my mind's made up and there's work on hand; so I said to the page:

"Now, Clarence, my boy—if that might happen to be your name—I'll get you to clear things up a bit, if you don't mind. What is the name of that queer fellow that brought me here?"

"My master and thine? That is the good knight and great lord Sir Kay, foster-brother to the king."

"Very good; go on, tell me everything."

He made a long story of it, but the part that had immediate interest for me was this: He said I was Sir Kay's prisoner, and that in the due course of custom I would be flung into a dungeon and left there on scant rations until my friends ransomed me, unless I chanced to rot, first. I saw that the last chance had the best show, but I didn't waste any bother about that; time was too precious. The page said, further, that dinner was about ended in the great hall by this time, and that as soon as the sociability and the heavy drinking should begin, Sir Kay would have me in and exhibit me before King Arthur and his knights seated at the Round Table, and would brag about capturing me, and would probably exaggerate the facts a little, but it wouldn't be good form for me to correct him, and not over-safe, either; and when I was done being exhibited, then ho for the dungeon; but he, Clarence, would find a way to come and see me every now and then, and cheer me up, and help me get word to my friends.

Get word to my friends! I thanked him; I couldn't do less; and about this time a servant came to say I was wanted; so Clarence led me in and took me off to one side and sat down by me.

Well, it was a curious kind of scene, and interesting. It was an immense place, and very high; there was a stone-railed gallery at each end, high up, with musicians in the one, and women, clothed in stunning colors, in the other. The floor was of big flat stones laid in black and white squares, rather battered by age and use, and needing repair. There was a fire-place big enough to camp in. Along the walls stood men-at-arms, rigid as statues.

In the middle of this arched and vaulted public square was an oak table which they called the Round

Table. It was as large as a circus-ring; and around it sat a great company of men dressed in such various and splendid colors that it hurt one's eyes to look at them. They wore their plumed hats right along, except that whenever one addressed himself directly to the king, he lifted his hat a trifle just as he was beginning his remark.

Mainly they were drinking—from entire ox horns; but a few were still munching bread or gnawing beef bones. There was about an average of two dogs to one man; and these sat waiting till a bone was flung to them, and then they went for it by brigades and divisions, with a rush, and there was a fight which filled the place with plunging heads and bodies and flashing tails, and the storm of howlings and barkings deafened all speech for the time; but that was no matter, for the dog-fight was always a bigger interest anyway. The men rose, sometimes, to observe it better and bet on it, and the ladies and the musicians stretched themselves out over their rails with the same object; and all broke into delighted shouts from time to time. In the end, the winning dog stretched himself out comfortably with his bone between his paws, and proceeded to growl over it, and gnaw it, and grease the floor with it, just as fifty others were already doing; and the rest of the court resumed their previous industries and entertainments.

As a rule, the speech and behavior of these people were gracious and courtly; and I noticed that they were good and serious listeners when anybody was telling anything—I mean in a dog-fightless interval. And plainly, too, they were a childlike and innocent lot, telling lies in a most gentle and winning way and ready and willing to listen to anybody else's lie, and believe it, too. It was hard to associate them with anything cruel or dreadful; and yet they dealt in tales of blood and suffering with a relish that made me almost forget to shudder.

I was not the only prisoner present. There were twenty or more. Poor devils, many of them were maimed, hacked, carved, in a frightful way; and their hair, their faces, their clothing, were caked with black and stiffened blood. They were suffering sharp physical pain, of course; and weariness, and hunger and thirst, no doubt; and none had given them the comfort of a wash, or even medicines for their wounds, yet you never heard them utter a moan or a groan, or saw them show any sign of restlessness, or any disposition to complain. The thought was forced upon me: "The rascals—*they* have served other people so in their day; it being their turn now, they were not expecting any better treatment than this; so their bearing is mere animal training."

CHAPTER III

KNIGHTS OF THE ROUND TABLE

Mainly the Round Table talk was of adventures in which prisoners were captured and their friends and backers killed and stripped of their horses and armor. As a general thing—as far as I could make out—these murderous adventures were not battles undertaken to get even for injuries, nor to settle old disputes or sudden fallings-out; no, as a rule they were simply duels between strangers—duels between people who had never even been introduced to each other, and between whom existed no cause of offense whatever. Many a time I had seen a couple of boys, strangers, meet by chance, and say at the same time, "I can lick you," and go at it on the spot; but I had always imagined until now that that sort of thing belonged to children only, and was a sign and mark of childhood; but here were these big boobies sticking to it and taking pride in it clear up into full age and beyond. Yet there was something very likable about these great simple-hearted creatures, something attractive and lovable. There did not seem to be brains enough in the entire Round Table, so to speak, to bait a fish-hook with; but you didn't seem to mind that, after a little, because you soon saw that brains were not needed in a society like that, and indeed would have spoiled it—perhaps made it impossible.

There was a fine manliness in almost every face; and in some a certain sweetness. A most noble kindness and purity marked the face of Sir Galahad, and likewise the king's also; and there was majesty and greatness in the giant frame and high bearing of Sir Launcelot of the Lake.

There was soon an incident which centered the general interest upon this Sir Launcelot. At a sign from a master of ceremonies, six or eight of the prisoners rose and came forward in a body and knelt on the floor and lifted up their hands toward the ladies' gallery and begged a word with the queen. She nodded her head in consent, and then the spokesman of the prisoners delivered himself and his fellows into her hands for free pardon, ransom, captivity, or death, as she might decide; and this, as he said, he was doing by command of Sir Kay, whose prisoners they were, he having vanquished them by his single might in sturdy conflict.

Surprise and astonishment flashed from face to face all over the house; the queen's pleased smile faded out at the name of Sir Kay, and she looked disappointed; and the page whispered in my ear with a scornful accent and manner:

"*Sir Kay, forsooth!* Oh, call me pet names, dearest, call me a marine! In two thousand years such a lie could not be matched."

Every eye was fastened upon Sir Kay. But he was equal to the occasion. He got up and played his hand like a major—and took every trick. He said he would state the case exactly according to the facts; he would tell the simple straightforward tale, "and then," said he, "if ye find glory and honor due, ye will give it unto him who is the mightiest man of his hands that ever bore shield or struck with sword—even him that sitteth there!" and he pointed to Sir Launcelot. It was a rattling good stroke. Then he went on and told how Sir Launcelot, seeking adventures, had killed seven giants at one sweep of his sword, and set a hundred and forty-two captive maidens free; and then went further and found him (Sir Kay) fighting a desperate fight against nine foreign knights, and took the battle solely into his own hands and conquered the nine; and that night Sir Launcelot dressed in Sir Kay's armor and took Sir Kay's horse and went away into distant lands, and vanquished sixteen knights in one pitched battle and thirty-four in another; and all these and the former nine he made to swear that about Whitsuntide they would ride to Arthur's court and yield them to Queen Guenever's hands as captives of Sir Kay; and now here were these half-dozen, and the rest would be along as soon as they might be healed of their desperate wounds.

Well, it was touching to see the queen blush and smile, and look embarrassed and happy, and fling shy glances at Sir Launcelot.

Everybody praised the courage of Sir Launcelot; and as for me, I was perfectly amazed that one man, all by himself, should have been able to beat down and capture such battalions of practised fighters. I said as much to Clarence, but this mocking feather-head only said :

"If Sir Kay had had time to get another drink into him, ye had seen the number doubled."

I looked at the boy in sorrow; and as I looked I saw his face sadden. I followed the direction of his eye, and saw that a very old and white-bearded man, clothed in a flowing black gown, had risen and was standing at the table upon unsteady legs, feebly swaying his ancient head and surveying the company with his watery and wandering eye. The same suffering look that was in the page's face was seen on all the faces around—the look of dumb creatures who know that they must endure and make no moan.

"We shall have it again," sighed the boy; "that same old weary tale that he hath told a thousand times in the same words, and that he *will* tell till he dieth. Would God I had died before I saw this day!"

"Who is it?"

"Merlin, the mighty liar and magician, Devil take him for the weariness he worketh with his one tale! But that men fear him for that he hath the storms and the lightnings and all the devils that be in hell at his beck and call, they would have killed him these many

Merlin told his long and tiresome tale.

years ago to squelch that tale. Misfortune take him. Good friend, wake me when the tale is done."

The boy nestled himself upon my shoulder and pretended to go to sleep. The old man began his tale, and presently the lad was asleep in reality; so also were the dogs, and the court, and the men-at-arms. The droning voice droned on; a soft snoring arose on all sides. Some heads were bowed upon folded arms, some lay back with open mouths and snored; the flies buzzed and bit, the rats swarmed softly out from a hundred holes, and pattered about, and made themselves at home everywhere; and one of them sat up like a squirrel on the king's head and held a bit of cheese in its hands and nibbled it, and dribbled the crumbs in the king's face. It was a calm scene, and restful to the weary eye and the tired spirit.

I was the only one who listened as Merlin told his long and tiresome tale of how on his adventures with King Arthur he had secured for him a sword with magic scabbard.

Sir Dinadan the Humorist was the first to awake, and he soon roused the rest with a practical joke. He tied some metal mugs to a dog's tail and turned him loose, and he tore around and around the place in a frenzy of fright, with all the other dogs bellowing after him and battering and crashing against everything that came in their way and making altogether a most deafening noise and confusion at which every man and woman laughed till the tears flowed, and some fell out of their chairs and wallowed on the floor in delight. It was just like so many children. Sir Dinadan was so proud of his joke that he could not keep from telling over and over again, to weariness, how the idea happened to occur to him. He was so set up that he decided to make a speech—of course a humorous speech. I think I never heard so many old played-out jokes strung together in my life. He was worse than the minstrels, worse than the clown in the circus. It seemed sad to sit here, thirteen hundred years before I was born, and listen again to poor, flat, worm-eaten jokes that had given me the dry gripes when I was a boy thirteen hundred years afterward. It about convinced me that there isn't any such thing as a new joke possible. Everybody laughed at these old jokes— but then they always do; I had noticed that, centuries later. However, the page didn't laugh. He said the most of Sir Dinadan's jokes were rotten and the rest were stale.

Now Sir Kay arose and began to tell his story to explain me. He told how he had met me in a far land of barbarians, who all wore the same ridiculous clothes that I did—clothes that were a work of enchantment, and intended to keep the wearer safe. However, he had overcome the force of the enchantment by prayer, and had killed my thirteen knights in a three hours' battle, and had taken me prisoner, sparing my life in order that so strange a curiosity as I was might be exhibited to the wonder and admiration of the king and the court. He spoke of me all the time, in the calmest way, as "this huge giant" and "this tusked and taloned man-devouring ogre," and everybody took in all this bosh, and never smiled or seemed to notice that there was any difference between this description and me. He said that in trying to escape from him I sprang into the top of a high tree at a single bound, but he dislodged me with a stone the size of a cow, which all but broke the most of my bones, and then swore me to appear at Arthur's court for sentence. He ended by condemning me to die at noon on the twenty-first; and was so little concerned about it that he stopped to yawn before he named the date.

I was in a dismal state by this time; indeed, I was hardly enough in my right mind to keep the run of a dispute that sprung up as to how I had better be killed, the possibility of the killing being doubted by some, because of the enchantment in my clothes. And yet it was nothing but an ordinary fifteen dollar suit.

They were so troubled about my enchanted clothes that they were mightily relieved, at last, when old Merlin swept the difficulty away for them with a common-sense hint. He asked them why they were so dull—why didn't it occur to them to strip me. In half a minute I was as naked as a pair of tongs! And dear, dear, to think of it: I was the only embarrassed person there. Everybody discussed me; and did it as unconcernedly as if I had been a cabbage. Queen Guenever was as interested as the rest, and said she had never seen anybody with legs just like mine before. It was the only compliment I got—if it was a compliment.

Finally I was carried off in one direction, and my dangerous clothes in another. I was shoved into a dark and narrow cell in a dungeon, with some scant remnants for dinner, some moldy straw for a bed, and no end of rats for company.

CHAPTER IV

AN INSPIRATION

I was so tired that even my fears were not able to keep me awake long.

When I next came to myself, I seemed to have been asleep a very long time. My first thought was, "Well, what an astonishing dream I've had! I reckon I've waked only just in time to keep from being hanged or drowned or burned or something. . . . I'll nap again till the whistle blows, and then I'll go down to the arms factory and have it out with Hercules."

But just then I heard the harsh music of rusty chains and bolts, a light flashed in my eyes, and that butterfly, Clarence, stood before me! I gasped with surprise; my breath almost got away from me.

"What!" I said, "you here yet? Go along with the rest of the dream! scatter!"

But he only laughed, in his light-hearted way, and fell to making fun of my sorry plight.

"All right," I said, "let the dream go on; I'm in no hurry."

"What dream?"

"What dream? Why, the dream that I am in Arthur's court—a person who never existed; and that I am talking to you, who are nothing but a work of the imagination."

25

"Oh, la, indeed! and is it a dream that you're to be burned tomorrow? Ho-ho—answer me that!"

The shock that went through me was distressing. I now began to reason that my situation was in the last degree serious, dream or no dream; for I knew by past experience of dreams, that to be burned to death, even in a dream, would be very far from being a jest, and was a thing to be avoided by any means, fair or foul, that I could manage. So I said beseechingly:

"Ah, Clarence, good boy, only friend I've got—for you *are* my friend, aren't you?—don't fail me; help me to plan some way of escaping from this place!"

"Now do but hear thyself! Escape? Why, man, the corridors are in guard and keep of men-at-arms."

"No doubt, no doubt. But how many, Clarence? Not many, I hope?"

"Full twenty. One may not hope to escape." After a pause—hesitatingly: "and there be other reasons— and weightier."

"Other ones? What are they?"

"Well, they say—oh, but I dare not, indeed I dare not!"

"Why, poor lad, what is the matter? Why do you tremble so?"

"Oh, in sooth, there is need! I do want to tell you, but—"

"Come, come, be brave, be a man—speak out, there's a good lad!"

He hesitated, pulled one way by desire, the other way by fear; then he stole to the door and peeped out, listening; and finally crept close to me and put his mouth to my ear and told me his fearful news in a whisper, and with all the fear of one who was venturing upon awful ground and speaking of things whose very mention might mean death.

"Merlin has woven a spell about this dungeon, and there is not a man in these kingdoms that would be desperate enough to try to cross its lines with you! Now God pity me, I have told it! Ah, be kind to me, be merciful to a poor boy who means thee well; for if thou betray me I am lost!"

I laughed the only really refreshing laugh I had had for some time, and shouted:

"Merlin has wrought a spell! *Merlin*, forsooth! That cheap old humbug? Bosh, pure bosh, the silliest bosh in the world! Why, it does seem to me that of all the childish, idiotic, chuckle-headed, chicken-livered superstitions that ev—oh, damn Merlin!"

But Clarence had slumped to his knees before I had half finished, and he was like to go out of his mind with fright.

"Oh, beware! These are awful words! Any moment these walls may crumble upon us if you say such things. Oh call them back before it is too late!"

Now this strange exhibition gave me a good idea and set me to thinking. If everybody about here was so honestly and sincerely afraid of Merlin's pretended

magic as Clarence was, certainly a superior man like
me ought to be shrewd enough to manage some way to
take advantage of such a state of things. I went on
thinking, and worked out a plan. Then I said:

"Get up. Pull yourself together; look me in the
eye. Do you know why I laughed?"

"No—but for our blessed Lady's sake, do it no
more."

"Well, I'll tell you why I laughed. Because I'm a
magician myself."

"Thou!" The boy fell back a step and caught his
breath, for the thing hit him rather sudden; but the
manner which he took on was very, very respectful.
I took quick note of that; it indicated that a humbug
didn't need to have a reputation in this asylum; people
stood ready to take him at his word, without that. I
went on.

"I've known Merlin seven hundred years, and he—"

"Seven hun—"

"Don't interrupt me. He has died and come alive
again thirteen times, and traveled under a new name
every time: Smith, Jones, Robinson, Jackson, Peters,
Haskins, Merlin—a new alias every time he turns up.
I knew him in Egypt three hundred years ago; I knew
him in India five hundred years ago—he is always
around in my way, everywhere I go; he makes me
tired. He doesn't amount to shucks as a magician; he
knows some of the old common tricks, but has never
got beyond the first steps, and never will. Dear me, *he*

oughtn't to set up for an expert—anyway not where there's a real artist. Now look here, Clarence, I am going to be your friend right along, and in return you must be mine. I want you to do me a favor. I want you to get word to the king that I am a magician myself —and the Supreme Grand High-yup-Muckamuck and head of the tribe, at that; and I want him to be made to understand that I am just quietly arranging a little trouble here that will make the fur fly if Sir Kay's project is carried out and any harm comes to me. Will you get that to the king for me?"

The poor boy was in such a state that he could hardly answer me. It was pitiful to see a creature so frightened, so unnerved. But he promised everything; and on my side he made me promise over and over again that I would remain his friend, and never turn against him or cast any enchantments upon him. Then he worked his way out, steadying himself with his hand along the wall, like a sick person.

Presently this thought occurred to me: how careless I have been! When the boy gets calm, he will wonder why a great magician like me should have begged a boy like him to help me get out of this place; he will put this and that together, and will see that I am a humbug.

I worried over that blunder for an hour, and called myself a great many hard names, meantime. But finally it occurred to me all of a sudden that these animals didn't reason, that *they* never put this and that together, that all their talk showed this. I was at rest, then.

But as soon as one is at rest, in this world, off he goes on something else to worry about. It occurred to me that I had made another blunder: I had sent the boy off to alarm his betters with a threat—I had expected to invent a disaster at my leisure; now the people who are the readiest and willingest to swallow miracles are the very ones who are hungriest to see you perform them; suppose I should be called on for a sample? Suppose I should be asked to name my disaster? Yes, I had made a blunder; I ought to have invented my disaster first. "What shall I do? What can I say to gain a little time?" I was in trouble again, in the deepest kind of trouble: . . . "There's a footstep!—they're coming. If I had only just a moment to think. . . . Good, I've got it. I'm all right."

You see, it was the eclipse. It came into my mind in the nick of time, how Columbus, or Cortez, or one of those people, played an eclipse as a saving trump once on some savages, and I saw my chance. I could play it myself, now.

Clarence came in, distressed, and said:

"I hurried the message to the king, and straightway he had me to his presence. He was frightened even to the bone, and was minded to give order for your instant freedom, and that you be dressed in fine clothing and lodged as befitted one so great; but then came Merlin and spoiled it all, for he persuaded the king that you are mad, and know not what you speak, and said your threat is but foolishness and idle talk. They disputed long, but in the end, Merlin said, 'Why hath he not *named* his brave disaster? Truly it is because he cannot.' This thrust did in a most sudden sort close the king's mouth, and he could offer nothing to turn the argument; and so, not willing to do you the discourtesy, he yet prayeth you to consider his perplexed case, as noting how the matter stands, and name the disaster—if you have determined the nature of it and the time of its coming. Oh, prithee delay not; to delay at such a time were to double the perils that already are about you. Oh, be thou wise— name the disaster!"

I waited a minute for effect, and then said:

"How long have I been shut up in this hole?"

"Ye were shut up when yesterday was well spent. It is nine of the morning now."

"No! Then I have slept well, sure enough. Nine in the morning now! And yet it is dark as midnight. This is the twentieth, then?"

"The twentieth—yes."

"And I am to be burned alive tomorrow." The boy shuddered.

"At what hour?"

"At high noon."

"Now then, I will tell you what to say." I paused, and stood over that frightened lad a whole minute in awful silence; then, in a voice deep and measured, I began, and rose by stages to my climax, which I delivered in as noble a way as ever I did such a thing in my life: "Go back and tell the king that at that hour I will smother the whole world in the dead blackness of midnight; I will blot out the sun, and he shall never shine again; the fruits of the earth shall rot for lack of light and warmth, and the peoples of the earth shall famish and die, to the last man!"

I had to carry the boy out myself, he sunk into such a collapse. I handed him over to the soldiers, and went back.

CHAPTER V

THE ECLIPSE

In the stillness and the darkness the knowledge that I was in deadly danger became deeper all the time and it turned me cold.

But at times like these, as soon as a man gets low enough, there comes a change and hope springs up, and cheerfulness along with it, and then he is in good shape to do something for himself, if anything can be done. When my hope came back, it came with a bound. I said to myself that my eclipse would be sure to save me, and make me the greatest man in the kingdom besides; and straightway my fears all vanished. I was as happy a man as there was in the world. I was even impatient for tomorrow to come, I so wanted to gather in that great triumph and be the center of all the nation's wonder and reverence. Besides, in a business way it would be the making of me; I knew that.

Meantime there was one thing which had got pushed into the background of my mind. That was the half-conviction that when the nature of my proposed disaster should be reported to those superstitious people, it would have such an effect that they would want to compromise. So, by and by when I heard footsteps coming, that thought was recalled to me,

33

and I said to myself, "As sure as anything, it's the compromise. Well, if it is good, all right, I will accept; but if it isn't, I mean to stand my ground and play my hand for all it is worth."

The door opened, and some men-at-arms appeared. The leader said:

"The stake is ready. Come!"

The stake! The strength went out of me, and I almost fell down. It is hard to get one's breath at such a time, such lumps come into one's throat; but as soon as I could speak, I said:

"But this is a mistake—the execution is tomorrow."

"Order changed; been set forward a day. Hurry!"

I was lost. There was no help for me. I had no command over myself; I only wandered purposelessly about, like one out of his mind; so the soldiers took hold of me and pulled me along with them, out of the cell and along the underground corridors, and finally into the daylight and the upper world. As we stepped into the vast inclosed court of the castle I got a shock; for the first thing I saw was the stake, standing in the center, and near it the piled wood and a monk. On all four sides of the court the seated multitudes rose rank above rank, forming sloping terraces that were rich with color. The king and the queen sat in their thrones, the most conspicuous figures there, of course.

To note all this took but a second. The next second Clarence had slipped from some place of hiding and was pouring news into my ear, his eyes beaming with triumph and gladness. He said:

"'Tis through *me* the change was brought about! And hard have I worked to do it, too. But when I told them the disaster in store, and saw how mighty was the terror it did cause, then saw I also that this was the time to strike! So I pretended that your power against the sun could not reach its full until the morrow; and so if any would save the sun and the world, you must be slain today, while your enchantments are but in the weaving and lack power. It was but a dull lie, but you should have seen them seize it and swallow it in their fright, as if it were salvation sent from heaven; and all the while was I laughing in my sleeve the one moment, to see them so cheaply deceived, and glorifying God the next, that He was content to let me be His instrument to the saving of thy life. Ah, how happy has the matter gone! You will not need to do the sun a *real* hurt—ah, forget not that, on your soul forget it not! Only make a little darkness—only the littlest little darkness, mind, and stop with that. It will be sufficient. They will see that I spoke falsely—being ignorant, as they will fancy—and with the falling of the first shadow of that darkness you shall see them go mad with fear; and they will set you free and make you great! Go to thy triumph, now! But remember—ah, good friend, I implore thee remember my prayer, and do the blessed sun no hurt. For *my* sake, thy true friend."

I choked out some words through my grief and misery; as much as to say I would spare the sun; for which the lad's eyes paid me back with such deep and loving gratitude that I had not the heart to tell him his good-hearted foolishness had ruined me and sent me to my death.

As the soldiers assisted me across the court the stillness was so deep that if I had been blindfolded I should have supposed I was alone. There was not a movement in those masses of humanity; they were as rigid as stone images, and as pale; and dread sat upon every face. This hush continued while I was being chained to the stake; it still continued while the wood was carefully piled about my ankles, my knees, my thighs, my body. Then there was a pause and a deeper hush, if possible, and a man knelt down at my feet with a blazing torch; the multitude strained forward, gazing, and parting slightly from their seats without knowing it; the monk raised his hands above my head and his eyes toward the blue sky, and began some words in Latin; in this attitude he droned on and on a little while, and then stopped. I waited two or three moments, and then looked up; he was standing there as if turned to stone. With a common impulse the multitude rose slowly up and stared into the sky. I followed their eyes; as sure as guns, there was my eclipse beginning! The life went boiling through my veins; I was a new man! The rim of black spread slowly into the sun's disk, my heart beat higher and higher, and still the crowd and the priest stared into the sky, motionless. I knew that this gaze would be turned upon me next. When it was, I was ready. I was in one of the most grand attitudes I ever struck, with my arm stretched up pointing to the sun. It was a noble effect. You could *see* the shudder sweep the mass like a wave. Two shouts rang out, one close upon the heels of the other:

"Apply the torch!"

"I forbid it!"

The one was from Merlin, the other from the king. Merlin started from his place—to apply the torch himself, I judged. I said:

"Stay where you are. If any man moves—even the king—before I give him leave, I will blast him with thunder, I will consume him with lightnings!"

The multitude sank meekly into their seats, as I was expecting they would. Merlin hesitated a moment or two, and I was on pins and needles during that little while. Then he sat down, and I took a good breath; for I knew I was master of the situation now. The king said:

"Be merciful, fair sir, and try no further in this dangerous matter lest disaster follow. It was reported to us that your powers could not reach their full strength until the morrow; but—"

"Your Majesty thinks the report may have been a lie? It *was* a lie."

That made an immense effect; up went appealing

hands everywhere, together with prayers to the king that I might be bought off at any price, and the disaster stopped. The king was eager to do as they wished. He said:

"Name any terms, reverend sir, even to the halving of my kingdom; but banish this disaster, spare the sun!"

My fortune was made; I would have taken him up in a minute, but *I* couldn't stop an eclipse; the thing was out of the question. So I asked time to consider. The king said:

"How long—ah, how long, good sir? Be merciful; look, it groweth darker, moment by moment. Prithee how long?"

"Not long. Half an hour—maybe an hour."

There were a thousand protests, but I couldn't shorten up any, for I couldn't remember how long a total eclipse lasts. I was in a puzzled condition, anyway, and wanted to think. Something was wrong about that eclipse, and the fact was very unsettling. If this wasn't the one I was after, how was I to tell whether this was the sixth century, or nothing but a dream? Dear me, if I could only prove it was the latter! Here was a glad new hope. If the boy was right about the date, and this was surely the twentieth, it *wasn't* the sixth century. I reached for the monk's sleeve, in considerable excitement, and asked him what day of the month it was.

Hang him, he said it was the *twenty-first!* It made

me turn cold to hear him. I begged him not to make any mistake about it; but he was sure; he knew it was the twenty-first. So, that feather-headed boy had botched things again! The time of the day was right for the eclipse; I had seen that for myself, in the beginning, by the dial that was near by. Yes, I *was* in King Arthur's court, and I might as well make the most of it I could.

The darkness was steadily growing, the people becoming more and more distressed. I now said:

"Sir King, for a lesson, I will let this darkness proceed and spread night in the world; but whether I blot out the sun for good, or restore it shall rest with you. These are the terms. You shall remain king over all your dominions, and receive all the glories and honors that belong to the kingship; but you shall appoint me your minister and executive, and give me for my services one per cent of such actual increase of income over and above its present amount as I may succeed in creating for the state. If I can't live on that, I shan't ask anybody to give me a lift. Is it satisfactory?"

There was a roar of applause, and out of the midst of it the king's voice rose, saying:

"Away with his bonds, and set him free! And do him honor, high and low, rich and poor, for he is become the king's right hand, is clothed with power and authority, and his seat is upon the highest step of the throne! Now sweep away this creeping night and bring the light and cheer again, that all the world may bless thee."

But I said:

"That a common man should be shamed before the world is nothing; but it were dishonor to the *king* if any that saw his minister naked should not also see him delivered from his shame. If I might ask that my clothes be brought again—"

"They are not fit," the king broke in. "Fetch clothing of another sort; clothe him like a prince!"

My idea worked. I wanted to keep things as they were till the eclipse was total; otherwise they would be trying again to get me to dismiss the darkness, and of course I couldn't do it. Sending for the clothes gained some delay, but not enough. So I had to make another excuse. I said it would be but natural if the king should change his mind and repent to some extent of what he had done under excitement; therefore I would let the darkness grow a while, and if at the end of a reasonable time the king had kept his mind the same, the darkness should be dismissed. Neither the king nor anybody else was satisfied with that arrangement, but I had to stick to my point.

It grew darker and darker and blacker and blacker, while I struggled with those awkward sixth-century clothes. It got to be pitch-dark at last, and the multitude groaned with horror to feel the cold night breezes fan through the place and see the stars come out and twinkle in the sky. At last the eclipse was total, and

I was very glad of it, but everybody else was in misery—which was quite natural. I said:

"The king, by his silence, still stands to the terms." Then I lifted up my hand—stood just so a moment— then I said, in the most solemn tones: "Let the enchantment dissolve and pass harmless away!"

There was no response for a moment, in that deep darkness and that graveyard hush. But when the silver rim of the sun pushed itself out a moment or two later, the crowd broke loose with a vast shout and came pouring down to smother me with blessings and gratitude; and Clarence was not the last one, to be sure.

CHAPTER VI

THE BOSS

Since I was now the second most important person in the kingdom, as far as political power and authority were concerned, much was made of me. My clothing was of silks and velvets and cloth-of-gold, and by consequence was very showy, and also uncomfortable. But habit would soon accustom me to my clothes; I was aware of that. I was given the choicest apartments in the castle, after the king's. They were bright with loud-colored silk hangings, but the stone floors had nothing but straw on them for a carpet. As for conveniences, properly speaking, there weren't any. I mean *little* conveniences; it is the little conveniences that make the real comfort of life. The big oak chairs, with rude carvings, were well enough, but that was the stopping-place. There was no soap, no matches, no looking-glass—except a metal one, about as powerful as a pail of water. And not a picture. No, even in my grand room of state, there wasn't anything in the nature of a picture except a thing the size of a bedquilt, which was either woven or knitted (it had darned places in it), and nothing in it was the right color or the right shape.

There wasn't even a bell or a speaking-tube in the castle. I had a great many servants, and those that were on duty waited in the anteroom; and when I wanted one of them I had to go and call for him. There was no gas, there were no candles; a bronze dish half full of boarding-house butter with a blazing rag floating in it was the thing that produced what was regarded as light. A lot of these hung along the walls and toned down the dark just enough to make it dismal. If you went out at night, your servants carried torches. There were no books, pens, paper or ink, and no glass in the openings they believed to be windows. It is a little thing—glass is—until it is absent, and then it becomes a big thing. But perhaps the worst of all was that there wasn't any sugar, coffee, tea, or tobacco. I saw that I was just another Robinson Crusoe cast away on an uninhabited island with no society but some more or less tame animals, and if I wanted to make life bearable I must do as he did— invent, contrive, create, reorganize things, set brain and hand to work, and keep them busy. Well, that was in my line.

One thing troubled me along at first—the great interest which people took in me. Apparently the whole nation wanted a look at me. I soon learned that the eclipse had scared the British world almost to death; that while it lasted the whole country, from one end to the other, was in a pitiable state of panic, and the churches, hermitages, and monkeries overflowed with praying and weeping poor creatures who thought the end of the world was come. Then had fol-

lowed the news that the producer of this awful event
was a stranger, a mighty magician at Arthur's court;
that he could have blown out the sun like a candle,
and was just going to do it when his mercy was pur-
chased, and he then dissolved his enchantments, and
was now recognized and honored as the man who had
by his unaided might saved the globe from destruction
and its peoples from extinction. Now if you consider
that everybody believed that, and not only believed
it, but never even dreamed of doubting it, you will
easily understand that there was not a person in all
Britain that would not have walked fifty miles to get
a sight of me. Of course I was all the talk—all other
subjects were dropped; even the king became suddenly a person of minor interest. Within twenty-four
hours the delegations began to arrive, and from that
time onward for two weeks they kept coming. The
village was crowded, and all the country-side. I had
to go out a dozen times a day and show myself to these
reverent and awe-stricken multitudes. It came to be
a great burden as to time and trouble, but of course
it was at the same time agreeable to be so celebrated
and such a center of attention. It turned Merlin green
with envy and spite, which was a great satisfaction to
me. But there was one thing I couldn't understand—
nobody had asked for an autograph. I spoke to Clarence about it. By George! I had to explain to him
what it was. Then he said nobody in the country could

read or write but a few dozen priests. Land! Think of that.

There was another thing that troubled me a little. Those multitudes presently began to ask for another miracle. That was natural. To be able to carry back to their far homes the boast that they had seen the man who could command the sun riding in the heavens, and be obeyed, would make them great in the eyes of their neighbors and envied by them all; but to be able also to say they had seen him work a miracle themselves—why, people would come a distance to see *them*. The pressure got to be pretty strong. Also, Clarence found that old Merlin was making himself busy on the sly among those people. He was spreading a report that I was a humbug, and that the reason I didn't accommodate the people with a miracle was because I couldn't. I saw that I must do something. I presently thought out a plan.

By my authority as executive I threw Merlin into prison—the same cell I had occupied myself. Then I gave public notice by herald and trumpet that I should be busy with affairs of state for two weeks, but about the end of that time I would take a moment and blow up Merlin's stone tower by fires from heaven; in the meantime, whoever listened to evil reports about me, let him beware. Furthermore, I would perform but this one miracle at this time, and no more; if it failed to satisfy and any murmured, I would turn

the murmurers into horses, and make them useful.
Quiet followed.

I took Clarence into my confidence to a certain
degree, and we went to work privately. I told him
that this was a sort of miracle that required a trifle
of preparation, and that it would be sudden death ever
to talk about these preparations to anybody. That
made his mouth safe enough. Secretly we made a few
bushels of first-rate blasting powder, and I super-
intended my armorers while they constructed a lightning-rod and some wires. This old stone tower was
very massive. It was Roman, and four hundred years
old; yes, and handsome, after a rude fashion, and
covered with ivy from base to top. It stood on a lonely
hill in good view from the castle, and about half a
mile away.

Working by night, we stowed the powder in the
tower—dug stones out on the inside, and buried the
powder in the walls themselves, which were fifteen
feet thick at the base. We put in a peck at a time in a
dozen places. We could have blown up the Tower of
London with these charges. When the thirteenth night
was come we put up our lightning-rod, bedded it in
one of the batches of powder, and ran wires from it
to the other batches. Everybody had shunned that
locality from the day of my announcement, but on
the morning of the fourteenth I thought best to warn
the people, through the heralds, to keep clear away—
a quarter of a mile away; then added, by command,

that at some time during the twenty-four hours I
would perform the miracle, but would first give a
brief notice by flags on the castle towers if in the daytime, by torch-baskets in the same places if at night.

Thunder-showers had been frequent of late, and
I was not much afraid of a failure; still, I shouldn't
have cared for a delay of a day or two; I should have
explained that I was busy with affairs of state yet,
and the people must wait.

Of course, we had a blazing sunny day—almost the
first one without a cloud for three weeks; things always happen so. I kept hidden and watched the
weather. Clarence dropped in from time to time and
said the public excitement was growing and growing
all the time, and the whole country filling up with human masses as far as one could see from the battlements. At last the wind sprang up and a cloud appeared—in the right quarter, too, and just at nightfall.
For a little while I watched that distant cloud spread
and blacken; then I judged it was time for me to appear. I ordered the torch-baskets to be lit, and Merlin
freed and sent to me. A quarter of an hour later I
climbed to the walls and there found the king and the
court gazing off in the darkness toward Merlin's
Tower. Already the darkness was so heavy that one
could not see far.

Merlin arrived in a gloomy mood. I said:

"You wanted to burn me alive when I had not done
you any harm, and lately you have been trying to

injure my professional reputation. Therefore I am
going to call down fire and blow up your tower, but it
is only fair to give you a chance; now if you think
you can break my enchantments and ward off the
fires, step to the bat; it's your innings."

"I can, fair sir, and will. Doubt it not."

He drew an imaginary circle on the stones of the
roof and burnt a pinch of powder in it, which sent
up a small cloud of smoke. Everybody fell back and
began to cross themselves and get uncomfortable.
Then he began to mutter and make passes in the air
with his hands. He worked himself up slowly and
gradually into a sort of frenzy, and got to thrashing
around with his arms like the sails of a windmill. By
this time the storm had about reached us; the gusts of
wind were flaring the torches and making the shadows
swash about, the first heavy drops of rain were falling,
the world abroad was black as pitch, the lightning
began to wink fitfully. Of course, my rod would be
loading itself now. In fact, things were ready to happen. So I said:

"You have had time enough. I have given you every
advantage, and not interfered. It is plain your magic
is weak. It is only fair that I begin now."

I made about three passes in the air, and then there
was an awful crash and that old tower leaped into
the sky in chunks, along with a vast volcanic fountain
of fire that turned night to noonday, and showed a

thousand acres of human beings hugging the ground in a general collapse of fright.

It was a great miracle and the people went home satisfied.

Merlin's stock was flat. The king wanted to stop his wages; he even wanted to banish him, but I interfered. I said he would be useful to work the weather and attend to small matters like that, and I would give him a lift now and then when his poor little parlor magic soured on him. There wasn't a rag of his tower left, but I had the government rebuild it for him. And as for being grateful, he never even said thank you. He was a rather hard lot, take him how you might; but then you couldn't fairly expect a man to be sweet that had been set back so.

To have enormous authority is fine, but to have the onlooking world consent to it is finer. The tower miracle had convinced the people and I was firm in my power. If any had been jealous and critical before that, they experienced a change of heart now. There was not anyone in the kingdom who would have considered it good judgment to meddle with my matters.

I was fast getting used to my situation and circumstances. For a time, I used to wake up, mornings, and smile at my "dream," and listen for the Colt's factory whistle; but that sort of thing played itself out, gradually, and at last I was fully able to realize that I was actually living in the sixth century, and

in Arthur's court, not a lunatic asylum. After that, I
was just as much at home in that century as I could
have been in any other; and I wouldn't have traded
it for the twentieth. Look at the opportunities here
for a man of knowledge, brains, pluck, and enterprise
to sail in and grow up with the country—the grandest field that ever was, and all my own: not a competitor, not a man who wasn't a baby to me in skills
and abilities; and what would I amount to in the twentieth century? I should be foreman of a factory, that
is about all, and could find any day a hundred better
men than myself.

What a jump I had made! I couldn't keep from
thinking about it, just as one does who has struck oil.

I was no shadow of a king; I was the real thing; the
king himself was the shadow. My power was great,
and it was not a mere name, as such things have generally been; it was the genuine article.

Well, it was a curious country, and full of interest.
And the people! They were the quaintest and simplest
and trustingest race; why, they were nothing but
rabbits. It was pitiful for a person born in a whole-
some free atmosphere to listen to their humble and
hearty outpourings of loyalty toward their king and
Church and nobility, as if they had any more occasion to love and honor king and Church and noble
than a slave has to love and honor the lash, or a dog
has to love and honor the stranger that kicks him!
Why, dear me, *any* kind of royalty, *any* kind of

aristocracy, is rightly an insult; but if you are born and brought up under that sort of arrangement you probably never find it out for yourself, and don't believe it when somebody else tells you. It is enough to make a body ashamed of his race to think of the sort of king that has always occupied its thrones without right or reason, and the seventh-rate people that have always figured as its aristocracies.

The most of King Arthur's British nation were slaves, pure and simple, and bore that name, and wore the iron collar on their necks; and the rest were slaves in fact, but without the name; they imagined themselves men and freemen, and called themselves so. The truth was, the nation as a body was in the world for one object, and only one: to bow before king and Church and noble; to slave for them, sweat blood for them, starve that they might be fed, work that they might play, drink misery to the dregs that they might be happy, go naked that they might wear silks and jewels, pay taxes that they might be spared from paying them. And for all this, the thanks they got were blows and contempt; and so poor-spirited were they that they took even this sort of attention as an honor.

Inherited ideas are a curious thing, and interesting to observe and examine. I had mine, the king and his people had theirs. In both cases they came from time and habit, and the man who should have proposed to change them by reason and argument would have had a big job. For instance, those people had inherited the idea that all men without title and a long pedigree, whether they had great natural gifts and acquirements or hadn't, were creatures of no more consideration than so many animals, bugs, insects; but I had inherited the idea that human beings who can consent to strut with inherited dignities and unearned titles, are of no good but to be laughed at. It seems to show that there isn't anything you can't stand, if you are only born and bred to it.

Here I was in King Arthur's kingdom, a man among children, a master intelligence among simple minds; by all reasonable measurement the one and only actually great man in that whole British world; and yet there and then, a man with a title was considered a better man than I was. There were times when *he* could sit down in the king's presence, but I couldn't. I could have got a title easily enough, and that would have raised me a large step in everybody's eyes, even in the king's, the giver of titles. But I didn't ask for it; and I declined it when it was offered. I couldn't have enjoyed such a thing with my notions; I couldn't have felt really and satisfactorily fine and proud and set-up over any title except one that should come from the nation itself, the only real source; and such a one I hoped to win; and in the course of years of honest and honorable endeavor, I did win it and did wear it with a high and clean pride. This title fell casually from the lips of a blacksmith, one day in a village, was caught up as a happy thought and tossed from mouth to mouth with a laugh and an affirmative vote; in ten days it had swept the kingdom, and was to become as familiar as the king's name. I was never known by any other name afterward, whether in the nation's talk or in grave debate upon matters of state at the council-board of the sovereign. This title, translated into modern speech, would be THE BOSS. Elected by the nation. That suited me.

Well, I liked the king, and *as king* I respected him —respected the office; at least respected it as much as I was capable of respecting anything unearned; but *as men* I looked down upon him and his nobles—privately. And he and they liked me, and respected my office; but as a person without birth or sham title, they looked down upon me.

CHAPTER VII

THE CHALLENGE

They were always having grand tournaments there at Camelot; and very stirring and ridiculous human bull-fights they were too, but just a little tiresome to the practical mind. However, I was generally on hand —for two reasons: a man must not hold himself away from the things which his friends like if he would be liked, especially as a statesman; and I wanted to study the tournament to see if I couldn't invent an improvement on it. That reminds me to remark that the very first official thing I did in my administration was to start a patent office.

Things ran along, a tournament nearly every week; and now and then the boys used to want me to take a hand—I mean Sir Launcelot and the rest—but I said I would by and by; no hurry yet, and too much government machinery to oil up and set to rights and start a-going.

We had one tournament which was continued from day to day during more than a week, and as many as five hundred knights took part in it, from first to last. They were weeks gathering. They came on horseback from everywhere, and many brought ladies, and all brought squires and troops of servants. It was a most gaudy and gorgeous crowd as to costumes, and very characteristic of the country and the time. It was fight or look on all day and every day; and sing, gamble, dance, half the night every night. They had a most noble good time. You never saw such people. Those beautiful ladies would see a knight sprawl from his horse with a lance-shaft the thickness of your ankle clean through him and the blood spouting, and instead of fainting they would clap their hands and crowd each other for a better view.

The noise at night would have been annoying to me ordinarily, but I didn't mind it in the present circumstances, because it kept me from hearing the quack doctors detaching legs and arms from the day's cripples. They ruined an uncommon good old cross-cut saw for me and broke the saw-buck, too, but I let it pass. And as for my ax—well, I made up my mind that the next time I lent an ax to a surgeon I would pick my century.

I not only watched this tournament from day to day, but detailed an intelligent priest from my Department of Public Morals and Agriculture, and ordered him to report it; for it was my purpose by and by, when I should have gotten the people along far enough, to start a newspaper. The first thing you want in a new country is a patent office; then work up your school system; and after that, out with your paper. A newspaper has its faults, but you can't bring to life a dead nation without it; there isn't any way. So I wanted to sample things, and be finding out what

sort of reporter-material I might be able to rake together out of the sixth century when I should come
to need it.

At the tournaments I sat in the box set aside for me
as the king's minister. One day I sat there watching
Sir Gareth in combat and listening to Sir Dinadan's
stale jokes. Just as Sir Dinadan pulled one of his
worst ones, he was called to enter the combat, and as
Sir Gareth gave him an awful welt, I said aloud, "I
hope to gracious he's killed!" Just then Sir Gareth
crashed with Sir Sagramor, who by ill luck caught
my words and thought I meant them for him. So he
challenged me to a duel and set the date three or four
years in the future as he was leaving to hunt for the
Holy Grail. The boys all took a flier at the Holy Grail
now and then. It was a several years' cruise. I don't
think any of them knew just what the Holy Grail was
or what they would do with it if they found it.

The Round Table soon heard of the challenge, and
of course it was a good deal discussed, for such things
interested the boys. The king thought I ought now to
set forth in search of adventures, so that I might gain
fame and be the more worthy to meet Sir Sagramor
when the several years should have rolled away. I ex-
cused myself for the present; I said it would take
me three or four years yet to get things well fixed up
and going smoothly; then I should be ready; all the
chances were that at the end of that time Sir Sagramor would still be out grailing, so no valuable time

So he challenged me to a duel.

would be lost by the postponement; I should then have been in office six or seven years, and I believed my system and machinery would be so well developed that I could take a holiday without its working any harm.

I was pretty well satisfied with what I had already accomplished. In various quiet nooks and corners I had the beginnings of all sorts of industries under way—beginnings of future vast factories. In these were gathered together the brightest young minds I could find, and I kept agents out raking the country for more all the time. I was training a crowd of ignorant folk into experts—experts in every sort of handiwork and scientific calling. These nurseries of mine went smoothly and privately along undisturbed in their country retreats, for nobody was allowed to come near them without a special permit—for I was afraid of the Church.

I had started a teacher-factory and a lot of Sunday-schools the first thing; as a result, I now had a fine system of graded schools in full blast in those places, and also a complete variety of Protestant congregations all in a prosperous and growing condition. Everybody could be any kind of a Christian he wanted to be.

All mines were royal property, and there were a good many of them. They had formerly been worked as savages always work mines—holes grubbed in the earth and the mineral brought up in sacks of hide by hand, at the rate of a ton a day; but I had begun to put the mining on a scientific basis as early as I could.

Yes, I had made pretty handsome progress when Sir Sagramor's challenge struck me.

Four years rolled by—and then! Well, you would never imagine it in the world. Unlimited power *is* the ideal thing when it is in safe hands and would be the absolutely perfect earthly government, if the despot, or absolute ruler, were the perfectest individual of the human race, and would live forever. But as a perishable perfect man must die and leave his power in the hands of an imperfect successor, despotism is not merely a bad form of government, it is the worst form that is possible.

My works showed what a despot could do with the resources of a kingdom at his command. Unsuspected by this dark land, I had the civilization of the nineteenth century booming under its very nose! It was fenced away from the public view, but there it was, a gigantic fact, and to be heard from yet, if I lived and had luck. My schools and churches were children four years before; they were grown up now; my shops of that day were vast factories now; where I had a dozen trained men then, I had a thousand now; where I had one brilliant expert then, I had fifty now. I stood with my hand on the switch, so to speak, ready to turn it on and flood the dark world with light at any moment. But I was not going to do the thing in that sudden way. It was not my policy. The people could not have stood it.

No, I had been going cautiously all the while. I had had confidential agents trickling through the country some time, whose office was to break down knighthood by degrees, and to gnaw a little at this and that and the other superstition, and so prepare the way gradually for a better order of things. I was turning on my light one candlepower at a time, and meant to continue to do so.

I had scattered some branch schools secretly about the kingdom, and they were doing very well. I meant to work this racket more and more, as time wore on, if nothing occurred to frighten me. One of my deepest secrets was my West Point—my military academy. I kept that most jealously out of sight, and I did the same with my naval academy which I had established at a remote seaport. Both were prospering to my satisfaction.

Clarence was twenty-two now, and was my head executive, my right hand. He was a darling; he was equal to anything; there wasn't anything he couldn't turn his hand to. Of late I had been training him for journalism, for the time seemed about right for a start in the newspaper line; nothing big, but just a small weekly for experimental circulation. He took to it like a duck; there was an editor concealed in him, sure. Already he had doubled himself in one way;

he talked sixth century and wrote nineteenth. His journalistic style was climbing steadily.

We had another large undertaking on hand, too. This was a telegraph and a telephone. Our first venture in this line. These wires were for a private service only, as yet, and must be kept private until a riper day should come. We had a gang of men on the road, working mainly by night. They were stringing ground-wires; we were afraid to put up poles, for they would attract too much inquiry. Ground-wires were good enough, in both instances, for my wires were protected by an insulation of my own invention which was perfect. My men had orders to lay the wires across country, avoiding the roads; they were to establish telephone and telegraph connections between all good-sized towns, and were to leave experts in each town to operate the apparatus. Nobody could tell you how to find any place in the kingdom, for nobody ever went intentionally to any place, but only struck it by accident in his wanderings, and then generally left it without thinking to inquire what its name was. At one time and another we had sent out expeditions to survey and map the kingdom, but the priests had always interfered and raised trouble. So we had given the thing up, for the present.

As for the general condition of the country, it was almost as it had been when I arrived in it. I had made changes, but they were necessarily slight, and they were not noticeable. Thus far, I had not even meddled with taxation, outside of the taxes which provided the royal revenues. I had systematized those and had put the service on an effective basis. As a result, these revenues were already four times as large, and yet the burden was so much more evenly distributed than before, that all the kingdom felt a sense of relief, and the praises of my administration were hearty and general.

Personally, I struck an interruption now, but I did not mind it; it could not have happened at a better time. Earlier it could have annoyed me, but now everything was in good hands and swimming right along. The king had reminded me several times, of late, that the postponement I had asked for, four years before, had about run out now. It was a hint that I ought to be starting out to seek adventures and get up a reputation of a size to make me worthy of the honor of breaking a lance with Sir Sagramor, who was still out grailing, but who was being hunted for by various relief expeditions, and might be found any year now. So you see I was expecting this interruption; it did not take me by surprise.

CHAPTER VIII

THE YANKEE IN SEARCH OF ADVENTURES

There never was such a country for wandering liars, and they were of both sexes. Hardly a month went by without one of these tramps arriving, generally loaded with a tale about some princess or other wanting help to get her out of some faraway castle where she was held in captivity by a lawless scoundrel, usually a giant. Now you would think that the first thing the king would do after listening to such a story from an entire stranger, would be to ask for proof—yes, and a pointer or two as to locality of castle, best route to it, and so on. But nobody ever thought of so simple and common-sense a thing as that. No, everybody swallowed these people's lies whole, and never asked a question of any sort about anything. Well, one day when I was not around, one of these people came along—it was a woman this time —and told a tale of the usual pattern. Her mistress was a captive in a vast and gloomy castle, along with forty-four other young and beautiful girls, pretty much all of them princesses; they had been in that cruel captivity for twenty-six years; the masters of the castle were three giant-like brothers, each with four arms and one eye—the eye in the center of the forehead and as big as a fruit. Sort of fruit not mentioned.

Would you believe it? The king and the whole Round Table were delighted over this crazy opportunity for adventure. Every knight of the Table jumped for the chance and begged for it; but the king gave it to me, who had not asked for it at all.

By an effort, I contained my joy when Clarence brought me the news. But he—he could not contain his. His mouth gushed delight and gratitude—delight in my good fortune, gratitude to the king for this splendid mark of his favor for me. He could keep neither his legs nor his body still, but danced about the place in the greatest happiness.

On my side, I could have cursed the kindness that gave me this favor, but I kept my vexation under the surface for policy's sake, and did what I could to let on to be glad. Indeed, I *said* I was glad. And in a way it was true; I was glad as a person is when he is scalped.

Well, one must make the best of things and not waste time with useless fretting, but get down to business and see what can be done; so I sent for the girl and she came. She was a pretty enough creature, and soft and modest, but, if signs went for anything, she didn't know much. I said:

"My dear, have you been questioned as to particulars?"

She said she hadn't.

"Well, I didn't expect you had, but I thought I would ask to make sure; it's the way I've been raised. Now you mustn't take it unkindly if I remind you that as we don't know you, we must go a little slow. You may be all right, of course, and we'll hope that you are; but to take it for granted isn't business. *You* understand that. I'm obliged to ask you a few questions; just answer up fair and square, and don't be afraid. Where do you live, when you are at home?"

"In the land of Moder, fair sir."

"Land of Moder. I don't remember hearing of it before. Parents living?"

"As to that, I know not if they be yet alive, since it is many years that I have lain shut up in the castle."

"Your name, please?"

"I am called the Demoiselle Alisande la Carteloise, if it please you."

"Do you know anybody here who can identify you?"

"That were not likely, fair lord, I being come hither now for the first time."

"Have you brought any letters—any documents—any proof that you are trustworthy and truthful?"

"Of a surety, no; and wherefore should I? Have I not a tongue, and cannot I say all that myself?"

"But *your* saying it, you know, and somebody else's saying it, is different."

"Different? How might that be? I fear me I do not understand."

"Don't *understand?* Land of—why, you see—you see—why great Scott, can't you understand a little thing like that? Can't you understand the difference between your— *why* do you look so innocent and idiotic!"

"I? In truth I know not, unless it is the will of God."

"Yes, yes, I reckon that's about the size of it. Don't mind my seeming excited; I'm not. Let us change the subject. Now as to this castle with forty-five princesses in it and three ogres at the head of it, tell me— where is it?"

"Oh, as to that, it is great and strong, and lieth in a far country. Yes, it is many leagues."

"How many?"

"Ah, fair sir, it were hard to tell, they are so many, and do so lap the one upon the other, and being made all in the same image and the same color, one may not know the one league from its fellow, nor how to count them except they be taken apart, and ye know well it were God's work to do that, being not within man's capacity; for ye will note—"

"Hold on, hold on, never mind about the distance; *whereabouts* does the castle lie? What's the direction from here?"

"Ah, please you sir, it hath no direction from here,

by reason that the road lieth not straight, but turneth evermore."

"Oh, never mind about the direction, hang the direction. Have you got such a thing as a map of that region about you? Now a good map—"

"Is it perhaps that manner of thing which of late the unbelievers have brought from over the great seas, which, being boiled in oil, and an onion and salt added thereto, doth—"

"What, a map? What are you talking about? Don't you know what a map is? There, there, never mind, don't explain; I hate explanations; they fog a thing up so that you can't tell anything about it. Run along, dear; good day; show her the way, Clarence."

Oh, well, it was reasonably plain now, why these donkeys didn't ask these liars for details. It may be that this girl had a fact in her somewhere, but I don't believe you could have pried it out with a crowbar or blasted it with anything short of dynamite. Why, she was a perfect fool; and yet the king and his knights had listened to her as if she had been a leaf out of the gospel. It kind of sizes up the whole party. And think of the simple ways of this court: this wandering girl hadn't any more trouble to see the king in his palace than she would have had to get into the poorhouse in my day and country. In fact, he was glad to see her, glad to hear her tale; with that adventure of hers to offer, she was as welcome as a corpse is to an undertaker.

Just as I was ending up these thoughts, Clarence

came back. I remarked upon the small result of my efforts with the girl; I hadn't got hold of a single point that could help me to find the castle. The youth looked a little surprised, or puzzled, or something, and hinted that he had been wondering to himself what I had wanted to ask the girl all those questions for.

"Why, great guns," I said, "don't I want to find the castle? And how else would I go about it?"

"La, sweet your worship, one may lightly answer that. She will go with thee. They always do. She will ride with thee."

"Ride with me? Nonsense!"

"But of a truth she will. She will ride with thee. Thou shalt see."

"What? She wander the hills and search the woods with me—alone—and I as good as engaged to be married? Why, it's scandalous. Think how it would look."

My, the dear face that rose before me! The boy was eager to know all about my engagement. I swore him to secrecy and then whispered her name—"Puss Flanagan." He looked disappointed, and said he didn't remember the countess. How natural it was for him to give her a rank. He asked me where she lived.

"In East Har—" I came to myself and stopped, a little confused; then I said, "Never mind, now; I'll tell you some time."

And might he see her? Would I let him see her some day?

It was but a little thing to promise—thirteen hundred years or so—and he so eager; so I said yes. But I sighed; I couldn't help it. And yet there was no sense in sighing, for she wasn't born yet. But that is the way we are made; we don't reason where we feel; we just feel.

My expedition was all the talk that day and that night, and the boys were very good to me and made much of me, and seemed to have forgotten their disappointment, and come to be as anxious for me to kill those ogres and set those old women loose as if it were themselves that had the contract. Well, they *were* good children, but just children, that is all. And they gave me no end of points about how to scout for giants, and how to scoop them in; and they told me all sorts of charms against enchantments, and gave me salves and other rubbish to put on my wounds. But it never occurred to one of them that if I was such a wonderful magician as I was pretending to be, I ought not to need salves or instructions, or charms against enchantments, and least of all, arms and armor in a battle of any kind—even against fire-spouting dragons and devils, let alone such poor opponents as these I was after, these commonplace ogres of the back settlements.

I was to have an early breakfast and start at dawn, for that was the usual way; but I had the devil's own time with my armor, and this delayed me a little. It is troublesome to get into, and there is so much detail. First you wrap a layer or two of blanket around your

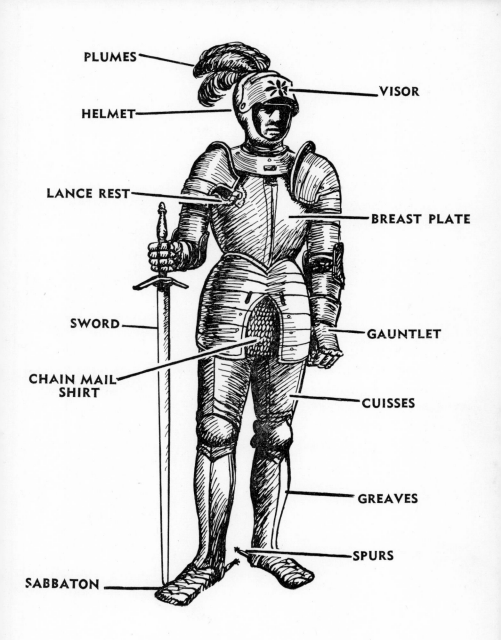

PLUMES

HELMET

VISOR

LANCE REST

BREAST PLATE

SWORD

GAUNTLET

CHAIN MAIL
SHIRT

CUISSES

GREAVES

SPURS

SABBATON

body, for a sort of cushion and to keep off the cold iron; then you put on your sleeves and shirt of chain mail—these are made of small steel links woven together, and they form a fabric so flexible that if you toss your shirt onto the floor, it slumps into a pile like a peck of wet fishnet; then you put on your shoes— flat-boats roofed over with interwoven bands of steel —and screw your clumsy spurs into the heels. Next you buckle your greaves on your legs, and your cuisses on your thighs; then come your back-plate and your breast-plate, and you begin to feel crowded; then you hitch onto the breast-plate the half-petticoat of broad overlapping bands of steel which hangs down in front but is scalloped out behind so you can sit down, and isn't any real improvement on an inverted coal-scuttle, either for looks or for wear, or to wipe your hands on; next you belt on your sword; then you put your stove-pipe joints onto your arms, your iron gauntlets onto your hands, your iron rat-trap onto your head, with a rag of steel web hitched onto it to hang over the back of your neck—and there you are, snug as a candle in a candle-mold. This is no time to dance.

The boys helped me, or I never could have got in. Just as we finished, Sir Bedivere happened in, and I saw that as like as not I hadn't chosen the most convenient outfit for a long trip. How stately he looked, and tall and broad and grand. He had on his head a conical steel helmet that came only down to his ears, and for visor had only a narrow steel bar that ex-

tended down to his upper lip and protected his nose;
and all the rest of him, from neck to heel, was flexible
chain mail, trousers and all. But pretty much all of
him was hidden under his outside garment, which of
course was of chain mail, as I said, and hung straight
from his shoulders to his ankles; and from his middle
to the bottom, both before and behind, was divided,
so that he could ride and let the skirts hang down on
each side. He was going grailing, and it was just the
outfit for it, too. I would have given a good deal for
that coat, but it was too late now to be fooling around.
The sun was just up, the king and the court were all
on hand to see me off and wish me luck; so it wouldn't
be polite for me to delay. You don't get on your horse
yourself; no, if you tried it you would get disappointed. They carry you out, just as they carry a sun-
struck man to the drug store, and put you on, and
help get you to rights, and fix your feet in the stir-
rups; and all the while you do feel so strange and
stuffy and like somebody else—like somebody that
has been married on a sudden, or struck by lightning,
or something like that, and hasn't quite come to yet,
and is sort of numb, and can't just get his bearings.
Then they stood up the mast they called a spear, in
its socket by my left foot, and I gripped it with my
hand; last they hung my shield around my neck, and I
was all complete and ready to up anchor and get to sea.
Everybody was as good to me as they could be, and a
maid of honor gave me the stirrup-cup her own self.

There was nothing more to do now, but for that girl to get up behind me, which she did, and put an arm or so around me to hold on.

And so we started, and everybody gave us a goodby and waved their handkerchiefs or helmets. And everybody we met, going down the hill and through the village, was respectful to us, except some shabby little boys on the outskirts. They said:

"Oh, what a guy!" And threw mud at us.

In my experience boys are the same in all ages. They don't respect anything; they don't care for anything or anybody.

CHAPTER IX

WAYS AND HIGHWAYS

Straight off, we were in the country. It was most lovely and pleasant in those lonely woods in the early cool morning in the first freshness of autumn. At times we left the world behind and entered into the rich gloom of the forest, where sly wild things scampered by and were gone before you could even get your eye on the place where the noise was. And by and by out we would swing again into the open.

About the third or fourth or fifth time that we swung out into the open—it was along there somewhere, a couple of hours or so after sun-up—it wasn't as pleasant as it had been. It was beginning to get hot. This was quite noticeable. We had a very long pull after that, without any shade. Now it is curious how little annoyances grow and multiply after they once get a start. Things which I didn't mind at all at first, I began to mind now—and more and more too, all the time. The first ten or fifteen times I wanted my handkerchief I didn't seem to care; I got along, and said never mind, it isn't any matter, and dropped it out of my mind. But now it was different; I wanted it all the time; it was nag, nag, nag, right along, and no rest; I couldn't get it out of my mind; and so at last I lost my temper and said hang a man that would make a suit of armor without any pockets in it. You see I had my handkerchief in my helmet; and some other things; but it was that kind of a helmet that you can't take off by yourself. That hadn't occurred to me when I put it there; and in fact I didn't know it. I supposed it would be particularly convenient there. And so now, the thought of its being there so handy and close by and yet not get-at-able, made it all the worse and the harder to bear. Yes, the thing that you can't get is the thing that you want, mainly; every-one has noticed that. Well, it took my mind off every-thing else, took it clear off and centered it in my hel-met; and mile after mile, there it stayed, imagining the handkerchief, picturing the handkerchief; and it was bitter and annoying to have the salt sweat keep trickling down into my eyes, and I couldn't get at it. It seems like a little thing, on paper, but it was not a little thing at all; it was the most real kind of misery. So we jogged along, and now and then we struck a stretch of dust, and it would tumble up in clouds and get into my nose and make me sneeze and cry; and of course I said things I oughtn't to have said; I don't deny that.

We couldn't seem to meet anybody in this lonesome Britain, not even an ogre; and, in the mood I was in then, it was well for the ogre; that is, an ogre with a handkerchief. Most knights would have thought of nothing but getting his armor; but so I got his hand-kerchief, he could keep his hardware, for all of me.

Meantime, it was getting hotter and hotter in there. You see, the sun was beating down and warming up the iron more and more all the time. Well, when you are hot that way, every little thing irritates you. When I trotted, I rattled like a crate of dishes, and that annoyed me; and moreover I couldn't seem to stand that shield slatting and banging, now about my breast, now around my back; and if I dropped into a walk my joints creaked and screeched in that wearisome way that a wheelbarrow does, and as we didn't create any breeze at that gait, I was like to get fried in that stove; and besides, the quieter you went the heavier the iron settled down on you and the more and more tons you seemed to weigh every minute. And you had to be always changing hands and passing your spear over to the other foot; it got so tiresome for one hand to hold it long at a time.

Well, you know, when you perspire that way, in rivers, there comes a time when you itch. You are inside, your hands are outside; so there you are; nothing but iron between. It is not a light thing, let it sound as it may. First it is one place, then another, then some more; and it goes on spreading and spreading, and nobody can imagine what you feel like, or how unpleasant it is. And when it had got to the worst, and it seemed to me that I could not stand anything more, a fly got in through the bars and settled on my nose, and the bars were stuck and wouldn't work, and I couldn't get the visor up; and I could only shake my head, which was baking hot by this time; and the fly—well, you know how a fly acts when he has got a certainty—he only minded the shaking enough to change from nose to lip, and lip to ear, and buzz and buzz all around in there, and keep on lighting and biting in a way that a person, already so distressed as I was, simply could not stand. So I gave in, and got Alisande (or Sandy, as I had nicknamed her) to take off the helmet and relieve me of it. Then she emptied it and fetched it full of water, and I drank and then stood up, and she poured the rest down inside the armor. One cannot think how refreshing it was. She continued to fetch and pour until I was well soaked and thoroughly comfortable.

It was good to have a rest—and peace. But nothing is quite perfect in this life, at any time. I had made a pipe awhile back, and also some pretty fair tobacco, not the real thing, but what some of the Indians use: the inside bark of the willow, dried. These comforts had been in the helmet, and now I had them again, but no matches.

Gradually, as the time wore along, one annoying fact was clear—that we were stuck. An inexperienced man in armor cannot mount his horse without help and plenty of it. Sandy was not enough, not enough for me, anyway. We had to wait until somebody should come along. Waiting in silence would have been agreeable enough, for I was full of matter for thought and wanted to give it a chance to work.

I wanted to try to think out how it was that reasonable men could ever have learned to wear armor, considering its inconveniences; and how they had managed to keep up such a fashion for generations when it was plain that what I had suffered today they had had to suffer all the days of their lives. I wanted to think that out; and moreover I wanted to think out some way to reform this evil and persuade the people to let the foolish fashion die out; but thinking was out of the question in the circumstances. You couldn't think, where Sandy was.

She was a quite friendly creature and good-hearted, but she had a flow of talk that was as steady as a mill, and made your head sore. If she had had a cork she would have been a comfort. But you can't cork that kind; they would die. Her tongue was going all day, and you would think something would surely happen to her works, by and by; but no, they never got out of order, and she never had to slack up for words. She could grind, and pump, and churn, and buzz by the week, and never stop to oil up or blow out. It was jaw, jaw, jaw, talk, talk, talk, jabber, jabber, jabber; but she was just as good as she could be. I hadn't minded her talk that morning, on account of having that hornets' nest of other troubles; but more than once in the afternoon I had to say:

"Take a rest, child; the way you are using up all the domestic air, the kingdom will have to go to importing it by tomorrow, and it's a low enough treasury without that."

It is strange how short a time a person can be contented. Only a little while back, when I was riding and suffering, what a heaven this peace, this rest, this sweet calm by this stream would have seemed, where I could keep perfectly comfortable all the time by pouring a dipper of water into my armor now and then; yet already I was getting dissatisfied, partly because I could not light my pipe—for, although I had long ago started a match factory, I had forgotten to bring matches with me—and partly because we had nothing to eat. A man in armor always trusted to chance for his food on a journey, and would have been shocked at the idea of hanging a basket of sandwiches on his spear. There was probably not a knight of all the Round Table combination who would not rather have died than have been caught carrying such a thing as that on his flagstaff. And yet there could not be anything more sensible. It had been my intention to smuggle a couple of sandwiches into my helmet, but I was interrupted in the act and had to make an excuse and lay them aside, and a dog got them.

Night approached, and with it a storm. The darkness came on fast. We must camp, of course. I found a good shelter for the girl under a rock, and went off and found another for myself. But I was obliged to remain in my armor, because I could not get it off by

myself and yet could not allow Sandy to help, because
it would have seemed so like undressing before folk.

With the storm came a change of weather; and the
stronger the wind blew and the wilder the rain lashed
around, the colder and colder it got. Pretty soon,
various kinds of bugs and ants and worms and things
began to flock in out of the wet and crawl down inside my armor to get warm; and while some of them
behaved well enough, and snuggled up amongst my
clothes and got quiet, the majority were of a restless,
uncomfortable sort, and never stayed still, but went
on prowling and hunting for they did not know what;
especially the ants, which went tickling along in wearisome procession from one end of me to the other by
the hour, and are a kind of creature which I never
wish to sleep with again. I said I would never wear
armor after this trip.

All those trying hours whilst I was frozen and yet
was in a living fire, as you may say, on account of
that swarm of crawlers, that same unanswerable
question kept circling and circling through my tired
head: How do people stand this miserable armor?
How have they managed to stand it all these generations? How can they sleep at night for dreading the
tortures of next day?

When the morning came at last, I was in a bad
enough way: seedy and drowsy from want of sleep,
weary from thrashing around, famished from long
fasting, pining to bathe and to get rid of the animals,

and crippled with rheumatism. And how had it fared with the nobly born, the titled aristocrat, the Demoiselle Alisande la Carteloise? Why, she was as fresh as a squirrel; she had slept like the dead; and as for a bath, probably neither she nor any other noble in the land had ever had one, and so she was not missing it. Measured by modern standards, they were merely modified savages, those people. This noble lady showed no impatience to get to breakfast—and that smacks of the savage, too. On their journeys those Britons were used to long fasts and knew how to bear them, and also how to fill up against probable fasts before starting, after the style of the Indian. As like as not, Sandy was loaded for a three-day stretch.

We were off before sunrise, Sandy riding and I limping along behind. In half an hour we came upon a group of ragged poor creatures who had assembled to mend the thing which was regarded as a road. They were as humble as animals to me; and when I proposed to breakfast with them, they were so flattered that at first they were not able to believe that I was in earnest. My lady put up her scornful lip and withdrew to one side; she said in their hearing that she would as soon think of eating with the other cattle —a remark which embarrassed these poor devils merely because it referred to them, and not because it insulted or offended them, for it didn't. And yet they were not slaves, but freemen.

They were freemen, but they could not leave the

estates of their lord or their bishop without his permission; they could not prepare their own bread, but
must have their corn ground and their bread baked
at his mill and his bakery, and pay roundly for the
same; they could not sell a piece of their own property without paying him a handsome percentage of
the proceeds, nor buy a piece of somebody else's without remembering him in cash for the privilege. They
had to harvest his grain for him without pay, and be
ready to come at a moment's notice, leaving their own
crop to destruction by the threatened storm; they
had to let him plant fruit trees in their fields, and then
keep their indignation to themselves when his heedless fruit-gatherers trampled the grain around the
trees; they had to smother their anger when his hunt-
ing-parties galloped through their fields laying waste
the result of their patient toil; they were not allowed
to keep doves themselves, and when the swarms from
my lord's dovecote settled on their crops they must
not lose their temper and kill a bird, for awful would
the penalty be. When the harvest was at last gathered,
then came the procession of robbers to levy their
blackmail upon it: first the Church carted off its fat
tenth, then the king's commissioner took his twentieth, then my lord's people took most of the remain-
der; after which, the skinned freeman had liberty to
put what was left in his barn, in case it was worth
the trouble. There were taxes, and taxes, and taxes,
and more taxes, and taxes again, and yet other taxes

—upon this free and independent pauper, but none upon his lord the baron or the bishop, none upon the wasteful nobility or the all-devouring Church; if the baron would sleep unvexed, the freeman must sit up all night after his day's work and whip the ponds to keep the frogs quiet; and finally, if the freeman, grown desperate with his tortures, found his life unendurable under such conditions, and sacrificed it and fled to death for mercy and refuge, the gentle Church condemned him to eternal fire, the gentle law buried him at midnight at the crossroads, with a stake through his back, and his master the baron or the bishop took all his property and turned his widow and his orphans out of doors.

And here were these freemen assembled in the early morning to work on their lord the bishop's road three days each, without pay; every head of a family, and every son of a family, three days each, without pay, and a day or so added for their servants.

These poor so-called freemen, who were sharing their breakfast and their talk with me, were as full of humble reverence for their king and Church and nobility as their worst enemy could desire. There was something pitifully funny about it. I asked them if they supposed a nation of people ever existed, who, with a free vote in every man's hand, would choose that a single family and its descendants should reign over it forever, whether gifted or boobies; and would also agree that a certain hundred families should be raised to high rank, and clothed with glories and privileges which the rest of the nation's families would not have.

They said they didn't know; they had never thought about it before; it had never occurred to them there could be a nation where everyone had a vote. I said I had seen one but only one man was interested and seemed to get the idea. He was a MAN and if I had had enough of his sort, it would have suited my nature to have resigned my boss-ship and struck for the welfare of the country by changing its system of government. But I knew you couldn't have a revolution until you had educated the people to want it; so I contented myself with giving the man a note to Clarence to put him in my man-factory and I promised him he would be taught to read and write. He was so overcome that he was ready to promise to be my slave and I had to cut him short and tell him he wasn't to be anybody's slave.

CHAPTER X

SANDY AND THE BOSS

MEET ADVENTURES

I paid three pennies for my breakfast, and a most extravagant price it was, too, seeing that one could have breakfasted a dozen persons for that money; but I was feeling good by this time, and I had always been a kind of spendthrift anyway; and then these people had wanted to give me the food for nothing, little as they had, and so it was a pleasure to show my appreciation and thankfulness with a good big financial lift where the money would do so much more good than it would in my helmet, where, these pennies being made of iron and heavy, my half-dollar's worth was a good deal of a burden to me. I spent money rather too freely in those days, it is true. One reason for it was that even yet, after so long a stay in Britain, I hadn't got along to where I was able absolutely to realize that a penny in Arthur's land and a couple of dollars in Connecticut were about one and the same thing. If my start from Camelot could have been delayed a very few days I could have paid these people in beautiful new coins from our own mint, and that would have pleased me and them too, not less. I had adopted the American values exclusively. In a week or two now, cents, nickels, dimes, quarters, and half-dollars, and also a trifle of gold, would be trickling in thin but steady streams all through the kingdom, and I looked to see this new blood freshen up its life.

The farmers were bound to throw in something whether I wanted it or not; so I let them give me a flint and steel; and as soon as they had comfortably bestowed Sandy and me on our horse, I lit my pipe. When the first blast of smoke shot out through the bars of my helmet, all those people broke for the woods, and Sandy went over backward and struck the ground with a dull thud. They thought I was one of those fire-belching dragons they had heard so much about from knights and other professional liars. I had great trouble to persuade those people to venture back within explaining distance. Then I told them that this was only a bit of enchantment which would work harm to none but my enemies. And I promised, with my hand on my heart, that if all who felt no enmity toward me would come forward and pass before me they should see that only those who remained behind would be struck dead. The procession moved with a good deal of promptness. There were no casualties to report, for nobody had curiosity enough to remain behind to see what would happen.

I lost some time now, for these big children, their fears gone, became so excited over my smoking that I had to stay there and smoke a couple of pipes out before they would let me go. However I had learned something from the delay, for their fright had given

I spouted a column of white smoke through the bars of my helmet.

me an idea. I was ready for any giant or any ogre that might come along, now.

We stayed with a holy hermit that night, and my opportunity came about the middle of the next afternoon. We were crossing a vast meadow by way of a short cut, and I was musing absently, hearing nothing, seeing nothing, when Sandy suddenly interrupted a remark which she had begun that morning, with the cry:

"Defend thee, lord!—peril of life is toward!"

And she slipped down from the horse and ran a little way and stood. I looked up and saw, far off in the shade of a tree, half a dozen armed knights and their squires; and straightway there was bustle among them and tightening of saddle-girths for the mount. My pipe was ready and would have been lit, if I had not been lost in thinking. I lit up at once, and by the time I had got a good head of reserved steam on, here they came. They came in a body, they came with a whir and a rush, they came like a volley from a battery; came with heads low down, plumes streaming out behind, lances advanced at a level. It was a handsome sight, a beautiful sight—for a man up a tree. I laid my lance in rest and waited, with my heart beating, till the iron wave was just ready to break over me, and then spouted a column of white smoke through the bars of my helmet. You should have seen the wave go to pieces and scatter! This was a finer sight than the other one.

But these people stopped two or three hundred yards away, and this troubled me. My satisfaction collapsed and fear came; I judged I was a lost man. But Sandy was radiant, and was going to be eloquent; but I stopped her and told her my magic had miscarried, somehow or other, and she must mount with all haste, and we must ride for life. No, she wouldn't. She said that my enchantment had disabled those knights; they were not riding on because they couldn't; wait, they would drop out of their saddles presently, and we would get their horses and harness. I could not deceive such trusting simplicity; so I said it was a mistake; that when my fireworks killed at all, they killed instantly; no, the men would not die; there was something wrong about my apparatus, I couldn't tell what; but we must hurry and get away, for those people would attack us again in a minute. Sandy laughed, and said:

"Lack-a-day, sir, they be not of that breed! Sir Launcelot will give battle to dragons, and will abide by them, and will assail them again, and yet again, and still again, until he do conquer and destroy them; and so likewise will Sir Pellinore and Sir Aglovale and Sir Carados, and maybe others, but there be none else that will venture it, let the idle say what the idle will. And, la, as to yonder base knights, think ye they have not their fill, but yet desire more?"

"Well, then, what are they waiting for? Why don't

they leave? Nobody's hindering. Good land, I'm willing to let bygones be bygones, I'm sure."

"Leave, is it? Oh, make thyself easy as to that. They dream not of it, no, not they. They wait to yield them."

"Come—really. If they want to, why don't they?"

"They would like to much; but if ye knew how dragons are esteemed, ye would not hold them blamable. They fear to come."

"Well, then, suppose I go to them instead, and—"

"Ah, they would not wait your coming. I will go."

And she did. She was a handy person to have along on a raid. I would have considered this a doubtful errand, myself. I presently saw the knights riding away and Sandy coming back. That was a relief. I judged she had somehow failed to get the first innings—I mean in the conversation; otherwise the interview wouldn't have been so short. But it turned out that she had managed the business well—in fact, admirably. She said that when she told those people I was The Boss, it struck them dumb: "smote them sore with fear and dread" were her words; and then they were ready to put up with anything she might require. So she swore them to appear at Arthur's court within two days and yield them, with horse and harness, and be my knights henceforth and subject to my command. How much better she managed that thing than I should have done it myself! She was a daisy.

"And so I'm proprietor of some knights," said I, as we rode off. "I shan't know what to do with them; unless I raffle them off. How many of them are there, Sandy?"

"Seven, please you sir, and their squires."

"It is a good haul. Who are they? Where do they hang out?"

"Where do they hang out?"

"Yes, where do they live?"

"Ah, I understood thee not. That will I tell thee."

Well I had set her going and I had to listen to her, though I knew she could go on for thirty days without getting down to any real facts. I listened and dozed and this is as much as I got of her long-winded story. The two knights Sir Gawaine and Sir Uwaine while riding in the forest saw twelve girls walking to and fro before a white shield on a tree, spitting at it and throwing mud on it. It seemed the shield was owned by a knight who was good enough in a fight but he hated women. This was their way of showing they didn't like it. The knight was Sir Marhaus, son of the king of Ireland. Well, Sir Gawaine and Sir Uwaine persuaded them to stop spitting on the shield and promised to meet the knight in a fight. They met him all right and the story of the fight was just like all the others I had heard—they came together and a spear was broken and one party went down—horse and man—and broke his neck. Then the next fellow rode in and broke his spear and shield and down he

We saw ahead the largest castle we had yet seen.

went—horse and man—and broke his neck, and this happened again and again until all the men were used up. You never can tell one fight from another nor who gets whipped, but it seems in this case, Sir Marhaus and the others made up and swore to live together as brothers. Then they all rode on together until they met three ladies and each knight took one behind him on his horse and one rode north, and one east, and the other south to seek adventure and meet again and tell lies after a year and a day.

That was as far as Sandy got when we saw ahead the largest castle we had yet seen, but she said it wasn't the one we were looking for.

As we approached the castle we met a horseman on the turn of the road. I saw he wore a plumed helmet and was otherwise clothed in steel. He had a curious addition which had grown out of an idea of my own—a kind of sandwich-board—which read "Persimmon's Soap—All the Prima Donnas Use It." It was part of my attempt to civilize these people. I had started out a number of the bravest knights with bulletin boards like this, bearing one sign or another. They were to spell out these gilt signs to lords and ladies they met and explain what soap was. If they were afraid of it, the knight was to get them to try it on a dog. If this didn't convince them, the knight was to try it on himself, and if this failed, to catch a hermit and try it on him. No knight was to give up until he had tried all these things. I had started a soap factory with only two hands, but business had grown so that I now had fifteen men and the factory was running night and day.

This knight we met was named La Cote Male Taile and he told us the castle was the home of Morgan le Fay, the sister of King Arthur and the wife of King Uriens, monarch of a kingdom so small you could stand in the middle of it and throw bricks into the next kingdom.

Well, Mrs. Le Fay had made everyone believe she was a great magician or sorceress. All her history was black with crime and among her crimes murder was common. To my surprise she was beautiful and looked so young she might have been a sister to her son, Sir Uwaine. She had a lovely voice and was full of pretty graces and I began to feel she had been lied about. But her handsome young page kneeling before her with something on a golden platter overdid his graces and lost his balance so that he fell lightly against her knee. She slipped a dagger into him in as matter of fact way as another person would have harpooned a rat. He slumped to the floor dead and Sir Uwaine called the servants to take the body out. She was a good housekeeper, for she watched the servants until they had cleaned up the last spot.

I happened to let drop a complimentary remark about King Arthur, having forgotten how she hated her brother. She clouded up like a storm and called to her guards, "Hale me these varmints to the dungeon."

Nothing occurred to me to say, but luckily Sandy had her wits about her and piped up, "Dost thou want destruction, maniac? It is The Boss." It worked like a charm and Le Fay pretended she had been joking to provoke some of my magic as she had known who I was.

CHAPTER XI

FROM BANQUET TO DUNGEON

Madame Le Fay, seeing me peaceful and unresentful, no doubt judged that I was deceived by her excuse; for her fright disappeared and she was soon so determined to have me give an exhibition and kill somebody, that the thing grew to be embarrassing. However, to my relief she was presently interrupted by the call to prayers. I will say this much for the nobility: that, tyrannical, murderous, and morally rotten as they were, they were deeply and enthusiastically religious. Nothing could keep them from the regular and faithful performance of the Church rites. More than once I had seen a noble who had gotten his enemy at a disadvantage, stop to pray before cutting his throat; more than once I had seen a noble, after ambushing and killing his enemy, retire to the nearest wayside shrine and humbly give thanks, without even waiting to rob the body. All the nobles of Britain, with their families, attended divine service morning and night daily in their private chapels, and even the worst of them had family worship five or six times a day besides.

After prayers we had dinner in a great banqueting-hall which was lighted by hundreds of grease-jets, and everything was as splendid as might become the royal degree of the hosts. At the head of the hall, on a raised platform, was the table of the king, queen, and their son, Prince Uwaine. Stretching down the hall from this, was the general table, on the floor. At this sat the visiting nobles and the grown members of their families—sixty-one persons; beyond sat minor officers of the household: altogether a hundred and eighteen persons sitting, and about as many servants standing behind their chairs, or serving in one way or another. It was a very fine show. In a gallery a band with cymbals, horns, harps, and other horrors, opened the proceedings with what seemed to be the crude first draft or original agony of the wail known to later centuries as "In the Sweet Bye and Bye." It was new, and ought to have been rehearsed a little more. For some reason or other the queen had the composer hanged after dinner.

After this music, the priest who stood behind the royal table said a noble long grace in Latin. Then the battalion of waiters broke away from their posts, and darted, rushed, flew, fetched and carried, and the mighty feeding began; no words anywhere, but absorbing attention to the business of eating. The mouths opened and shut in unison, and the sound of it was like the muffled hum of machinery.

The confusion continued an hour and a half, and unimaginable was the destruction of food. Of the chief feature of the feast—the huge wild boar that lay stretched out so imposing at the start—almost nothing was left; and the same thing had happened to all the other dishes.

With the pastries and so on, the heavy drinking began—and the talk. Gallon after gallon of wine and beer disappeared, and everybody got comfortable, then happy, then sparklingly joyous—both sexes—and by and by pretty noisy. Men told anecdotes that were terrific to hear, and the crowd let go with a horse-laugh that shook the fortress.

By midnight everybody was tired out and sore with laughing; and, as a rule, drunk; some weepingly, some affectionately, some hilariously, some quarrelsomely, some dead and under the table.

Suddenly, even while the priest was lifting his hands, and all conscious heads were bowed in reverent expectation of the coming blessing, there appeared under the arch of the far-off door at the bottom of the hall an old and bent and white-haired lady, leaning upon a crutch-stick; and she lifted the stick and pointed it toward the queen and cried out:

"The wrath and curse of God fall upon you, woman without pity, who have slain the page, mine innocent grandchild, and made desolate this old heart that had neither chick, nor friend, nor comfort in all this world but him!"

Everybody crossed himself in fright, for a curse was an awful thing to those people; but the queen rose up majestic, with the death-light in her eye, and flung back this ruthless command:

"Lay hands on her! To the stake with her!"

The guards left their posts to obey. It was a shame; it was a cruel thing to see. What could be done? Sandy gave me a look; I knew she had another inspiration. I said:

"Do what you choose."

She was up and facing toward the queen in a moment. She indicated me, and said:

"Madame, *he* says this may not be. Recall the order, or he will dissolve the castle and it shall vanish away like a dream!"

Confound it, what a crazy contract to pledge a person to! What if the queen—

But my panic passed off; for the queen, all in a collapse, took back her order and sunk into her seat. When she reached it she was sober. So were many of the others. The crowd rose and rushed for the door like a mob, overturning chairs, smashing crockery, tugging, struggling, shouldering, crowding—anything to get out before I should change my mind and puff the castle into space. Well, well, well, they *were* a superstitious lot.

The poor queen was so scared and humbled that she was even afraid to hang the composer without first consulting me. I was very sorry for her; indeed, anyone would have been, for she was really suffering; so I was willing to do anything that was reasonable, and had no desire to carry things to the limit. I therefore considered the matter thoughtfully, and ended

by having the musicians ordered into our presence to
play that Sweet Bye and Bye again, which they did.
Then I saw that she was right, and gave her permission to hang the whole band. This little relaxation of
sternness had a good effect upon the queen.

Now that the queen was at ease in her mind once
more and measurably happy, she began to feel the
wine. I mean it set her tongue going again. Dear me,
she was a master talker. It would not become me to
suggest that it was pretty late and that I was a tired
man and very sleepy. I wished I had gone off to bed
when I had the chance. Now I must stick it out; there
was no other way. So she tinkled along and along, in
the otherwise ghostly hush of the sleeping castle, until by and by there came, as if from deep down under
us, a far-away sound, as of a muffled shriek, with an
expression of agony about it that made my flesh crawl.
The queen stopped, and her eyes lighted with pleasure; she tilted her graceful head as a bird does when
it listens. The sound bored its way up through the
stillness again.

"What is it?" I said.

"It is truly a stubborn soul, and endureth long. It
is many hours now."

"Endureth what?"

"The rack. Come—ye shall see a merry sight. If he
yield not his secret now, ye shall see him torn asunder."

What a silky smooth devil she was, and so composed and serene, when the cords all down my legs were hurting in sympathy with that man's pain. Conducted by mailed guards bearing flaring torches, we tramped along echoing corridors and down stone stairways, dark and dripping and smelling of mold —a chill, uncanny journey and a long one. It was not made the shorter or the cheerier by the queen's talk, which was about this sufferer and his crime. He had been accused by an unnamed informer of having killed a deer in the royal forests. I said:

"Anonymous testimony isn't just the right thing, your Highness. It were fairer to confront the accused with the accuser."

"I had not thought of that, it being but of small consequence. But if I would, I could not, for the accuser came masked by night, and told the forester, and straightway got him hence again, and so the forester knoweth him not."

"Then is this Unknown the only person who saw the deer killed?"

"Marry, *no* man *saw* the killing, but this Unknown saw this hardy wretch near to the spot where the deer lay, and came with right loyal zeal and betrayed him to the forester."

"So the Unknown was near the dead deer, too? Isn't it just possible that he did the killing himself? His loyal zeal—in a mask—looks just a shade suspicious. But what is your Highness's idea for racking the prisoner? Where is the profit?"

"He will not confess, else; and then were his soul lost. For his crime his life is forfeited by the law—and of a surety will I see that he payeth it!—but it were peril to my own soul to let him die unconfessed and unabsolved. Nay, I were a fool to fling me into hell for *his* accommodation."

"But, your Highness, suppose he has nothing to confess?"

"As to that, we shall see anon. If I rack him to death and he confess not, it will perhaps show that he had indeed naught to confess—ye will grant that? Then shall I not be damned for an unconfessed man that had nothing to confess; wherefore, I shall be safe."

It was the stubborn unreasoning of the time. It was useless to argue with her. Arguments have no chance against such training.

As we entered the rack-cell I caught a picture that will not go from me; I wish it would. A native young giant of thirty or thereabouts lay stretched upon the frame on his back, with his wrists and ankles tied to ropes which led over windlasses at either end. There was no color in him; sweat-drops stood upon his forehead. A priest bent over him on each side; the executioner stood by; guards were on duty; smoking torches stood in sockets along the walls; in a corner crouched a poor young creature, her face drawn with pain, a half-wild and hunted look in her eyes, and in her lap lay a little child asleep. Just as we stepped across the threshold the executioner gave his machine a slight turn, which wrung a cry from both the prisoner and the woman; but I shouted, and the executioner released the strain without waiting to see who spoke. I could not let this horror go on; it would have killed me to see it. I asked the queen to let me clear the place and speak to the prisoner privately; and when she was going to object I spoke in a low voice and said I did not want to make a scene before her servants, but I must have my way, for I was King Arthur's representative and was speaking in his name. She saw she had to yield. I asked her to approve me to these people and then leave me. It was not pleasant for her, but she even went further than I was meaning to require. I only wanted the backing of her own authority, but she said:

"Ye will do in all things as this lord shall command. It is The Boss."

It was certainly a good word to play with; you could see it by the squirming of these rats. The queen's guards fell into line, and she and they marched away, with their torch-bearers. I had the prisoner taken from the rack and placed upon his bed, and medicine applied to his hurts, and wine given him to drink. The woman crept near and looked on, eagerly, lovingly, but fearfully; indeed, she tried slyly to touch the man's forehead, and jumped back, the picture of fright, when I turned unconsciously toward her. It was pitiful to see.

"Lord," I said, "stroke him, lass, if you want to. Do anything you're a mind to; don't mind me."

Why, her eyes were as grateful as an animal's when you do it a kindness that it understands. The baby was out of her way and she had her cheek against the man's in a minute, with her hands fondling his hair, and her happy tears running down. The man revived, and caressed his wife with his eyes, which was all he could do. I judged I might clear the den now, and I did; cleared it of all but the family and myself. Then I said:

"Now, my friend, tell me your side of this matter; I know the other side."

The man moved his head in sign of refusal. But the woman looked pleased—as it seemed to me—pleased with my suggestion. I went on:

"You know of me?"

"Yes. All do, in Arthur's realms."

"If my reputation has come to you right and straight, you should not be afraid to speak."

The woman broke in, eagerly:

"Ah, fair my lord, do thou persuade him! Thou canst if thou wilt. Ah, he suffereth so; and it is for me—for *me!* And how can I bear it? I would I might see him die—a sweet, swift death; oh, my Hugo, I cannot bear this!"

And she fell begging at my feet. Begging what?

The man's death? I could not quite get the bearings of the thing. But Hugo interrupted her and said:

"Peace! Ye know not what ye ask. Shall I starve whom I love, to win a gentle death? I thought thou knewest me better."

"Well," I said, "I can't quite make this out. It is a puzzle. Now—"

"Ah, dear my lord, if ye will but persuade him! Consider how his tortures wound me! Oh, and he will not speak!—whereas, the healing, the comfort that lie in a blessed swift death—"

"What *are* you jabbering about? He's going out from here a free man and whole—he's not going to die."

The man's white face lit up, and the woman flung herself at me in a most surprising joy, and cried out:

"He is saved!—for it is the king's word by the mouth of the king's servant—Arthur, the king whose word is gold!"

"Well, then you do believe I can be trusted, after all. Why didn't you before?"

"Who doubted? Not I, indeed, and not she."

"Well, why wouldn't you tell me your story, then?"

"Ye had made no promise, else had it been otherwise."

"I see, I see. . . . And yet I believe I don't quite see, after all. You stood the torture and refused to confess, which shows plain enough to even the dullest understanding that you had nothing to confess—"

"*I*, my lord? How so? It was I that killed the deer!"

"You did? Oh, dear, this is the most mixed-up business that ever—"

"Dear lord, I begged him on my knees to confess, but—"

"You *did!* It gets thicker and thicker. What did you want him to do that for?"

"Since it would bring him a quick death and save him all this cruel pain."

"Well, yes, there is reason in that. But *he* didn't want the quick death."

"He? Why, of a surety he *did.*"

"Well, then, why in the world *didn't* he confess?"

"Ah, sweet sir, and leave my wife and chick without bread and shelter?"

"Oh, heart of gold, now I see it! The bitter law takes the convicted man's estate and beggars his widow and his orphans. They could torture you to death, but without conviction or confession they could not rob your wife and baby. You stood by them like a man; and *you*—true wife and true woman that you are—you would have bought him release from torture at the cost to yourself of slow starvation and death. Well, it humbles a body to think what your sex can do when it comes to self-sacrifice. I'll book you both for my colony; you'll like it there; it's a factory where I'm going to turn slaves into *men.*"

Well, I arranged all that, and I had the man sent to his home. The queen was a good deal put out next morning, when she found she was going to have neither Hugo's life nor his property. But I told her she must bear this, as in Arthur the king's name I had pardoned him.

I had had enough of this place by this time and wanted to leave, but I couldn't because I had something on my mind that my conscience kept hurting me about, and wouldn't let me forget. If I had the re-making of man, he wouldn't have any conscience.

There was something I wanted to do before leaving, but it was a disagreeable matter and I hated to go at it. Well, it bothered me all the morning. I could have mentioned it to the old king, but what would be the use? He had been active in his time, but his time was past, this good while. He was nothing, this so-called king; the queen was the only power here, and you couldn't tell what she would do.

However, I braced up and placed my matter before her royal Highness. I said I had been having a general jail delivery at Camelot and among neighboring castles, and with her permission I would like to ex-amine her collection—that is to say, her prisoners. She resisted but she finally consented. I was expecting that, but not so soon. She called her guards and torches, and we went down into the dungeons. These were down under the castle's foundations, and mainly were small cells hollowed out of the living rock. Some of these cells had no light at all. In one of them was a woman in foul rags, who sat on the ground and would not answer a question or speak a word, but only looked up at us once or twice through a cobweb of tangled hair, as if to see what thing it might be that was disturbing the meaningless dull dream that had become her life; after that, she sat bowed and gave no further sign. This poor rack of bones seemed to be a woman of middle age, but was only twenty-seven. She was a commoner who had been sent here on her bridal night by a neighboring lord who had demanded her for himself. The young husband had interfered and the lord had had both of them thrown in this dungeon, since his own was full. They had passed nine dark years within fifty feet of each other, yet neither knew the other was there nor indeed whether the other was alive or not. I asked to see the man. He was thirty-four and looked sixty. He sat upon a squared block of stone with his head bent down, his long hair hanging like a fringe before his face, muttering to himself. He raised his head and looked at us dully, and then dropped it again and fell to muttering as before. I could not rouse him and so I said I would take him to her—to the bride who had been the fairest thing on earth to him. The sight of her would surely set his blood racing. It was a disappointment. They sat together looking dimly into each other's eyes for a while, then dropped their eyes and were away again in some land of dreams and shadows. I had them taken out and sent to their friends.

Dear me, for what trifling offenses the most of

those men and women were shut up there—forty-seven of them. Indeed, some were there for no distinct offense at all, but only because of somebody's spite; and not always the queen's by any means, but sometimes a friend's. The newest prisoner's crime was a mere remark which he had made. He said he believed that men were about all alike, and one man as good as another, barring clothes. He said he believed that if you were to strip the nation naked and send a stranger through the crowd, he couldn't tell the king from a quack doctor, nor a duke from a hotel clerk. Apparently, here was a man whose brains had not been reduced to mush by idiotic training. I set him loose and sent him to the factory.

Some of the cells carved in the living rock were just behind the face of the precipice, and in each of these an arrow-slit had been pierced outward to the daylight, and so the captive had a thin ray from the blessed sun for his comfort. The case of one of these poor fellows was particularly hard. From the hole high up in that vast wall of native rock he could peer out through the arrow-slit and see his own home off yonder in the valley; and for twenty-two years he had watched it, with heartache and longing, through that crack. He could see the lights shine there at night, and in the daytime he could see figures go in and come out —his wife and children, some of them no doubt, though he could not make out at that distance. In the course of years he noted festivities there, and tried to rejoice, and wondered if they were weddings or what they might be. And he noted funerals, and they wrung his heart. He could make out the coffin, but he could not determine its size, and so could not tell whether it was wife or child. He had left behind him five children and a wife; and in nineteen years he had seen five funerals pass. So he had lost five of his family; there must still be one remaining—one now infinitely, unspeakably precious—but *which* one, wife or child? That was the question that tortured him, by night and by day, asleep and awake. Well, to have an interest of some sort, and half a ray of light when you are in a dungeon, is a great support to the body and preserver of the intellect. This man was in pretty good condition yet. By the time he had finished telling me his distressful tale, I was in the same state of mind that you would have been in yourself, if you have got average human curiosity; that is to say, I was as burning up as he was to find out which member of the family it was that was left. So I took him over home myself; and an amazing kind of surprise party it was, too. We found the one-time young wife 50 years old, and the babies all men and women, and some of them married and experimenting familywise themselves—for not a soul of the tribe was dead! Imagine the devilishness of that queen: she had a special hatred for this prisoner, and she had *invented* all those funerals herself to scorch his heart; and the stroke of genius of the whole thing was leaving the family a funeral *short,* so as to let him wear his poor old soul out guessing.

But for me, he never would have got out. Morgan le Fay hated him with her whole heart, and she never would have softened toward him. And yet his crime was committed more in thoughtlessness than wickedness. He had said she had red hair.

Consider it: among these forty-seven captives there were five whose names, offenses, and dates of imprisonment were no longer known! One woman and four men, all bent and wrinkled, with minds gone. They themselves had long ago forgotten these details; at any rate, they had mere vague theories about them, nothing definite and nothing that they repeated twice in the same way. The priests had stories about them but nothing more. Even by the help of these stories the only thing that could be proven was that none of the five had seen daylight for thirty-five years; how much longer this had lasted was not guessable. The king and queen knew nothing about these poor creatures, except that they were inherited, along with the throne, from the former firm. Nothing of their history had been given with their persons, and so the inheriting owners had considered them of no value, and had felt no interest in them. I said to the queen:

"Then why in the world didn't you set them free?"

The question was a puzzler. She didn't know *why* she hadn't; the thing had never come up in her mind.

When I brought my procession of human bats up into the open world, they were a sight to look at—skeletons, scarecrows, goblins, pathetic frights, every one. I muttered absently:

"I wish I could photograph them!"

You have seen those kinds of people who will never let on that they don't know the meaning of a new big word. The more ignorant they are, the more pitifully certain they are to pretend you haven't shot over their heads. The queen was just one of that sort and was always making the stupidest blunders by reason of it. She hesitated a moment; then her face brightened up with sudden understanding, and she said she would do it for me.

I thought to myself: She? why what can she know about photography? But it was a poor time to be thinking. When I looked around, she was moving on the procession with an ax!

Well, she certainly was a curious one, was Morgan le Fay. I have seen a good many kinds of women in my time, but she beat them all for variety. And how like her this act was. She had no more idea than a horse of how to photograph a procession; but being in doubt, it was just like her to try to do it with an ax.

CHAPTER XII

THE OGRE'S CASTLE

Sandy and I were on the road again next morning, bright and early. It was so good to open up one's lungs and take in fresh air after being for two days in that intolerable place.

Between six and nine we made ten miles, which was plenty for a horse carrying triple—man, woman, and armor; then we stopped for a long noon under some trees by a brook.

By and by a knight came riding; and as he drew near he made sad moan, and by the words of it I perceived that he was cursing and swearing; yet nevertheless was I glad of his coming, for I saw that he bore a bulletin-board whereon in letters all of shining gold was written:

"USE PETERSON'S PROPHYLACTIC TOOTH-
BRUSH—ALL THE GO"

I was glad of his coming, for even by this token I knew him for knight of mine. It was Sir Madok de la Montaine, a burly great fellow whose chief distinction was that he had come within an ace of sending Sir Launcelot down over his horse-tail once. He was never long in a stranger's presence without finding some excuse or other to let out that great fact. But there was another fact of nearly the same size, which

115

he never pushed upon anybody unasked, and yet never withheld when asked: that was, that the reason he didn't quite succeed, was that he was interrupted and sent down over horse-tail himself. This innocent lubber did not see any particular difference between the two facts. I liked him, for he was earnest in his work, and very valuable. He was so fine to look at, with his broad mailed shoulders, and the grand lion-like set of his plumed head, and his big shield with its quaint device of a hand clutching a prophylactic toothbrush, with motto: "Try Noyoudont." This was a toothwash that I was introducing.

He was aweary he said, and indeed he looked it; but he would not alight. He said he was after the stove-polish man, and with this he broke out cursing anew. The bulletin-boarder referred to was Sir Ossaise of Surluse, a brave knight, and of considerable fame on account of his having met in a tournament, once, with no less a knight than Sir Gaheris himself— although not successfully. He was of a light and laughing disposition, and to him nothing in this world was serious. It was for this reason that I had chosen him to work up a stove-polish sentiment. There were no stoves yet, and so there could be nothing serious about stove-polish. All that the agent needed to do was skilfully and by degrees to prepare the public for the great change, and have them ready for the time when the stove would appear upon the stage.

Sir Madok was very bitter. He said he had cursed

his soul to rags; and yet he would not get down from his horse, neither would he take any rest, nor listen to any comfort, until he should have found Sir Ossaise and settled this account. It appeared, by what I could piece together of his statement, that he had chanced upon Sir Ossaise at dawn of the morning, and been told that if he would make a short cut across the fields and swamps and broken hills and glades, he could head off a company of travelers who would be rare customers for prophylactics and toothwash. With characteristic zeal Sir Madok had plunged away at once upon this quest, and after three hours of awful cross-lot riding had overhauled his game. And behold, it was the five old prisoners that had been released from the dungeons the evening before! Poor old creatures, it was all of twenty years since any one of them had known what it was to be equipped with any remaining snag or remnant of a tooth.

"Blank-blank-blank him," said Sir Madok, "if I do not stove-polish him if I find him, leave it to me; for never a knight that is called Ossaise or anything else may do this to me and live if I find him."

And with these words and others, he lightly took his spear and rode on. In the middle of the afternoon we came upon one of those very same released prisoners ourselves, in the edge of a poor village. He was enjoying the love of relatives and friends whom he had not seen for fifty years; and about him and caressing him were also descendants of his own body whom he had never seen at all till now, but to him these were all strangers; his memory was gone, his mind was gone. It seemed incredible that a man could outlast half a century shut up in a dark hole like a rat, but here were his old wife and some old comrades to testify to it. They could remember him as he was in the freshness and strength of his young manhood, when he kissed his child and delivered it to its mother's hands and went away into that long imprisonment. The people at the castle could not tell within half a generation the length of time the man had been shut up there for his unrecorded and forgotten offense; but his old wife knew; and so did her old child, who stood there among her married sons and daughters trying to realize a father who had been to her a name, a thought, all her life, and now was suddenly actual flesh and blood before her face.

It was a curious situation; yet it is not on that account that I have made room for it here, but on account of a thing which seemed to me still more curious: That is, that this dreadful matter brought from these downtrodden people no outburst of rage against these oppressors. They had been subjects of cruelty and outrage so long that nothing could have startled them but a kindness. Yes, here was a curious revelation, indeed, of the depth to which these people had been sunk in slavery. Their entire being was reduced to a monotonous dead level of patience, resignation, dumb uncomplaining acceptance of whatever might befall them in this life. Their very imagination was dead. When you can say that of a man, he has struck bottom, I reckon; there is no lower deep for him.

I rather wished I had gone some other road. This was not the sort of experience for a statesman to encounter who was planning out a peaceful revolution in his mind. For it could not help bringing up the fact that no people in the world ever did achieve their freedom by goody-goody talk and moral persuasion; all revolutions that will succeed must *begin* in blood, whatever may answer afterward. If history teaches anything, it teaches that. What this folk needed, then, was a Reign of Terror and a guillotine, and I was the wrong man for them.

Two days later, toward noon, Sandy began to show signs of excitement. She said we were approaching the ogre's castle. I was surprised into an uncomfortable shock. The object of our search had gradually dropped out of my mind; and now it seemed quite a real and startling thing for a moment, and roused up in me a smart interest. Sandy's excitement increased every moment; and so did mine, for that sort of thing is catching. My heart got to thumping. You can't reason with your heart; it has its own laws, and thumps about things which the mind scorns. Presently, when Sandy slid from the horse, motioned me to stop, and went creeping quietly, with her head bent nearly to her knees, toward a row of bushes that bordered a valley, the thumpings grew stronger and quicker. And they kept it up while she was gaining her ambush and getting her glimpse over the valley, and also while I was creeping to her side on my knees. Her eyes were burning now, as she pointed with her finger, and said in a panting whisper:

"The castle! The castle! Lo, where it looms!"

What a welcome disappointment I experienced! I said:

"Castle? It is nothing but a pigsty, a pigsty with a fence around it."

She looked surprised and distressed. The excitement faded out of her face; and during many moments she was lost in thought and silent. Then:

"It was not enchanted before," she said as if to herself. "And how strange is this marvel, and how awful —that to the one it is enchanted and appears base and shameful; yet to the other it is not enchanted, has suffered no change, but stands firm and stately still, with its moat, and waving its banners in the blue air from its towers."

I saw my cue. The castle was enchanted to *me*, not to her. It would be wasted time to try to argue her out of the idea; it couldn't be done; I must just humor it. So I said:

"This is a common case—the enchanting of a thing to one eye and leaving it in its proper form to another. You have heard of it before, Sandy, though you haven't happened to experience it. But no harm is done. In fact, it is lucky the way it is. If these ladies were hogs to everybody and to themselves, it would be necessary to break the enchantment, and that might be impossible if one failed to find out the particular process of the enchantment. And dangerous, too; for in attempting a disenchantment without the true key, you are liable to make a mistake, and turn your hogs into dogs, and the dogs into cats, the cats into rats, and so on. But here, by good luck, no one's eyes but mine are under the enchantment, and so it is of no consequence to dissolve it. These ladies remain ladies to you, and to themselves, and to everybody else; and at the same time they will suffer in no way from my mistaken idea, for when I know that what looks like a hog is a lady, that is enough for me; I know how to treat her."

"Thanks, oh, sweet my lord, thou talkest like an angel. And I know that thou wilt deliver them, for thou art as strong a knight and as brave as any that is alive."

"I will not leave a princess in the sty, Sandy. Are those three yonder that to my eyes are starving swineherds—"

"The ogres? Are *they* changed also? It is most wonderful. Now am I fearful; for how canst thou strike with sure aim when five of their fifteen feet of height are to thee invisible? Ah, go carefully, fair sir; this is a mightier task than I knew."

"You be easy, Sandy. All I need to know is, how

much of an ogre is invisible; then I know how to locate his vitals. Don't you be afraid, I will make short work of these bunco-steerers. Stay where you are."

I left Sandy kneeling there, corpse-faced but plucky and hopeful, and rode down to the pigsty and struck up a trade with the swineherds. I won their gratitude by buying out all the hogs at the lump sum of sixteen pennies, which was rather above latest quotations. I was just in time; for the Church, the lord of the manor, and the rest of the tax-gatherers would have been along next day and swept off pretty much all the stock, leaving the swineherds very short of hogs and Sandy out of princesses. But now the tax people could be paid in cash, and there would be a stake left besides.

I sent the three men away, and then opened the sty gate and beckoned Sandy to come—which she did, not leisurely, but with the rush of a prairie fire. And when I saw her fling herself upon those hogs, with tears of joy running down her cheeks, and strain them to her heart, and kiss them, and caress them, and call them reverently by grand princely names, I was ashamed of her, ashamed of the human race.

We had to drive those hogs home—ten miles; and no ladies were ever more fickle-minded or contrary. They would stay in no road, no path; they broke out through the brush on all sides, and flowed away in all directions, over rocks, and hills, and the roughest places they could find. And they must not be struck or roughly handled; Sandy could not bear to see them treated in ways unbecoming their rank. The trouble-somest old sow of the lot had to be called my Lady, and your Highness, like the rest. It is annoying and difficult to scour around after hogs, in armor. There was one small countess, with an iron ring in her snout and hardly any hair on her back, that was the devil for contrariness. She gave me a race of an hour, over all sorts of country, and then we were right where we had started from, having made not a rod of real progress. I seized her at last by the tail, and brought her along squealing. When I overtook Sandy she was horrified, and said it was in the last degree indelicate to drag a countess by her train.

We got the hogs home just at dark—most of them. The princess Nerovens de Morganore was missing, and two of her ladies in waiting: namely, Miss Angela Bohun, and the Demoiselle Elaine Courtemains, the former of these two being a young black sow with a white star in her forehead, and the latter a brown one with thin legs and a slight limp in the forward shank on the starboard side—a couple of the trying-est animals to drive that I ever saw. Also among the missing were several mere baronesses—and I wanted them to stay missing; but no, all that sausage-meat had to be found; so servants were sent out with torches to scour the woods and hills to that end.

Of course, the whole drove was housed in the house, and, great guns!—well, I never saw anything like it, nor ever heard anything like it. And I never smelled anything like it.

CHAPTER XIII

THE PILGRIMS

When I did get to bed at last I was unspeakably tired; the stretching-out and the relaxing of the long-tense muscles, how luxurious, how delicious! But that was as far as I could get—sleep was out of the question for the present. The ripping and tearing and squealing of the nobility up and down the halls and corridors kept me broad awake. Being awake, my thoughts were busy, of course; and mainly they busied themselves with Sandy's curious idea. Here she was, as sane a person as the kingdom could produce; and yet, from my point of view she was acting like a crazy woman. My land, the power of training! of influence! of education! It can bring a body up to believe anything. I had to put myself in Sandy's place to realize that she was not crazy. Yes, and put her in mine, to show how easy it is to seem crazy to a person who has not been taught as you have been taught. If I had told Sandy I had seen a wagon, without enchantment, spin along fifty miles an hour; had seen a man, unequipped with magic powers, get into a basket and soar out of sight among the clouds; and had listened, without any magician's help, to the conversation of a person who was several hundred miles away, Sandy would not merely have supposed me to be crazy, she would have thought she knew it. Everybody around her believed in enchantments; nobody had any doubts; to doubt that a castle could be turned into a sty, and its occupants into hogs, would have been the same as my doubting, among Connecticut people, the reality of the telephone and its wonders—and in both cases would be absolute proof of a diseased mind, an unsettled reason. Yes, Sandy was sane; that must be admitted. If I wished Sandy also to think me sane, I must keep my information about locomotives, balloons, and telephones to myself. Also, I believed that the world was not flat, and hadn't pillars under it to support it, nor a roof over it to keep off water that occupied all space above; but as I was the only person in the kingdom with such opinions, I recognized that it would be good wisdom to keep quiet about this matter, too, if I did not wish to be suddenly shunned and forsaken by everybody as a madman.

The next morning Sandy gathered the swine in the dining-room and gave them their breakfast, waiting upon them personally and showing in every way the deep reverence which the natives of her island, ancient and modern, have always felt for rank. I could have eaten with the hogs if I had had birth approaching my lofty official rank; but I hadn't, and so accepted the slight and made no complaint. Sandy and I had our breakfast at the second table. The family were not at home. I said:

"How many are in the family, Sandy, and where do they keep themselves?"

"Family?"

"Yes."

"Which family, good my lord?"

"Why, this family; your own family."

"Sooth to say, I understand you not. I have no family."

"No family? Why, Sandy, isn't this your home?"

"Now how indeed might that be? I have no home."

"Well, then whose house is this?"

"Ah, I would surely tell you if I knew myself."

"Come, you don't even know these people? Then who invited us here?"

"None invited us. We but came; that is all."

"Why, woman, this a most extraordinary performance. The boldness of it is beyond admiration. We march into a man's house and cram it full of the only really valuable nobility the sun has yet discovered in the earth, and then it turns out that we don't even know the man's name. Why did you ever take this extravagant liberty? I supposed, of course, it was your home. What will the man say?"

"What will he say? Forsooth what can he say but give thanks?"

"Thanks for what?"

Her face was filled with a puzzled surprise:

"Verily, thou troublest mine understanding with strange words. Do ye dream that one of his position is like to have the honor twice in his life to entertain company such as we have brought to grace his house?"

"Well, no—when you come to that. No, it's an even

bet that this is the first time he has had a treat like this."

"Then let him be thankful, and show the same by grateful speech."

To my mind, the situation was uncomfortable. It might become more so. It might be a good idea to muster the hogs and move on. So I said:

"The day is wasting, Sandy. It is time to get the nobility together and be moving."

"Wherefore, fair sir and Boss?"

"We want to take them to their home, don't we?"

"La, but list to him! They be of all the regions of the earth! Each must go to her own home. Life is too short for us to take all the journeys."

"Who is to take the aristocracy home?"

"Even their friends. These will come for them from the far parts of the earth."

This was lightning from a clear sky, for unexpectedness; and the relief of it was like pardon to a prisoner. She would remain to deliver the goods, of course.

"Well, then, Sandy, as our enterprise is handsomely and successfully ended, I will go home and report; and if ever another one—"

"I also am ready; I will go with thee."

This was recalling the pardon.

"How? You will go with me? Why should you?"

"Will I be traitor to my knight, dost think? That were dishonor. I may not part from thee until some stronger champion shall fairly win me. I would be to blame if I thought that that might ever happen."

"Elected for the long term," I sighed to myself. "I may as well make the best of it." So then I spoke up and said:

"All right, let us make a start."

While she was gone to cry her farewells over the pork, I gave all the nobility away to the servants. And I asked them to take a duster and dust around a little where the nobilities had mainly lodged and walked about; but they considered that that would be hardly worth while, and would moreover be unusual, and therefore likely to make talk. That settled it; it was a nation capable of committing any crime but the unusual. The servants said they would follow the fashion, a fashion grown sacred through long custom; they would scatter fresh rushes in all the rooms and halls, and then the evidence of the aristocratic visit would be no longer visible.

The first thing we struck that day was a procession of pilgrims. It was not going our way but we joined it, nevertheless; for I saw that if I would govern this country wisely, I must be posted in the details of its life, and not at second hand, but by personal observation.

This company of pilgrims had in it a sample of about all the upper occupations and professions the country could show, and a corresponding variety of costume. There were young men and old men, young women and old women, lively folk and grave folk. They rode upon mules and horses.

Sandy knew the goal and purpose of this pilgrimage, and she told me.

"They journey to the Valley of Holiness, to be blessed by the godly hermits and drink of the miraculous waters and be cleansed from sin."

"Where is this watering-place?"

"It lieth a two-day journey hence, by the borders of the land called the Cuckoo Kingdom."

"Tell me about it. Is it a celebrated place?"

"Oh, of a truth, yes. There be none more so. Of old time there lived there an abbot and his monks. There were none in the world more holy than these; for they studied pious books, and spoke not the one to the other, or indeed to any, and ate decayed herbs and nothing else; and slept hard, and prayed much, and washed never; also they wore the same garment until it fell from their bodies. So came they to be known to all the world by reason of their holiness, and visited by rich and poor, and reverenced."

"Proceed."

"But always there was lack of water there. Whereas, upon a time, the holy abbot prayed, and for answer a great stream of clear water burst forth by miracle in a desert place. Now were the fickle monks tempted, and they begged their abbot that he would construct a bath; and when he was weary and couldn't refuse to give in to them, he granted their request. These monks did enter into the bath and come thence washed as white as snow; and lo, in that moment God's sign appeared in miraculous rebuke! for His insulted waters ceased to flow, and utterly vanished away."

"They fared mildly, Sandy, considering how that kind of crime is regarded in this country."

"Perhaps; but it was their first sin; and they had been of perfect life for long. Prayers, tears, torturings of the flesh—all was vain to cause that water to flow again. Even processions, even burnt offerings, even candles to the Virgin did fail all of them; and all in the land did marvel. And so upon a time, after a year and a day, the good abbot destroyed the bath. And behold, God's anger was in that moment satisfied, and the waters gushed richly forth again, and even unto this day they have not ceased to flow in that generous measure."

"Then I take it nobody has washed since."

"He that would try it would be hung."

"The community has prospered since?"

"Even from that very day. The fame of the miracle went abroad into all lands. From every land came monks to join; they came even as the fishes come, in shoals; and the monastery added building to building, and yet others to these, and so spread wide its arms and took them in. And nuns came also, and more again, and yet more, and built over against the monastery on the other side of the valley and added building to building, until mighty was that nunnery. And these were friendly unto those, and they joined their loving labors together, and together they built a fair great orphan asylum midway of the valley between."

"You spoke of some hermits, Sandy."

"These have gathered there from the ends of the earth. A hermit thrives best where there be multitudes of pilgrims. Ye shall not find a hermit of any sort wanting. If any shall mention a hermit of a kind he thinketh new and not to be found but in some far strange land, let him but scratch among the holes and caves and swamps that line that Valley of Holiness, and whatsoever be his breed, it matters not, he shall find a sample of it there."

Early in the afternoon we overtook another procession of pilgrims; but in this one was no merriment, no jokes, no laughter, no playful ways, nor any happy giddiness, whether of youth or age. Yet both were here, both age and youth; gray old men and women, strong men and women of middle age, young husbands, young wives, little boys and girls, and three babies at the breast. Even the children were smileless; there was not a face among all these half a hundred people but was cast down, and bore that set expression of hopelessness which comes from long and hard trials and despair. They were slaves. Chains led from their fettered feet and their bound hands to a leather belt about their waists; and all except the children were also linked together in a file, six feet apart, by a single chain which led from collar to collar all down the line. They were on foot, and had tramped three hundred miles in eighteen days, upon the cheapest odds and ends of food, and stingy rations of that. They had slept in these chains every night, bundled togther like swine. They had upon their bodies some poor rags, but they could not be said to be clothed. Their irons had chafed the skin from their ankles and made sores which were ulcerated and wormy. Their naked feet were torn, and none walked without a limp. Originally, there had been a hundred of these unfortunates, but about half had been sold on the trip. The trader in charge of them rode a horse and carried a whip with a short handle and a long heavy lash divided into several knotted tails at the end. With this whip he cut the shoulders of any that tottered from weariness and pain, and straightened them up. He did not speak; the whip was enough. None of these poor creatures looked up as we rode along by; they showed no consciousness of our presence. And they made no sound but one: that was the dull and awful clank of their chains from end to end of the long file, as forty-three burdened feet rose and fell together. The file moved in a cloud of its own making.

All these faces were gray with a coating of dust. I noticed the faces of some of the women, young mothers carrying babes that were near to death, how a something in their hearts was written in the dust upon their faces, plain to see, and lord, how plain to read! for it was the track of tears. One of these young mothers was but a girl, and it hurt me to the heart to see such misery in one that should not yet know trouble.

She stumbled just then with fatigue, and down came the lash and flicked a flake of skin from her naked shoulder. It stung me as if I had been hit instead. The master halted the file and jumped from his horse. He stormed and swore at this girl and said she had made trouble enough with her laziness, and as this was the last chance he should have, he would settle the account now. She dropped on her knees and put up her hands and began to beg, and cry, and implore, in a passion of terror, but the master gave no attention. He snatched the child from her, and then made the men-slaves who were chained before and behind her throw her on the ground and hold her there and expose her body; and then he laid on with his lash like a madman till her back was flayed, she shrieking and struggling the while piteously. One of the men who was holding her turned away his face, and for this was flogged.

All our pilgrims looked on and commented—on the expert way in which the whip was handled. They were too much hardened by lifelong every-day familiarity with slavery to notice that there was anything wrong in this. This was what slavery could do;

for these pilgrims were kind-hearted people, and they would not have allowed that man to treat a horse like that.

I wanted to stop the whole thing and set the slaves free, but that would not do. I must not interfere too much and get myself a name for riding over the country's laws and the citizen's rights rough-shod. If I lived and prospered I would be the death of slavery, that I was resolved upon; but I would try to fix it so that when I became its executioner it should be by command of the nation.

Just here was the wayside shop of a smith; and now arrived a landed proprietor who had bought this girl a few miles back deliverable here where her irons could be taken off. They were removed; then there was a squabble between the gentleman and the dealer as to which should pay the blacksmith. The moment the girl was delivered from her irons, she flung herself, all tears and frantic sobbings, into the arms of the slave who had turned away his face when she was whipped. He strained her to his breast and smothered her face and the child's with kisses, and washed them with the rain of his tears. I suspected. I inquired. Yes, I was right; it was husband and wife. They had to be torn apart by force; the girl had to be dragged away, and she struggled and fought and shrieked like one gone mad till a turn of the road hid her from sight; and even after that, we could still make out the fading shrieks. And the husband and father, with his wife and child gone, never to be seen by him again in life?—well, the look of him one might not bear at all, and so I turned away; but I knew I should never get his picture out of my mind again, and there it is to this day, to wring my heart-strings whenever I think of it.

We put up at the inn in a village just at nightfall, and when I rose next morning and looked abroad, I saw a knight come riding in the golden glory of the new day, and recognized him for knight of mine—Sir Ozana le Cure Hardy. He was in the gentlemen's furnishing line, and his specialty was plug-hats. He was clothed all in steel, in the beautifulest armor of the time—up to where his helmet ought to have been; but he hadn't any helmet; he wore a shiny stove-pipe hat, and was as ridiculous a sight as one might want to see. It was another of my schemes for ending knighthood by making it absurd. Sir Ozana's saddle was hung about with leather hat-boxes, and every time he overcame a wandering knight he swore him into my service and fitted him with a hat and made him wear it. I dressed and ran down to welcome Sir Ozana and get his news.

"How is trade?" I asked.

"Ye will note that I have but these four left; yet were they sixteen when I left Camelot."

"Why, you have certainly done nobly, Sir Ozana. Where have you been of late?"

"I am but now come from the Valley of Holiness, please you sir."

"I am headed for that place myself. Is there anything stirring in the monkery, more than common?"

"Sir, it is startling news I bring, and—be these pilgrims? Then ye may not do better, good folk, than gather and hear the tale I have to tell, since it concerns you. Something has happened, the like of which has not been seen but once this two hundred years— the fountain hath ceased to flow."

"The miraculous fountain hath ceased to flow!" This shout burst from twenty pilgrim mouths at once.

"Ye say well, good people."

"Has somebody been washing again?"

"Nay, it is suspected, but none believe it. It is thought to be some other sin, but none know what."

"How are they feeling about the disaster?"

"None may describe it in words. The fountain is these nine days dry. The prayers that did begin then, and the holy processions have not ceased night nor day; and so the monks and the nuns and the orphans be all exhausted, and do hang up prayers written upon parchment, since no strength is left in man to lift up voice. And at last they sent for thee, Sir Boss, to try magic and enchantment; and if you could not come, then was the messenger to fetch Merlin, and he is there these three days now, and says he will fetch that water though he burst the globe and wreck its kingdoms to accomplish it; and right bravely doth he work his magic and call upon his helpers to come to him, but not a whiff of moisture hath he started yet."

Breakfast was ready. As soon as it was over I

showed to Sir Ozana these words which I had written on the inside of his hat: *Chemical Department, Laboratory extension, Section G. Pxxp. Send two of first size, two of No. 3, and six of No. 4, together with the proper complementary details—and two of my trained assistants.* And I said:

"Now get you to Camelot as fast as you can fly, brave knight, and show the writing to Clarence, and tell him to have these required matters in the Valley of Holiness with all possible haste."

"I will well, Sir Boss," and he was off.

CHAPTER XIV

THE HOLY FOUNTAIN

The pilgrims were human beings. Otherwise they would have acted differently. They had come a long and difficult journey, and now when the journey was nearly finished, and they learned that the main thing they had come for had ceased to exist, they didn't do as horses or cats or angleworms would probably have done—turn back and get at something profitable; no, anxious as they had before been to see the miraculous fountain, they were as much as forty times as anxious now to see the place where it had used to be. There is no accounting for human beings.

We made good time, and a couple of hours before sunset we stood upon the edge of the Valley of Holiness, and our eyes swept it from end to end. There were three masses of buildings that seemed in the distance like toy constructions in the lonely waste of what seemed a desert—and was. Such a scene is always mournful; it is so still, and looks so death-like. But there was a sound here which interrupted the stillness only to add to its mournfulness; this was the faint far sound of tolling bells which floated fitfully to us on the passing breeze, and so faintly, so softly, that we hardly knew whether we heard it with our ears or with our spirits.

We reached the monastery before dark, and there the males were given lodging, but the women were sent over to the nunnery. The bells were close at hand now, and their solemn booming fell upon the ear like a message of doom. A superstitious despair possessed the heart of every monk and showed in his ghastly face. Everywhere, these black-robed, soft-sandaled, pale-faced ghosts appeared, flitted about and disappeared, noiseless as the creatures of a troubled dream.

The old abbot's joy to see me was pathetic, even to tears; but he did the shedding himself. He said:

"Delay not, son, but get to thy saving work. If we bring not the water back again, and soon, we are ruined, and the good work of two hundred years must end. And see thou do it with enchantments that be holy, for the Church will not endure that work in her cause be done by devil's magic."

"When I work, Father, be sure there will be no devil's work connected with it. I shall use no arts that come of the devil, and no elements not created by the hand of God. But is Merlin working strictly on pious lines?"

"Ah, he said he would, my son, he said he would, and took oath to make his promise good."

"Well, in that case, let him proceed."

"But surely you will not sit idle by, but help?"

"It will not answer to mix methods, Father; neither would it be professional courtesy. Two of a trade must not underbid each other. We might as well cut rates and be done with it; it would arrive at that in the end. Merlin has the contract; no other magician can touch it till he throws it up."

"But I will take it from him; it is a terrible emergency and the act is thereby justified. And if it were not so, who will give law to the Church? The Church giveth law to all; and what she wills to do, that she may do, hurt whom it may. I will take it from him; you shall begin upon the moment."

"It may not be, Father. No doubt, as you say, where power is supreme, one can do as one likes and suffer no injury; but we poor magicians are not so situated. Merlin is a very good magician in a small way, and has quite a neat local reputation. He is struggling along, doing the best he can, and it would not be etiquette for me to take his job until he himself abandons it."

The abbot's face lighted.

"Ah, that is simple. There are ways to persuade him to abandon it."

"No, no, Father, it will not do. If he were persuaded against his will, he would load that well with a malicious enchantment which would balk me until I found out its secret. It might take a month. I could set up a little enchantment of mine which I call the telephone, and he could not find out its secret in a hundred years. Yes, you perceive, he might block me for a month. Would you like to risk a month in a dry time like this?"

"A month! The mere thought of it maketh me to shudder. Have it thy way, my son. But my heart is heavy with this disappointment. Leave me, and let me wear my spirit with weariness and waiting, even as I have done these ten long days, pretending to rest."

Of course, it would have been best, all round, for Merlin to waive etiquette and quit and call it half a day, since he would never be able to start that water, for he was a true magician of the time; which is to say, the big miracles, the ones that gave him his reputation, always had the luck to be performed when nobody but Merlin was present; he couldn't start this well with all this crowd around to see; a crowd was as bad for a magician's miracle in that day as it was for a spiritualist's miracle in mine; there was sure to be some doubting person on hand to spoil everything. But I did not want Merlin to retire from the job until I was ready to take hold of it effectively myself; and I could not do that until I got my things from Camelot, and that would take two or three days.

My presence gave the monks hope, and cheered them up a good deal; insomuch that they ate a square meal that night for the first time in ten days. As soon as their stomachs had been properly filled with food, their spirits began to rise fast; when the drink began to go round they rose faster. By the time everybody was half-seas over, the holy community was in good shape to make a night of it; so we stayed by the board and put it through on that line. Matters got to be very jolly. Good old stories were told that made the tears run down and mouths stand wide and the round bellies shake with laughter; and songs were bellowed out in a mighty chorus that drowned the boom of the tolling bells.

At last I ventured a story myself, and great was the success of it. Not right off, of course, for the native of those islands does not, as a rule, see the joke at first; but the fifth time I told it, they began to crack in places; the eighth time I told it, they began to crumble; the twelfth they fell apart in chunks; and at the fifteenth they went to pieces, and I got a broom and swept them up.

I was at the well next day. Merlin was there, enchanting away like a beaver, but not raising the moisture. He was not in a pleasant humor, and every time I hinted that perhaps this contract was a shade too hefty for a beginner he cursed.

Matters were about as I expected to find them. The "fountain" was an ordinary well; it had been dug in the ordinary way, and stoned up in the ordinary way. There was no miracle about it. Even the lie that had created its reputation was not miraculous; I could have told it myself, with one hand tied behind me. The well was in a dark chamber which stood in the center of a cut-stone chapel, whose walls were hung with pious pictures of angels.

The well-chamber was dimly lighted by lamps; the water was drawn with a windlass and chain by monks, and poured into troughs which delivered it into stone reservoirs outside in the chapel—when there was water to draw, I mean—and none but monks could enter the well-chamber. I entered it, for I had temporary authority to do so, by courtesy of Merlin. But he hadn't entered it himself. He did everything by prayers; he never worked his mind. If he had stepped in there and used his eyes instead of his disordered mind, he could have cured the well by natural means, and then turned it into miracle in the customary way; but no, he was an old numbskull, a magician who believed in his own magic; and no magician can thrive who is handicapped with a superstition like that.

I had an idea that the well had sprung a leak, that some of the wall stones near the bottom had fallen and exposed cracks that allowed the water to escape. I measured the chain—ninety-eight feet. Then I called in a couple of monks, locked the door, took a candle, and made them lower me in the bucket. When the chain was all paid out, the candle showed me I was right; a considerable section of the wall was gone, exposing a good big crack.

I almost regretted that my theory about the well's trouble was correct, because I had another one that had a showy point or two about it for a miracle. I remembered that in America, many centuries later, when an oil-well ceased to flow, they used to blast it out with a dynamite torpedo. If I should find this well dry and no explanation of it, I could astonish these people most nobly by having a person of no especial value drop a dynamite bomb into it. It was my idea to appoint Merlin. However, it was plain that there was no occasion for the bomb. One cannot have everything the way he would like it.

When I was above ground again, I turned out the monks, and let down a fishline; the well was a hundred and fifty feet deep, and there was forty-one feet of water in it! I called in a monk and asked:

"How deep is the well?"

"That, sir, I know not, having never been told."

"How does the water usually stand in it?"

"Near to the top, these two centuries, as we have always been told."

It was true—as to recent times at least—for there was witness to it, and better witness than a monk; only about twenty or thirty feet of the chain showed wear and use, the rest of it was unworn and rusty. What had happened when the well gave out that other time? Without doubt some practical person had come along and mended the leak, and then had come up and told the abbot he had discovered by magic that if the sinful bath were destroyed the well would flow again. The leak had occurred again now, and these children would have prayed, and marched, and rung their bells for heavenly help till they all dried up and blew away, and no innocent of them all would ever have thought to drop a fishline into the well or go down in it and find out what was really the matter.

Old habit of mind is one of the toughest things to get away from in the world; and for a man, in those days, to have had an idea that his ancestors hadn't had, would have brought him under suspicion. I said to the monk:

"It is a difficult miracle to restore water in a dry well, but we will try, if my brother Merlin fails. Brother Merlin is a very good magician, but only in the parlor-magic line, and he may not succeed; in fact, is not likely to succeed. But I can do this miracle; I shall do this miracle; yet I do not try to conceal from you that it is a miracle to tax the magic powers to the last strain."

"None knows that truth better than the brotherhood, indeed; for it was dangerous and difficult the time before and took a year. Nevertheless God send you good success, and to that end will we pray."

As a matter of business it was a good idea to get the notion around that the thing was difficult. Many a small thing has been made large by the right kind of advertising. That monk was filled up with the difficulty of this job; he would fill up the others. In two days anxiety would be booming.

On my way home at noon, I met Sandy. She had been sampling the hermits. I said:

"I would like to do that myself. This is Wednesday. Is there a matinée?"

"A which, please you, sir?"

"Matinée. Do they keep open afternoons?"

"Who?"

"The hermits, of course."

"Keep open?"

"Yes, keep open. Isn't that plain enough? Do they knock off at noon?"

"Knock off?"

"Knock off—yes, knock off. What is the matter with knock off? I never saw such a dunderhead; can't you understand anything at all? In plain terms, do they shut up shop, draw the game, bank the fires—"

"Shut up shop, draw—"

"There, never mind, let it go; you make me tired. You can't seem to understand the simplest thing."

"I would I might please thee, sir, and I am sorry that I fail, but I am but a simple girl and not taught. I would that I could understand thee and pray your mercy that I cannot."

I saw it was not fair to expect this girl of the sixth century to understand the nineteenth, so I apologized and we went together to see the hermits. They were a strange group.

The chief idea among them seemed to be to see which could manage to be the uncleanest and have the most fleas. Their manners and attitudes were the last expression of self-satisfied self-righteousness. It was one hermit's pride to lie naked in the mud and let the insects bite him and blister him. It was another's to lean against a rock all day long, conspicuous to the admiration of the throng of pilgrims and pray; it was another's to go naked and crawl around on all fours; it was another's to drag about with him, year in and year out, eighty pounds of iron; it was another's never to lie down when he slept, but to stand among the thornbushes and snore when there were pilgrims around to look; a woman, who had the white hair of age, and no other apparel, was black from crown to heel with forty-seven years of refusal to use water. Groups of gazing pilgrims stood around all of these strange objects, lost in wonder, and envious of the holiness which these pious acts had won for them from an exacting heaven.

By and by we went to see one of the supremely great ones—a stylite. He was a mighty celebrity; his fame had spread to all Christendom; the noble and the renowned journeyed from the remotest lands on the globe to pay him reverence. His stand was in the center of the widest part of the valley, and it took all that space to hold his crowds.

His stand was a pillar sixty feet high, with a broad platform on the top of it. He was now doing what he had been doing every day for twenty years up there —bowing his body ceaselessly and rapidly almost to his feet. It was his way of praying. I timed him with a stop-watch, and he made twelve hundred and forty-four revolutions in twenty-four minutes and forty-six seconds. It seemed a pity to have all this power going to waste. It was one of the most useful motions in mechanics, the pedal movement; so I made a note in my memorandum-book, planning some day to apply a system of elastic cords to him and run a sewing-machine with it. I afterward carried out that scheme, and got five years' good service out of him; in which time he turned out upward of eighteen thousand first-rate linen shirts, which was ten a day. I worked him Sundays and all; he was going Sundays the same as week-days, and it was no use to waste the power. These shirts cost me nothing but just the mere trifle for the materials—I furnished those myself; it would not have been right to make him do that—and they sold like smoke to pilgrims at a dollar and a half apiece, which was the price of fifty cows or a blooded race-horse in Arthurdom. They were regarded as a perfect protection against sin, and advertised as such by my knights everywhere. There was not a cliff or a boulder or a dead wall in England but you could read on it at a mile distance:

"Buy the only genuine St. Stylite Shirt; patronized by the Nobility. Patent applied for."

There was more money in the business than one knew what to do with. As it extended, I brought out a line of goods suitable for kings, and a snappy thing for duchesses and that sort.

But about that time I noticed that the hermit had taken to standing on one leg, and I found that there was something the matter with the other one; so I sold the business.

CHAPTER XV

RESTORATION OF THE FOUNTAIN

Saturday noon I went to the well and looked on a while. Merlin was still burning smoke-powders, and pawing the air, and muttering gibberish as hard as ever, but looking pretty downhearted, for of course he had not started even a drop of water in that well yet. Finally I said:

"How does the thing promise by this time, partner?"

"Behold, I am even now busied with trial of the powerfulest enchantment known to the princes of the magic arts in the lands of the East; if it fails me nothing can help. Peace, until I finish."

He raised a smoke this time that darkened all the region, and must have made matters uncomfortable for the hermits, for the wind was their way, and it rolled down over their dens in a dense and billowy fog. He poured out volumes of speech to match, and twisted his body and sawed the air with his hands in a most extraordinary way. At the end of twenty minutes he dropped down panting and about exhausted. Now arrived the abbot and several hundred monks and nuns, and behind them a multitude of pilgrims and a couple of acres of orphans, all drawn by the great smoke, and all in a grand state of excitement. The abbot inquired anxiously for results. Merlin said:

"If any labor of mortal might break the spell that binds these waters, this which I have just tried had done it. It has failed; whereby I do now know that that which I had feared is a truth; the sign of this failure is that the most powerful spirit known to the magicians of the East, and whose name none may utter and live, has laid his spell upon this well. The mortal does not breathe, nor ever will, who can find the secret of that spell, and without that secret none can break it. The water will flow no more forever, good Father. I have done what man could. Let me go."

Of course this threw the abbot into a good deal of distress. He turned to me with the signs of it in his face, and said:

"Ye have heard him. Is it true?"

"Part of it is."

"Not all, then, not all! What part is true?"

"That that spirit with the Russian name has put his spell upon the well."

"Then are we ruined!"

"Possibly."

"But not certainly? Ye mean, not certainly?"

"That is it."

"Wherefore, ye also mean that when he says none can break the spell—"

"Yes, when he says that, he says what isn't neces-

Merlin was burning smoke-powders and pawing the air.

sarily true. There are conditions under which an effort to break it may have some chance—that is, some small, some trifling chance—of success."

"The conditions—"

"Oh, they are nothing difficult. Only these: I want the well and the surroundings for the space of half a mile, entirely to myself from sunset today until I remove the ban—and nobody allowed to cross the ground but by my authority."

"Are these all?"

"Yes."

"And you have no fear to try?"

"Oh, none. One may fail, of course; and one may also succeed. One can try, and I am ready to chance it. I have my conditions?"

"These and all others ye may name. I will issue an order to that effect."

"Wait," said Merlin, with an evil smile. "Ye know that he that would break this spell must know that spirit's name?"

"Yes, I know his name."

"And know you also that to know it is not enough, but ye must likewise pronounce it? Ha-ha! Knew ye that?"

"Yes, I knew that, too."

"You had that knowledge! Art a fool? Are ye minded to utter that name and die?"

"Utter it? Why certainly. I would utter it if it was Welsh."

"Ye are even a dead man, then; and I go to tell Arthur."

"That's all right. Take your gripsack and get along. The thing for *you* to do is to go home and work the weather, John W. Merlin."

It was a home shot, for he was the worst weather failure in the kingdom. Whenever he ordered up the danger-signals along the coast there was a week's dead calm, sure, and every time he prophesied fair weather it rained brickbats. But I kept him in the weather bureau right along, to undermine his reputation. However, that shot made him mad, and instead of starting home to report my death, he said he would remain and enjoy it.

My two experts arrived in the evening, and pretty worn out, for they had traveled night and day. They had pack-mules along, and had brought everything I needed—tools, pump, lead pipe, sheaves of big rockets, Roman candles, colored fire sprays, electric apparatus, and a lot of sundries—everything necessary for the stateliest kind of a miracle. They got their supper and a nap, and about midnight we took possession of the well and its surroundings. My boys were experts in all sorts of things, from the stoning-up of a well to the constructing of a mathematical instrument. An hour before sunrise we had that leak mended in shipshape fashion, and the water began to rise. Then we stowed our fireworks in the chapel, locked up the place, and went home to bed.

Before the noon mass was over, we were at the well again; for there was a deal to do yet, and I was determined to spring the miracle before midnight for business reasons: for whereas a miracle worked for the Church on a week-day is worth a good deal, it is worth six times as much if you get it on a Sunday. In nine hours the water had risen to its customary level; that is to say, it was within twenty-three feet of the top. We put in a little iron pump, one of the first turned out by my works near the capital; we bored into a stone reservoir which stood against the outer wall of the well-chamber and inserted a section of lead pipe that was long enough to reach to the door of the chapel and project beyond the threshold, where the gushing water would be visible to the two hundred and fifty acres of people I was intending should be present on the flat plain in front of this little holy hill at the proper time.

We knocked the head out of an empty barrel and hoisted this to the flat roof of the chapel, where we clamped it down fast, poured in gunpowder till it lay loosely an inch deep on the bottom, then we stood up rockets in the barrel as thick as they could loosely stand. We grounded the wire of a pocket electrical battery in that powder, we placed a whole magazine of flares on each corner of the roof—blue on one corner, green on another, red on another, and purple on the last—and grounded a wire in each.

About two hundred yards off, in the flat, we built

a pen about four feet high and laid planks on it, and so made a platform. We covered it with swell drapes borrowed for the occasion, and topped it off with the abbot's own throne. When you are going to do a miracle for an ignorant race, you want to get in every detail that will count; you want to make it impressive to the public eye; you want to make matters comfortable for your head guest; then you can turn yourself loose and play your effects for all they are worth. I know the value of these things, for I know human nature. You can't throw too much style into a miracle. It costs trouble and work and sometimes money, but it pays in the end. Well, we brought the wires to the ground at the chapel, and then brought them under the ground to the platform and hid the batteries there. We put a rope fence a hundred feet square around the platform to keep off the common multitude, and that finished the work. My idea was, doors open at ten-thirty, performance to begin at eleven-twenty-five sharp. I wished I could charge admission, but of course that wouldn't answer. I instructed my boys to be in the chapel as early as ten, before anybody was around, and to be ready to man the pumps at the proper time, and make the fur fly. Then we went home to supper.

The news of the disaster to the well had traveled far by this time, and now for two or three days a steady stream of people had been pouring into the valley. The lower end of the valley had become one huge camp; we should have a good crowd, no question about that. Criers went the rounds early in the evening and announced the coming attempt, which put every pulse up to fever-heat. They gave notice that the abbot and his officials would move in state and occupy the platform at ten-thirty, up to which time all the region which was to be closed off must be clear; the bells would then cease tolling, and this sign should be permission to the multitudes to close in and take their places.

I was at the platform and all ready to do the honors when the abbot's solemn procession came in sight— which it did not do till it was nearly to the rope fence, because it was a starless black night and no torches permitted. With it came Merlin, and took a front seat on the platform; he was as good as his word for once. The moment the bells stopped, the masses of people broke and poured over the line like a vast black wave, and for as much as a half-hour it continued to flow, and you could have walked upon a pavement of human heads to—well, miles.

We had a solemn stage-wait now, for about twenty minutes—a thing I had counted on for effect; it is always good to let your audience have a chance to work itself up. At length, out of the silence a noble Latin chant—men's voices—broke and swelled up and rolled away into the night, a majestic tide of melody. I had put that up, too, and it was one of the best effects I ever invented. When it was finished I stood up on the platform and extended my hands abroad, for two minutes, with my face uplifted—that always produces a dead hush—and then slowly pronounced this ghastly word with a kind of awfulness which caused hundreds to tremble, and many women to faint:

"Constantinopolitanischerdukelsackspfeifenmachersgeselschafft!"

Just as I was moaning out the closing hunks of that word, I touched off one of my electric connections, and all that murky world of people stood revealed in a hideous blue glare! It was immense—that effect! Lots of people shrieked, women curled up and quit in every direction, orphans collapsed. The abbot and the monks crossed themselves and their lips fluttered with prayers. Merlin held his grip, but he was astonished clear down to his corns; he had never seen anything to compare with that, before. Now was the time to pile in the effects. I lifted my hands and groaned out this word—as it were in agony:

"NIHILISTENDYNAMITTHEATERKAEST-CHENSSPRENGUNGSATTENTAETSVERSU-CHUNGEN!"

—and turned on the red fire! You should have heard that sea of people moan and howl when that crimson joined the blue! After sixty seconds I shouted:

"TRANSVAALTRUPPENTROPENTRANS-PORTTRAMPELTHIERTREIBERTRAUUNGS-THRAENENTRAGEDIE!"

—and lit up the green fire! After waiting only forty

seconds this time, I spread my arms abroad and thundered out the syllables of this word of words:

"MEKKAMUSELMANNENMASSENMENCH-
ENMOERDERMOHRENMUTTERMARMOR-
MOUNMENTENMACHER!"

—and whirled on the purple glare! There they were, all going at once, red, blue, green, purple!—four furious volcanoes pouring vast clouds of radiant smoke aloft, and spreading a blinding rainbowed noonday to the furthest parts of that valley. In the distance one could see that fellow on the pillar standing rigid against the background of sky, his see-saw stopped for the first time in twenty years. I knew the boys were at the pump now and ready. So I said to the abbot:

"The time is come, Father. I am about to pronounce the dread name and command the spell to dissolve. You want to brace up and take hold of something." Then I shouted to the people: "Behold, in another minute the spell will be broken, or no mortal can break it. If it break, all will know it, for you will see the sacred water gush from the chapel door!"

I stood a few moments, then waved my arms and shouted:

"Lo, I command the dread spirit that possesses the holy fountain to discharge now into the skies all the fires that still remain in him, and straightway dissolve his spell and flee hence to the pit, there to lie bound a thousand years. By his own dread name I command it—BGWJJILLIGKKK!"

Then I touched off the barrel of rockets, and a vast fountain of dazzling lances of fire shot toward the heavens with a hissing rush, and burst in mid-sky into a storm of fiery stars! One mighty groan of terror started up from the massed people—then suddenly broke into a wild hosannah of joy—for there, fair and plain in the glare, they saw the freed water leaping forth! The old abbot could not speak a word, for tears and the chokings in his throat; without utterance of any sort, he folded me in his arms and mashed me. It was more eloquent than speech. And harder to get over, too, in a country where there were really no doctors that were worth a damaged nickel.

You should have seen those acres of people throw themselves down in that water and kiss it; kiss it, and pet it, and fondle it, and talk to it as if it were alive, and welcome it back with the dear names they gave their darlings, just as if it had been a friend who was long gone away and lost, and was come home again. Yes, it was pretty to see, and made me think more of them than I had done before.

I sent Merlin home on a shutter. He had caved in and gone down like a landslide when I pronounced that fearful name, and had never come to since. He never had heard that name before—neither had I— but to him it was the right one. Any jumble would have been the right one. He admitted afterward that

that spirit's own mother could not have pronounced that name better than I did. He never could understand how I survived it, and I didn't tell him. It is only young magicians that give away a secret like that. Merlin spent three months working enchantments to try to find out the deep trick of how to pronounce that name and outlive it. But he didn't arrive.

When I started to the chapel, the people fell back reverently to make a wide way for me, as if I had been some kind of a superior being—and I was. I was aware of that. I took along a night shift of monks and taught them the mystery of the pump, and set them to work, for it was plain that a good part of the people out there were going to sit up with the water all night; consequently it was but right that they should have all they wanted of it. To those monks that pump was a good deal of a miracle itself, and they were full of wonder over it—and of admiration, too, of the exceeding effectiveness of its performance.

It was a great night, an immense night. There was reputation in it. I could hardly get to sleep for glorying over it.

CHAPTER XVI

A RIVAL MAGICIAN

My influence in the Valley of Holiness was something great now. It seemed worth while to try to turn it to some valuable account. The thought came to me the next morning, and was suggested by my seeing one of my knights who was in the soap line come riding in. According to history, the monks of this place two centuries before had been wordly-minded enough to want to wash. It might be that there was a little of this unrighteousness still remaining. So I sounded a Brother:

"Wouldn't you like a bath?"

He shuddered at the thought—the thought of the peril of it to the well—but he said with feeling:

"One needs not to ask that of a poor body who has not known that blessed refreshment since he was a boy. Would God I might wash! But it may not be, fair sir, tempt me not; it is forbidden."

And then he sighed in such a sorrowful way that I was resolved he should have at least one layer of his real estate removed, if it sized up my whole influence and bankrupted the pile. So I went to the abbot and asked for a permit for this Brother. He paled at the idea—I don't mean that you could see him pale for of

162

course you couldn't see it without you scraped him. He said:

"Ah, son, ask aught else thou wilt, and it is thine, and freely granted out of a grateful heart—but this, oh, this! Would you drive away the blessed water again?"

"No, Father, I will not drive it away. I have mysterious knowledge that there was an error that other time when it was thought the bath banished the fountain." A large interest began to show up in the old man's face.

"These are brave words—but—but right welcome, if they be true."

"They are true, indeed. Let me build the bath again, Father. Let me build it again, and the fountain shall flow forever."

"You promise this? Say the word—say you promise it!"

"I do promise it."

"Then will I have the first bath myself! Go, get ye to your work. Wait not, wait not, but go."

I and my boys were at work, straight off. The ruins of the old bath were there yet in the basement of the monastery, not a stone missing. They had been left just so all these lifetimes, and avoided with a pious fear as things accursed. In two days we had it all done and the water in—a large pool of clear pure water that a body could swim in. It was running water, too. It came in and went out through the ancient pipes. The old abbot kept his word and was the first to try it. He went down black and shaky, leaving the whole black community above troubled and worried and full of fear; but he came back white and joyful, and the game was made! another triumph scored.

It was a good campaign that we made in that Valley of Holiness, and I was very well satisfied and ready to move on now, but I struck a disappointment. I caught a heavy cold, and it started up an old rheumatism of mine.

When at last I got out, I was a shadow. But everybody was full of attentions and kindnesses, and these brought cheer back into my life, and were the right medicine to help me swiftly up toward health and strength again; so I gained fast.

Sandy was worn out with nursing, so I made up my mind to turn out and go on a cruise alone, leaving her at the nunnery to rest up. My idea was to disguise myself as a freeman of peasant degree and wander through the country a week or two on foot. This would give me a chance to eat and lodge with the lowliest and poorest class of free citizens on equal terms. There was no other way to inform myself perfectly of their every-day life. If I went among them as a gentleman, I would be shut out from their private joys and troubles, and I should get no further than the outside shell.

One morning I was out on a long walk to get up muscle for my trip, and had climbed the ridge which bordered the northern edge of the valley, when I came upon an artificial opening in the face of a low cliff, and recognized it by its location as a hermitage which had often been pointed out to me from a distance as the den of a hermit of great fame for dirt and holiness. I knew he had lately been offered a situation in the Great African desert, where lions and sandflies made the hermit life peculiarly attractive and difficult, and had gone there to take possession, so I thought I would look in and see how the atmosphere of this den agreed with its reputation.

My surprise was great; the place was newly swept and scoured. Then there was another surprise. Back in the gloom of the cavern I heard the clink of a little bell, and then this exclamation:

"Hello, Central! Is this you, Camelot? If you have faith to believe wonderful news—here stands The Boss. With your own ears you can hear him speak."

The telephone clerk stepped into the light, and I recognized one of my young fellows. I said:

"How long has this office been established here, Ulfius?"

"But since midnight, fair Sir Boss, if it please you. We saw many lights in the valley, and so judged it well to make a station, for where there were so many lights must be a town of goodly size."

"Quite right. It isn't a town in the customary sense, but it's a good stand, anyway. Do you know where you are?"

"Of that I have had no time to make sure; for when my comrades moved hence upon their labors, leaving me in charge, I took some needed rest, expecting to inquire when I waked, and report the place's name to Camelot for record."

"Well, this is the Valley of Holiness."

It didn't take; I mean, he didn't start at the name, as I had supposed he would. He merely said:

"I will so report it."

"Why, the surrounding regions are filled with the noise of late wonders that have happened here! You didn't hear of them?"

"Ah, ye will remember we move by night, and avoid speech with all. We learn nothing except what we get by the telephone from Camelot."

"Why *they* know all about this thing. Haven't they told you anything about the great miracle of the restoration of a holy fountain?"

"Oh, *that?* Indeed yes. But the name of *this* valley differs from the name of *that* one; indeed to differ wider were not pos—"

"What was that name, then?"

"The Valley of Hellishness."

"*That* explains it. Confound a telephone, anyway. It is the very devil for mixing up sounds. But no matter, you know the name of the place now. Call up Camelot."

He did it, and had Clarence sent for. It was good to hear my boy's voice again. It was like being home. After some affectionate greetings, and some account of my late illness, I said:

"What is new?"

"The king and queen and many of the court do start even in this hour, to go to your valley to do honor to the waters ye have restored, and cleanse themselves of sin, and see the place where the fiendish spirit spouted true hell-flames to the clouds—if ye listen sharply ye may hear me wink and hear me likewise smile a smile, since 'twas I that made selection of those flames from out our stock and sent them by your order."

"Does the king know the way to this place?"

"The king—no, nor to any other in his kingdom; but the lads that helped you with your miracle will be his guide and lead the way, and appoint the places for rests at noon and sleeps at night."

"This will bring them here—when?"

"Mid-afternoon or later, the third day."

"Anything else in the way of news?"

"The king hath begun the raising of the standing army ye suggested to him; one regiment is complete and officered."

"The mischief! I wanted a main hand in that myself. There is only one body of men in the kingdom that are fitted to officer a regular army."

"Yes—and now ye will marvel to know there's not so much as one West-Pointer in that regiment."

"What are you talking about? Are you in earnest?"

"It is truly as I have said."

"Why, this makes me uneasy. Who were chosen, and what was the method? By examination?"

"Indeed, I know nothing of the method. I but know this—these officers are all of noble family, and are born—what is it you call it?—chuckle-heads."

"There's something wrong, Clarence."

"Comfort yourself, then; for two candidates for a lieutenancy do travel hence with the king—young nobles both—and if you but wait where you are you will hear them questioned."

"That is news to the purpose. I will get one West-Pointer in, anyway. Mount a man and send him to that school with a message; let him kill horses, if necessary, but he must be there before sunset tonight and say—"

"There is no need. I have laid a ground-wire to the school. Prithee let me connect you with it."

It sounded good! In this atmosphere of telephones and lightning communication with distant regions, I was breathing the breath of life again.

I gave my order to the superintendent of the Academy personally. I also asked him to bring me some paper and a fountain-pen and a box or so of safety matches. I was getting tired of doing without these conveniences. I could have them now, as I wasn't going to wear armor any more at present, and therefore could get at my pockets.

When I got back to the monastery, I found a thing of interest going on. The abbot and his monks were assembled in the great hall, observing with childish wonder and faith the performances of a new magician, a fresh arrival. His dress was as showy and foolish as the sort of thing an Indian medicine-man wears. He was mumbling and waving his arms, and drawing mystical figures in the air and on the floor—the regular thing, you know. He was a famous magician from Asia—so he said, and that was enough. That sort of evidence was as good as gold, and was believed everywhere.

How easy and cheap it was to be a great magician on this fellow's terms. His specialty was to tell you what any individual on the face of the globe was doing at the moment, and what he had done at any time in the past, and what he would do at any time in the future. He asked if any would like to know what the Emperor of the East was doing now? The sparkling eyes and the delighted rubbing of hands was his answer—this crowd *would* like to know what that monarch was at, just at this moment. The fraud went through some more mummery, and then made grave announcement:

"The high and mighty Emperor of the East doth

at this moment put money in the palm of a holy begging friar—one, two, three pieces, and they be all of
silver."

A buzz of admiring exclamations broke out all
around:

"It is marvelous! Wonderful!" "What study, what
labor, to have acquired a so amazing power as this!"

Would they like to know what the Supreme Lord
of India was doing? Yes. He told them what the
Supreme Lord of India was doing. Then he told
them what the Sultan of Egypt was at; also what the
King of the Remote Seas was about. And so on and
so on; and with each new marvel the astonishment at
his accuracy rose higher and higher. They thought
he must surely strike an uncertain place some time;
but no, he never had to hesitate; he always knew. I
saw that if this thing went on I should lose my su-
premacy; this fellow would capture my following;
I should be left out in the cold. I must put a cog in
his wheel and do it right away, too. I said:

"If I might ask, I should very greatly like to know
what a certain person is doing."

"Speak, and freely. I will tell you."

"It will be difficult—perhaps impossible."

"My art knoweth not that word. The more difficult
it is, the more certainly will I reveal it to you."

You see, I was working up the interest. It was getting pretty high, too. So now I brought it to a head:

"If you make no mistake—if you tell me truly

what I want to know—I will give you two hundred silver pennies."

"The fortune is mine! I will tell you what you would know."

"Then tell me what I am doing with my right hand."

"Ah-h!" There was a general gasp of surprise. It had not occurred to anybody in the crowd—that simple trick of inquiring about somebody who wasn't ten thousand miles away. The magician was hit hard; it was an emergency that had never happened in his experience before, and it stopped him; he didn't know how to meet it. He looked stunned, confused; he couldn't say a word. "Come," I said, "What are you waiting for? Is it possible you can answer up, right off, and tell what anybody on the other side of the earth is doing, and yet can't tell what a person is doing who isn't three yards from you? Persons behind me know what I am doing with my right hand—they will tell you if you are correct." He was still dumb. "Very well, I'll tell you why you don't speak up and tell; it is because you don't know. *You* a magician! Good friends, this tramp is a mere fraud and liar."

This distressed the monks and terrified them. They were not used to hearing these awful beings called names, and they did not know what might be the consequence. There was a dead silence now; superstitious fear was in every mind. The magician began to pull his wits together, and when he presently smiled an easy smile, it spread a mighty relief around. He said:

"It hath struck me speechless, the lightness of this person's speech. Let all know, if perhaps there be any who know it not, that enchanters of my degree do not concern themselves with the doings of any but kings, princes, emperors, them that be born in the purple and them only. Had ye asked me what Arthur the great king is doing, it were another matter, and I had told ye; but the doings of a subject interest me not."

"Oh, I misunderstood you. I thought you said 'anybody,' and so I supposed 'anybody' included—well, anybody; that is, everybody."

"It does—anybody that is of noble birth, and the better if he be royal."

"That, it meseemeth, might well be," said the abbot, who saw his opportunity to smooth things and keep off disaster, "for it were not likely that so wonderful a gift as this would be given for the revealing of the concerns of lesser beings than such as be born near to greatness. Our Arthur the king—"

"Would you know of him?" broke in the enchanter.

"Most gladly, yea, and gratefully."

Everybody was full of awe and interest again right away, the idiots. They watched the magician absorbingly, and looked at me with a "There, now, what can you say to that?" air, when the announcement came:

"The king is weary with the chase, and lieth in his palace these two hours sleeping a dreamless sleep."

"God's blessing upon him!" said the abbot, and

crossed himself. "May that sleep be to the refreshment of his body and his soul."

"And so it might be, if he were sleeping," I said, "but the king is not sleeping; the king rides."

Here was trouble again—a conflict of authority. Nobody knew which of us to believe; I still had some reputation left. The magician's scorn was stirred, and he said:

"Lo, I have seen many wonderful soothsayers and prophets and magicians in my life days, but none before that could sit idle and see to the heart of things with never a spell to help."

"You have lived in the woods, and lost much by it. I use spells myself, as this good brotherhood are aware—but only on occasions of moment."

When it comes to sarcasm, I reckon I know how to keep my end up. That jab made this fellow squirm. The abbot inquired after the queen and the court, and got this information:

"They be all asleep, being overcome by fatigue, like as to the king."

I said:

"That is merely another lie. Half of them are about their amusements, the queen and the other half are not sleeping; they ride. Now perhaps you can spread yourself a little, and tell us where the king and queen and all that are this moment riding with them are going?"

"They sleep now, as I said; but on the morrow they will ride, for they go a journey toward the sea."

"And where will they be the day after tomorrow in the evening?"

"Far to the north of Camelot, and half their journey will be done."

"That is another lie, by the space of a hundred and fifty miles. Their journey will not be merely half done; it will be all done, and they will be *here*, in this valley."

That was a noble shot! It set the abbot and the monks in a whirl of excitement, and it rocked the enchanter to his base. I followed the thing right up:

"If the king does not arrive, I will have myself ridden on a rail: if he does I will ride you on a rail instead."

Next day I went up to the telephone office and found that the king had passed through two towns that were on the line. I spotted his progress on the succeeding day in the same way. I kept these matters to myself. The third day's reports showed that if he kept up his speed he would arrive by four in the afternoon. There seemed to be no preparations in the making to receive him in state, a strange thing, truly. Only one thing could explain this: that other magician had been cutting under me, sure. This was true. I asked a friend of mine, a monk, about it; and he said, yes, the magician had tried some further enchantments and found out that the court had concluded to make no journey at all, but stay at home. Think of that! Observe how much a reputation was worth in such a country. These people had seen me do the very showiest bit of magic in history, and the only one within their memory that had a positive value, and yet here they were, ready to take up with an adventurer who could offer no evidence of his powers but his mere word.

However, it was not good politics to let the king come without any fuss and feathers at all; so I went down and drummed up a procession of pilgrims and smoked out a batch of hermits and started them out at two o'clock to meet him. And that was the sort of state he arrived in. The abbot was helpless with anger when I brought him out on a balcony and showed him the head of the state marching in and never a monk on hand to offer him welcome. He took one look and then flew to rouse out his forces. The next minute the bells were ringing furiously, and out of the various buildings came monks and nuns, who went swarming in a rush toward the coming procession; and with them went that magician—and he was on a rail, too, by the abbot's order; and his reputation was in the mud and mine was in the sky again.

CHAPTER XVII

A COMPETITIVE EXAMINATION

When the king traveled for change of air, or visited a distant noble whom he wished to bankrupt with the cost of his keep, part of the administration moved with him. It was a fashion of the time. The commission charged with the examination of candidates for posts in the army came with the king to the Valley, though they could have handled their business just as well at home. And although this expedition was strictly a holiday excursion for the king, he kept some of his business functions going just the same. As usual, he touched for the evil—that is, he laid hands on the sick to cure them; he held court in the gate at sunrise; he tried cases, for he was himself Chief Justice of the King's Bench.

He shone very well in this latter office. He was a wise and humane judge, and he clearly did his honest best and fairest, according to his lights. Of course, whenever there was a dispute between a noble or gentleman and a person of lower degree, the king's leanings and sympathies were for the former class always, whether he suspected it or not. It was impossible that this should be otherwise, since the system had blunted his feelings and had convinced him he was a superior being and that his class was superior and was therefore right. Cases which he tried that day which were between nobles and commons all ended with the noble top dog. You couldn't beat the system.

King Arthur had hurried up the army business more than I expected. I had not supposed he would move in the matter while I was away; and so I had not mapped out a scheme for determining the merits of officers; I had only remarked that it would be wise to submit every candidate to a sharp and searching examination; and privately I meant to put together a list of military qualifications that nobody could answer but my West-Pointers. That ought to have been attended to before I left; for the king was so taken with the idea of a standing army that he couldn't wait but must get about it at once, and get up as good a scheme of examination as he could invent out of his own head.

I was impatient to see what this was; and to show, too, how much better was the one which I should display to the Examining Board. I hinted this gently to the king, and it fired his curiosity. When the Board was assembled, I followed him in, and behind us came the candidates. One of these candidates was a bright young West-Pointer of mine, and with him were a couple of West Point professors.

When I saw the Board, I did not know whether to cry or to laugh. The head of it was the officer known to later centuries as Norroy King-at-Arms! The two other members were chiefs of bureaus in his department; and all three were priests, of course; all officials who had to know how to read and write were priests.

My candidate was called first, out of courtesy to me, and the head of the Board opened on him with official solemnity:

"Name?"

"Mal-ease."

"Son of?"

"Webster."

"Webster—Webster. H'm—I—my memory faileth to recall the name. Condition?"

"Weaver."

"Weaver!—God keep us!"

The king was staggered, from his head to his toes; one clerk fainted, and the others came near it. The chairman pulled himself together and said indignantly:

"It is sufficient. Get you hence."

But I appealed to the king. I begged that my candidate might be examined. The king was willing, but the Board, who were all well-born folk, implored the king to spare them from examining the weaver's son. I knew they didn't know enough to examine him anyway; so I joined my prayers to theirs and the king turned the duty over to my professors. I had had a blackboard prepared, and it was put up now, and the circus began. It was beautiful to hear the lad lay out the science of war, and wallow in details of battle and siege, of supply, transportation, mining and counter-mining, grand tactics, big strategy and little strategy, signal service, infantry, cavalry, artillery, and all about siege-guns, field-guns, Gatling guns, rifled guns, smooth bores, musket practice, revolver practice— and not a solitary word of it all could these catfish make head or tail of, you understand. It was hand-some to see him chalk off mathematical nightmares on the blackboard that would stump the angels them-selves, and do it like nothing, too—all about eclipses, and comets, and sun and stars, and mean time, and sidereal time, and dinner-time, and bedtime, and every other imaginable thing above the clouds or under them that you could bullyrag an enemy with and make him wish he hadn't come. When the boy made his military salute and stood aside at last, I was proud enough to hug him, and all those other people were so dazed they looked partly petrified, partly drunk, and wholly caught out and snowed under. I judged that we had won, and by a large majority.

Education is a great thing. This was the same youth who had come to West Point so ignorant that when I asked him, "If a general officer should have a horse shot under him on the field of battle, what ought he to do?" answered up and said:

"Get up and brush himself."

One of the young nobles was called up now. I thought I would question him a little myself. I said.

"Can your lordship read?"

His face flushed indignantly, and he fired this at me:

"Takest me for a clerk? I hope I am not of a blood that—"

"Answer the question!"

He crowded his wrath down and made out to answer "No."

"Can you write?"

He wanted to resent this, too, but I said:

"You will confine yourself to the questions and make no comments. Can you write?"

"No."

"Do you know the multiplication table?"

"I know not what ye refer to."

"How much is nine times six?"

"It is a mystery that is hidden from me by reason that the emergency requiring the understanding of it hath not in my life-days occurred, and so, not having need to know this thing, I do not know it!"

"If A trade a barrel of onions to B, worth twopence the bushel, in exchange for sheep worth fourpence and a dog worth a penny, and C kill the dog before delivery, because bitten by the same, who mistook him for D, what sum is still due to A from B, and which party pays for the dog, C or D, and who gets the money? If A, is the penny sufficient, or may

he claim damages in the form of additional money to
represent the possible profit which might have come
from the dog?"

"Verily, in the all-wise and unknowable providence
of God, who moveth in mysterious ways His wonders
to perform, have I never heard the fellow to this question for confusion of the mind and mixing-up of
thought. Wherefore I beseech you let the dog and the
onions and these people of the strange and godless
names work out their several salvations from their
piteous and wonderful difficulties without help of
mine!"

"What do you know of the laws of attraction and
gravitation?"

"If there be such, mayhap his grace the king did
make them whilst that I lay sick about the beginning
of the year and thereby failed to hear his proclamation."

"What do you know of the science of optics?"

"I know of governors of places, and of castles, and
sheriffs of counties, and many like small offices and
titles of honor, but him you call the Science of Optics
I have not heard of before; perhaps it is a new dignity."

"Yes, in this country."

Try to conceive of this man gravely applying for
an official position of any kind under the sun! After
nagging him a little more, I let the professors loose
on him and they turned him inside out on the line of

scientific war, and found him empty, of course. He knew something about the warfare of the time— hunting around for ogres, and bull-fights in the tournament ring, and such things—but otherwise he was empty and useless. Then we took the other young noble in hand, and he was as ignorant as the first one. I delivered them into the hands of the chairman of the Board with the comfortable consciousness that they would fail. I sat back to enjoy their examination.

"Name, so please you?"

"Pertipole, son of Sir Pertipole, Baron of Barley Mash."

"Grandfather?"

"Also, Sir Pertipole, Baron of Barley Mash."

"Great-grandfather?"

"The same name and title."

"Great-great-grandfather?"

"We had none, worshipful sir, the line failing before it had reached so far back."

"It mattereth not. It is a good four generations, and fulfilleth the requirements of the rule."

"Fulfills what rule?" I asked.

"The rule requiring four generations of nobility or else the candidate is not eligible."

"A man is not eligible for a lieutenancy in the army unless he can prove four generations of noble descent?"

"Even so; neither lieutenant nor any other officer may be commissioned without that qualification."

"Oh, come, this is a strange thing. What good is such a qualification as that?"

The king said:

"Why, truly I see nothing about it that is strange. All places of honor and of profit do belong, by natural right, to them that be of noble blood."

The chairman resumed as follows:

"By what great achievement for the honor of the Throne and state did the founder of your great line lift himself to the sacred dignity of the British nobility?"

"He built a brewery."

"Sire, the Board finds this candidate perfect in all the requirements and qualifications for military command, and doth hold his case open for decision after due examination of his competitor."

The competitor came forward and proved exactly four generations of nobility himself, but his great grandmother was proved to have greater nobility than Sir Pertipole's and the lieutenancy was therefore given to him.

I was down in the bottomless pit. I had promised myself an easy triumph, and this was the outcome!

I was almost ashamed to look my poor disappointed cadet in the face. I told him to go home and be patient; this wasn't the end.

I had a private audience with the king, and made a proposition. I said it was quite right to officer that regiment with nobilities, and he couldn't have done a wiser thing. It would also be a good idea to add five hundred officers to it; in fact, add as many officers as there were nobles and relatives of nobles in the country, even if there should finally be five times as many officers as privates in it; and thus make it the crack regiment, the envied regiment, the King's Own regiment, entitled to fight on its own hook and in its own way, and go whither it would and come when it pleased in time of war, and be utterly swell and independent. This would make that regiment the heart's desire of all the nobility, and they would all be satisfied and happy. Then we would make up the rest of the standing army out of commonplace materials, and officer it with nobodies, as was proper—nobodies selected on a basis of mere ability—and we would make this regiment toe the line, allow it no freedom, and force it to do all the work to the end that whenever the King's Own was tired and wanted to go off for a change and rummage around amongst ogres and have a good time, it could go without uneasiness, knowing that matters were in safe hands behind it, and business going to be continued at the old stand, same as usual. The king was charmed with the idea.

CHAPTER XVIII

THE YANKEE AND THE KING

TRAVEL IN DISGUISE

I had decided I was going out disguised as a commoner to tour the country and learn how the common people lived. When I told the king, he was all afire with the novelty of the thing in a minute, and was bound to take a chance in the adventure himself; nothing should stop him; he would drop everything and go along; it was the prettiest idea he had run across for many a day. He wanted to glide out the back way and start at once, but I showed him that that wouldn't do.

He was billed to "touch for the king's evil" and it wouldn't have been right to disappoint the crowd expecting him. There was a very good lay-out for the king's evil business. The king sat under a canopy of state surrounded by priests. Marinel, a hermit of the quack doctor kind, was there to introduce the sick, about eight hundred of whom had gathered. The king touched the sick and gave a coin to each one which was supposed to cure whatever ailed them. Would you think that would cure them? It certainly did. Of course anything would have if the patient's faith was strong enough.

Well, after this had been going on for about three hours, I heard a call outside which roused me and seemed to put me back in the nineteenth century. "Camelot Weekly Hosannah & Literary Volcano— latest irruption—only two cents—all about the big miracle in the Valley of Holiness." It was my news-boy. I dropped a nickel out the window and got my paper and the first newsboy of the world went around the corner to get my change and is still around the corner. It was delicious to get a newspaper again, but I was a little shocked by the tone of the paper, due no doubt to the fact that I had now lived in this atmos-phere of reverence and respect so long that modern lack of it seemed out of place.

HIGH TIMES IN THE VALLEY
OF HOLINESS!

THE WATER-WORKS CORKED!

BROTHER MERLIN WORKS HIS ARTS, BUT GETS
LEFT?

But the Boss scores on his first Innings!

*The Miraculous Well Uncorked amid
awful outbursts of*
INFERNAL FIRE AND SMOKE
AND THUNDER!

THE BUZZARD-ROOST ASTONISHED!

UNPARALLELED REJOICINGS!

—and so on, and so on. Yes, it was too loud. Once I could have enjoyed it and would have seen nothing out of the way about it, but now its note was wrong. There were a good many of the following kind of items, and they bothered me:

Local Smoke and Cinders.

Sir Launcelot met up with old King Agrivance of Ireland unexpectedly last weok over on the moor south of Sir Balmoral le Merveilleuse's hog dasture. The widow has been notified.

Expedition No. 3 will start adout the first of mext-mgnth-on a search f8r Sir Sagramour le Desirous. It is in com- and of the renowned Knight of the Red Lawns, assisted by Sir Persant of Inde, who is compete9t. intelligent, courte- ous, and in every may a brick, and fur- tHer assisted by Sir Palamides and Sara- cen, who is no huckleberry hinself. This is no pic-nic, these boys *M*ean businine'S.

The Demoiselle Irene Dewlap, of South Astolat, is visting her uncle, the popular host of the Cattlemen's Board- ing Ho&se, Liver Lane, this city.

Young Barker the bellows-mender is hoMe again, and looks much improved by his vacation round-up among the out- lying smithies. See his ad.

Of course it was good enough journalism for a be- ginning; I knew that quite well, and yet it was some- how disappointing. The "Court Circular" pleased me better, its simple and dignified respectfulness was a distinct refreshment to me. But even it could have been improved. It needed variety.

COURT CIRCULAR

On Monday, the King rode in the park.
" Tuesday,   "   "   "
" Wednesday "   "   "
" Thursday   "   "   "
" Friday,   "   "   "
" Saturday   "   "   "
" Sunday,   "   "   "

However, take the paper by and large, I was vastly pleased with it. Little errors of a mechanical sort could be seen here and there, but there were not enough of them to amount to anything, and it was good enough proof-reading anyhow, and better than was needed in Arthur's day and kingdom. As a rule, the grammar was leaky and the construction more or less lame, but I did not much mind these things.

I was hungry enough for literature to want to take down the whole paper at this one meal, but I got only a few bites, and then had to postpone it, because the monks around me had so many questions: What is this curious thing? What is it for? Is it a handkerchief?—saddle-blanket?—part of a shirt? What is it made of? How thin it is, and how dainty and frail; and how it rattles. Will it wear, do you think, and won't the rain injure it? Is it writing that appears on it, or is it only ornamentation? They suspected it was writing, because those among them who knew how to read Latin and had a smattering of Greek, recognized some of the letters, but they could make nothing out of the result as a whole. I put my information in the simplest form I could:

"It is a public journal; I will explain what that is another time. It is not cloth; it is made of paper; some time I will explain what paper is. The lines on it are reading-matter, and not written by hand, but printed; by and by I will explain what printing is. A thousand of these sheets have been made, all exactly like this, in every detail—they can't be told apart." Then they all broke out with exclamations of surprise and admiration:

"A thousand! Verily a mighty work—a year's work for many men."

"No—merely a day's work for a man and a boy."

They crossed themselves.

"Ah-h—a miracle, a wonder! Dark work of enchantment."

I let it go at that. Then I read in a low voice to as many as could crowd their shaven heads within hearing distance, part of the account of the miracle of the restoration of the well, and was accompanied by astonished and reverent exclamations all through: "Ah-h-h!" "How true!" "Amazing, amazing!" "These be the very haps as they happened, in marvelous exactness!" And might they take this strange thing in their hands and feel of it and examine it?—they would be very careful. Yes. So they took it, handling it as cautiously as if it had been some holy thing, and gently felt of its texture, caressed its pleasant smooth surface, and gazed at the mysterious characters with fascinated eyes.

My paper traveled from group to group all up and down and about that huge hall, and my happy eye was upon it always, and I sat motionless, steeped in satisfaction, drunk with the enjoyment of having my work so appreciated.

About bedtime I took the king to my private quarters to cut his hair and help him get the hang of the lowly clothes he was to wear on his trip with me. The high classes wore their hair banged across the forehead but hanging to the shoulders the rest of the way around, while commoners were banged fore and aft both; the slaves were bangless, and allowed their hair free growth. So I inverted a bowl over his head and cut away all the locks that hung below it. I also trimmed his whiskers and mustache until they were only about a half-inch long. When he got his big sandals on, and his long robe of coarse brown linen cloth, which hung straight from his neck to his ankle-bones, he was no longer the handsomest man in his kingdom, but one of the unhandsomest and most commonplace and unattractive. We were dressed and barbered alike, and could pass for small farmers, or farm bailiffs, or shepherds, or carters—yes, or for village mechanics, if we chose, our costume being in effect worn by all the poor, because of its strength and cheapness. I don't mean that it was really cheap to a very poor person, but I do mean that it was the cheapest material there was for male dress.

We slipped away an hour before dawn, and by broad sun-up had made eight or ten miles, and were in the midst of a thinly settled country. I had a pretty heavy knapsack; it was loaded with provisions—provisions for the king to get used to gradually till he could take to the coarse fare of the country without damage.

I found a comfortable seat for the king by the roadside, and then gave him a bite or two to stay his stomach with. Then I said I would find some water for him, and strolled away. Part of my project was to get out of sight and sit down and rest a little myself. It had always been my custom to stand when in his presence, even at the council board, except upon those rare occasions when the sitting was a very long one, extending over hours; then I had a trifling little backless chair which was as comfortable as the toothache. I didn't want to break him in suddenly, but do it by degrees. We should have to sit together now when in company, or people would notice; but it would not be good politics for me to be playing equality with him when there was no necessity for it.

I found the water some three hundred yards away, and had been resting about twenty minutes, when I heard voices. That is all right, I thought—peasants going to work; nobody else likely to be stirring this early. But the next moment these comers jingled into sight around a turn of the road—smartly clad people of quality, with luggage-mules and servants in their train! I was off like a shot, through the bushes by the shortest cut. For a while it did seem that these people would pass the king before I could get to him; but desperation gives you wings, you know, and I bent my body forward, and held my breath and flew. I arrived. And in plenty good enough time, too.

"Pardon, my king, but it's no time for ceremony—jump! Jump to your feet—some quality are coming!"

"Is that a marvel? Let them come."

"But my lord! You must not be seen sitting. Rise! —and stand humbly while they pass. You are a peasant, you know."

"True—I had forgot it, so lost was I in planning a huge war with Gaul." He was up by this time, but a farm could have got up quicker, if there was any kind of a boom in real estate.

"A humbler attitude, my lord the king—and quick! Duck your head!—more!—still more! droop it!"

He did his honest best, but lord, it was no great thing. Indeed, it was such a thundering poor success that it raised wondering scowls all along the line, and a gorgeous flunkey at the tail end of it raised his whip; but I jumped in time and was under it when it fell; and under cover of the coarse laughter which followed, I spoke up sharply and warned the king to take no notice. He mastered himself for the moment, but it was hard work; he wanted to eat up the procession. I said:

"It would end our adventures at the very start; and we, being without weapons, could do nothing with that armed gang. If we are going to succeed in our undertaking, we must not only look the peasant but act the peasant."

"It is wisdom; none can deny it. Let us go on, Sir Boss. I will take note and learn, and do the best I may."

He kept his word. He did the best he could, but I've seen better. If you have ever seen an active heedless child going busily out of one mischief and into another all day long, and an anxious mother at its heels all the while, just saving it by a hair from drowning itself or breaking its neck with each new experiment, you've seen the king and me.

If I could have foreseen what the thing was going to be like, I should have said, No, if anybody wants to make his living exhibiting a king as a peasant, let him do it, not me. During the first three days I never allowed him to enter a hut or other dwelling. If he could get by anywhere during those first days, it would be in small inns and on the road; so to these places we confined ourselves. Yes, he certainly did the best he could, but what of that? He didn't improve a bit that I could see.

He was always frightening me, always breaking

out in new and unexpected places. Toward evening on the second day, what does he do but calmly take out a dagger from inside his robe!

"Great guns, my lord, where did you get that?"

"From a smuggler at the inn, yester eve."

"What in the world possessed you to buy it?"

"We have escaped various dangers by wit—thy wit —but I thought that it were but wisdom if I bore a weapon, too. Thine might fail thee in some pinch."

"But people of our condition are not allowed to carry arms. What would a lord say—yes, or any other person—if he caught a peasant with a dagger on his person?"

It was a lucky thing for us that nobody came along just then. I persuaded him to throw the dagger away; and it was as easy as persuading a child to give up some bright fresh new way of killing itself. We walked along, silent and thinking. Finally the king said:

"When ye know that I think a thing inconvenient, or that hath a danger in it, why do you not warn me to cease from that project?" It was a startling question and a puzzler. I didn't quite know how to take hold of it or what to say and so, of course, I ended by saying the natural thing:

"But, sire, how can *I* know what your thoughts are?"

The king stopped dead in his tracks, and stared at me.

"I believed thou wert greater than Merlin; and

truly in magic thou art. But prophecy is greater than magic. Merlin is a prophet."

I saw I had made a blunder. I must get back my lost ground. After deep thought and careful planning, I said:

"Sire, I have been misunderstood. I will explain. There are two kinds of prophecy. One is the gift to foretell things that are but a little way off, the other is the gift to fortell things that are whole ages and centuries away. Which is the mightier gift, do you think?"

"Oh, the last, most surely!"

"True. Does Merlin possess it?"

"Partly, yes. He foretold mysteries about my birth and future kingship that were twenty years away."

"Has he ever gone beyond that?"

"He would not claim more, I think."

"It is probably his limit. All prophets have their limit. The limit of some of the great prophets has been a hundred years."

"These are few, I suppose."

"There have been two still greater ones, whose limit was four hundred and six hundred years, and one whose limit was even seven hundred and twenty."

"Gramercy, it is marvelous!"

"But what are these in comparison with me? They are nothing."

"What? Canst thou truly look beyond even so vast a stretch of time as—"

"Seven hundred years? My lord, as clear as the vision of an eagle does my prophetic eye see into and lay bare the future of this world for nearly thirteen centuries and a half!"

My land, you should have seen the king's eyes spread slowly open, and lift the earth's entire atmosphere as much as an inch! That settled Merlin. One never had any occasion to prove his facts, with these people; all he had to do was to state them. It never occurred to anybody to doubt the statement.

"Now, then," I continued, "I *could* work both kinds of prophecy—the long and the short—if I chose to take the trouble to keep in practice; but I seldom exercise any but the long kind, because the other is beneath my dignity. It is properer to Merlin's sort. Of course, now and then I give out a minor prophecy, but not often. You will remember that there was great talk, when you reached the Valley of Holiness, about my having prophesied your coming and the very hour of your arrival, two or three days beforehand."

"Indeed, yes, I remember it now."

"Well, I could have done it as much as forty times easier, and piled on a thousand times more detail into the bargain, if it had been five hundred years away instead of two or three days."

"How amazing that it should be so!"

"Yes, a genuine expert can always foretell a thing that is five hundred years away easier than he can a thing that's only five hundred seconds off."

"And yet in reason it should clearly be the other way; it should be five hundred times as easy to foretell the last as the first."

Well, I had convinced the king; now he was as hungry to find out everything that was going to happen during the next thirteen centuries as if he were expecting to live in them. From that time out, I prophesied myself bald-headed trying to supply the demand. I have done some foolish things in my day, but this thing of playing myself for a prophet was the worst. Still, it had its advantages. A prophet doesn't have to have any brains. They are good to have, of course, for the ordinary happenings of life, but they are no use in professional work.

Every day a knight or so came along, and the sight of them fired the king's warlike spirit every time. He would have forgotten himself, sure, and said something to them in a style a suspicious shade or so above his peasant's degree, and so I always got him well out of the road in time. Then he would stand and look with all his eyes; and a proud light would flash from them, and his nostrils would inflate like a war-horse's, and I knew he was longing for a brush with them. But about noon of the third day I had stopped in the road to take a precaution which had been suggested by the whip-stroke that had fallen to my share two days before; a precaution which I had afterward decided to leave untaken, I so hated to do it; but now I had just had a fresh reminder: while striding heed-

lessly along, I stubbed my toe and fell sprawling. I
was so pale I couldn't think for a moment; then I got
softly and carefully up and unstrapped my knapsack.
I had a dynamite bomb in it, done up in wool in a
box. It was a good thing to have along; the time would
come when I could do a valuable miracle with it,
maybe, but it was a nervous thing to have about me,
and I didn't like to ask the king to carry it. Yet I must
either throw it away or think up some safe way to get
along with it. I got it out and slipped it into my bag,
and just then here came a couple of knights.

The king stood, stately as a statue, gazing toward
them—had forgotten himself again, of course—and
before I could get a word of warning out, it was time
for him to skip, and well that he did it, too. He supposed they would turn aside. Turn aside to avoid
trampling peasant dirt under foot? When had he
ever turned aside himself—or ever had the chance to
do it, if a peasant saw him or any other noble knight
in time to save him the trouble? The knights paid no
attention to the king at all; it was his place to look out
himself, and if he hadn't skipped he would have been
calmly ridden down, and laughed at besides.

The king was in a flaming fury, and shouted a challenge and cursed with royal vigor. The knights were
some little distance by now. They halted, greatly surprised, and turned in their saddles and looked back,
as if wondering if it might be worth while to bother
with such scum as we. Then they wheeled and started

It resembled a steamboat explosion on the Mississippi.

for us. Not a moment must be lost. I started for *them*. I passed them at a rattling speed, and as I went by I flung out a hair-lifting soul-scorching thirteen-jointed insult which made the king's effort poor and cheap by comparison. I got it out of the nineteenth century where they know how. They had such headway that they were nearly to the king before they could check up; then, frantic with rage, they stood up their horses on their hind hoofs and whirled them around, and the next moment here they came, breast to breast. I was seventy yards off, then, and scrambling up a great rock at the roadside. When they were within thirty yards of me they let their long lances droop to a level, bent their mailed heads, and so, with their horse-hair plumes streaming straight out behind, most gallant to see, this lightning express came tearing for me! When they were within fifteen yards, I sent that bomb with a sure aim, and it struck the ground under the horses' noses.

Yes, it was a neat thing, very neat and pretty to see. It resembled a steamboat explosion on the Mississippi; and during the next fifteen minutes we stood under a steady drizzle of fragments of knights and hardware and horse-flesh. I say we, for the king joined the audience, of course, as soon as he had got his breath again. There was a hole there which would afford steady work for all the people in that region for some years to come—in trying to explain it, I mean.

But I explained it to the king myself. I said it was done with a dynamite bomb. This information did him no damage, because it left him as intelligent as he was before. However, it was a noble miracle, in his eyes, and was another settler for Merlin. I thought it well enough to explain that this was a miracle of so rare a sort that it couldn't be done except when the atmospheric conditions were just right. Otherwise he would be asking for it every time we had a good subject, and that would be inconvenient, because I hadn't any more bombs along.

CHAPTER XIX

THE SMALLPOX HUT

On the morning of the fourth day, when it was just sunrise, and we had been tramping an hour in the chill dawn, I came to a resolution: the king *must* be drilled; things could not go on so; he must be taken in hand and deliberately drilled, or we couldn't ever venture to enter a dwelling; the very cats would know this masquerader for a humbug and no peasant. So I called a halt and said:

"Sire, as between clothes and face, you are all right, but as between your clothes and your bearing, you are all wrong. Your soldierly walk, your lordly bearing—these will not do. You stand too straight, your looks are too high, too confident. The cares of a kingdom do not stoop the shoulders, they do not droop the chin, they do not put doubt and fear in the heart and hang out the signs of them in slouching body and unsure step. It is the cares of the lowly born that do these things. You must learn the trick; you must imitate the trade-marks of poverty, misery, oppression, and insult. Pray try to walk like this."

The king took careful note, and then tried an imitation.

"Pretty fair—pretty fair. Chin a little lower, please —there, very good. Eyes too high; pray don't look at the horizon, look at the ground, ten steps in front of you. Ah—that is better, that is very good. Wait, please; you show too much vigor, too much decision; you want more of a shuffle. Look at me, please—this is what I mean. . . . Now you are getting it; that is the idea—at least, it sort of approaches it. . . . Yes, that is pretty fair. *But!* There is a great big something wanting; I don't quite know what it is. Please walk thirty yards, so that I can look you over. . . . Now, then—your head's right, speed's right, shoulders right, eyes right, chin right, walk and general style right—everything's right! And yet the fact remains, the whole is wrong. Do it again, please . . . *now* I think I begin to see what it is. Yes, I've struck it. You see, the genuine spiritlessness is wanting; that's what's the trouble. It's all *amateur*—mechanical details all right, almost to a hair; everything about perfect, except that it won't fool anyone."

"What, then, must one do?"

"Let me think. . . . I can't quite seem to get at it. In fact, there isn't anything that can right the matter but practice. This is a good place for it: roots and stony ground to break up your stately walk, a region not liable to interruption, only one field and one hut in sight, and they so far away that nobody could see us from there. It will be well to move a little off the road and put in the whole day drilling you, sire."

After the drill had gone on a little while, I said:

"Now, sire, imagine that we are at the door of the hut yonder, and the family are before us. Proceed, please—address the head of the house."

The king unconsciously straightened up like a monument and said, with frozen stiffness:

"Varlet, bring a seat; and serve to me what cheer ye have."

"Ah, your grace, that is not well done."

"In what does it lack?"

"These people do not call *each other* varlets."

"Nay, is that true?"

"Yes; only those above them call them so."

"Then must I try again. I will call him villein."

"No-no; for he may be a freeman."

"Ah, so. Then perhaps I should call him goodman."

"That would answer, your grace, but it would be still better if you said friend, or brother."

"Brother!—to dirt like that?"

"Ah, but *we* are pretending to be dirt like that, too."

"It is even true. I will say it. Brother, bring a seat, and thereto what cheer ye have, withal. *Now* 'tis right."

"Not quite, not wholly right. You have asked for one, not *us*—for one, not both; food for one, a seat for one."

The king looked puzzled—he wasn't a very heavy weight when it came to brains.

"Would *you* have a seat also—and sit?"

"If I did not sit, the man would see that we were only pretending to be equals."

"It is well and truly said! How wonderful is truth, come it in whatsoever unexpected form it may! Yes, he must bring out seats and food for both, and in serving us present not plate and napkin with more show of respect to the one than to the other."

"And there is even yet a detail that needs correcting. He must bring nothing outside; we will go in—in among the dirt, and possibly other unsightly things —and take the food with the household, and after the fashion of the house, and all on equal terms, except the man be of the slave class; and finally there will be no plate and no napkin, whether he be slave or free. Please walk again, my lord. There—it is better—it is the best yet; but not perfect. The shoulders have known no worse burden than iron mail, and they will not stoop."

"Give me, then, the bag. I will learn the spirit that goeth with burdens that have not honor. It is the spirit that stoopeth the shoulders, I suppose, and not the weight; for armor is heavy, yet it is a proud burden, and a man standeth straight in it. . . . Nay, offer me no objections. I will have the thing. Strap it upon my back."

He was complete now with that knapsack on, and looked as little like a king as any man I had ever seen. But it was an obstinate pair of shoulders; they could not seem to learn the trick of stooping with any sort of naturalness. The drill went on, I prompting and correcting:

"Now, make believe you are in debt, and eaten up by creditors; you are out of work—which is horse-shoeing, let us say—and can get none; and your wife is sick, your children are crying because they are hungry—"

And so on, and so on. I drilled him as representing in turn all sorts of people out of luck and suffering need and misfortunes. But lord, it was only just words, words—they meant nothing in the world to him; I might just as well have whistled. Words mean nothing, unless you have suffered in your own person the thing which the words try to describe.

When we arrived at that hut at mid-afternoon, we saw no signs of life about it. The field near by had been harvested some time before, and had a skinned look. Fences, sheds, everything had a ruined look. No animal was around anywhere, no living thing in sight. The stillness was awful; it was like the stillness of death. The cabin was a one-story one, black with age, and ragged from lack of repair.

The door stood a trifle open. We approached it on tiptoe and at half-breath—for that is the way one's feeling makes him do at such a time. The king knocked. We waited. No answer. Knocked again. No answer. I pushed the door softly open and looked in. I made out some dim forms, and a woman started up from the ground and stared at me, as one does who is awakened from sleep. Presently she found her voice:

"Have mercy!" she pleaded. "All is taken, nothing is left."

"I have not come to take anything, poor woman."

"You are not a priest?"

"No."

"Nor come not from the lord of the manor?"

"No, I am a stranger."

"Oh, then, for the fear of God, who visits with misery and death such as be harmless, stay not here, but fly! This place is under his curse—and his Church's."

"Let me come in and help you—you are sick and in trouble."

I was better used to the dim light now. I could see her hollow eyes fixed upon me. I could see how thin she was.

"I tell you the place is under the Church's ban. Save yourself—and go, before someone see thee here, and report it."

"Give yourself no trouble about me; I don't care anything for the Church's curse. Let me help you."

"Now all good spirits—if there be any such—bless thee for that word. Would God I had a cup of water! —but hold, hold, forget I said it, and fly; for there is that here that even he that feareth not the Church must fear: this disease whereof we die. Leave us, thou brave, good stranger, and take with thee such whole and sincere blessing as them that be accursed can give."

But before this I had picked up a wooden bowl and was rushing past the king on my way to the brook. It was ten yards away. When I got back and entered, the king was within and was opening the shutter that closed the window-hole, to let in air and light. The place was full of a foul smell. I put the bowl to the woman's lips, and as she gripped it with her eager fingers the shutter came open and a strong light flooded her face. Smallpox!

I sprang to the king, and said in his ear:

"Out of the door on the instant, sire! The woman is dying of that disease that almost destroyed Camelot two years ago."

He did not budge.

"Of a truth I shall remain—and likewise help."

I whispered again:

"King, it must not be. You must go."

"Ye mean well, and ye speak not unwisely. But it were shame that a king should know fear, and shame that belted knight should withhold his hand when there be such as need help. Peace, I will not go. It is you who must go. The Church's ban is not upon me, but it forbiddeth you to be here, and she will deal with you with a heavy hand if word come to her of your disobedience."

It was a desperate place for him to be in, and might

cost him his life, but it was no use to argue with him. If he considered his knightly honor at stake here, that was the end of argument. And so I dropped the subject. The woman spoke:

"Fair sir, of your kindness will ye climb the ladder there, and bring me news of what ye find? Be not afraid to report, for times can come when even a mother's heart is past breaking, being already broke."

"Stay," said the king, "and give the woman to eat. I will go." And he put down the knapsack.

I turned to start, but the king had already started. He halted, and looked down upon a man who lay in a dim light, and had not noticed us thus far, or spoken.

"Is it your husband?" the king asked.

"Yes."

"Is he asleep?"

"He is dead."

"Dead?"

"Yes, what triumph it is to know it! None can harm him, none insult him more. He is in heaven now, and happy; or if not there, he bides in hell and is content. We were boy and girl together; we were man and wife these five-and-twenty years, and never separated till this day. Think how long that is to love and suffer together. This morning was he out of his mind, and in his fancy we were boy and girl again and wandering in the happy fields; and so in that innocent glad dream he died."

There was a slight noise from the direction of the dim corner where the ladder was. It was the king descending. I could see that he was bearing something in one arm, and assisting himself with the other. He came forward into the light; upon his breast lay a slender girl of fifteen. She was but half conscious; she was dying of smallpox. Here was heroism at its best; this was challenging death in the open field unarmed, and no admiring world in silks and cloth-of-gold to gaze and applaud; and yet the king's bearing was as serenely brave as it had always been in those cheaper contests where knight meets knight in equal fight, clothed in protecting steel. He was great now, sublimely great.

He laid the girl down by her mother, who poured out words and caresses from an overflowing heart, and one could see a flickering faint light of response in the child's eyes, but that was all. The mother hung over her, kissing her, petting her, and begging her to speak, but the lips only moved and no sound came. I snatched my liquor flask from my knapsack, but the woman forbade me, and said:

"No, she does not suffer; it is better so. It might bring her back to life. None that be so good and kind as ye are would do her that cruel hurt. For look you— what is left to live for? Her brothers are gone, her father is gone, her mother goeth, the Church's curse is upon her, and none may shelter or befriend her even though she lay perishing in the road. She is desolate. I have not asked you, good heart, if her sister be still alive here overhead; I had no need; ye had gone back, else, and not left the poor thing forsaken—"

"She is at peace," interrupted the king in a subdued voice.

"I would not change it. How rich is this day in happiness! Ah, my Annis, thou shalt join thy sister soon —thou'rt on thy way, and these be merciful friends that will not hinder."

And so she fell to murmuring and cooing over the girl again, softly stroking her face and hair, and kissing her and calling her by affectionate names; but there was scarcely sign of response now in the glazing eyes. I saw tears rise in the king's eyes and trickle down his face. The woman noticed them too, and said:

"Ah, I know that sign: thou'st a wife at home, poor soul, and you and she have gone hungry to bed, many's the time, that the little ones might have your crust; you know what poverty is, and the daily insults of your betters, and the heavy hand of the Church and the king."

The king winced under this accidental home-shot, but kept still; he was learning his part; and he was playing it well, too, for a pretty dull beginner. I changed the subject and offered the woman food and liquor, but she refused both. She would allow nothing to come between her and death. Then I slipped away and brought the dead child from aloft, and laid it by her. This broke her down again, and there was another scene that was full of heartbreak. By and by I persuaded her to tell her story.

"Ye know it well yourselves, having suffered it, for truly none of our condition in Britain escape it. It is the old, weary tale. We fought and struggled and succeeded, meaning by success, that we lived and did not die; more than that is not to be claimed. No troubles came that we could not outlive, till this year brought them; then came they all at once, as one might say, and overwhelmed us. Years ago the lord of the manor planted certain fruit-trees on our farm, in the best part of it, too—a grievous wrong and shame—"

"But it was his right," interrupted the king.

"None denieth that, indeed; if the law mean anything, what is the lord's is his, and what is mine is his also. Our farm was ours by lease; therefore 'twas likewise his, to do with it as he would. Some little time ago, three of those trees were found cut down. Our three grown sons ran frightened to report the crime. Well, in his lordship's dungeon they lie. He says there shall they lie and rot till they confess. They have naught to confess, being innocent; therefore there will they remain until they die. Ye know that right well. Think how this left us—a man, a woman, and two children—to gather a crop that was planted by so much greater number; yes, and protect it night and day from pigeons and prowling animals that be sacred and must not be hurt by any of our sort. When my lord's crop was nearly ready for the harvest, so also was ours; when his bell rang to call us to his fields to harvest his crop for nothing, he would not allow that I and my two girls should count for our three captive sons, but for only two of them; so, for the lacking one were we daily fined. All this time our own crop was perishing through neglect; and so both the priest and his lordship fined us because their shares of it were suffering through damage. In the end the fines ate up our crop, and they took it all; they took it all and made us harvest it for them, without pay or food, and we starving. Then the worst came when I, in my despair, uttered a deep curse— oh, a thousand of them!—against the Church and the Church's ways. It was ten days ago. I had fallen sick with this disease, and it was to the priest I said the words, for he was come to scold me because I had complained. He carried the story of my wickedness to his betters; I was stubborn; wherefore, presently upon my head and upon all heads that were dear to me, fell the curse of Rome.

"Since that day we are avoided, shunned with horror. None has come near this hut to know whether we live or not. The rest of us were taken ill. Then I got up, as wife and mother will. It was little they could have eaten in any case; it was less than little they had to eat. But there was water, and I gave them that. How they wanted it! and how they blessed it! But the end came yesterday; my strength broke down. Yesterday was the last time I ever saw my husband and this youngest child alive. I have lain here all these hours—these ages, ye may say—listening, listening for any sound up there that—"

She gave a sharp quick glance at her eldest daughter, then cried out, "Oh, my darling!" and feebly gathered the stiffening form to her sheltering arms. She had recognized the death-rattle.

CHAPTER XX

THE TRAGEDY OF THE MANOR-HOUSE

At midnight all was over, and we sat in the presence of four corpses. We covered them with such rags as we could find, and started away, fastening the door behind us. Their home must be these people's grave, for they could not have Christian burial, or be admitted to sacred ground.

We had not moved four steps when I caught a sound as of footsteps upon gravel. My heart flew to my throat. We must not be seen coming from that house. I plucked at the king's robe and we drew back and took shelter behind the corner of the cabin.

"Now we are safe," I said, "but it was a close call, so to speak. If the night had been lighter he might have seen us; he seemed to be so near."

"Perhaps it is but a beast and not a man at all."

"True. But man or beast, it will be wise to stay here a minute and let it get by and out of the way."

"Hark! It comes hither."

True again. The steps were coming toward us, straight toward the hut. It must be a beast, then, and we might as well have saved our fear. I was going to step out, but the king laid his hand upon my arm. There was a moment of silence; then we heard a soft knock on the cabin door. It made me shiver. Presently the knock was repeated, and then we heard these words in a guarded voice:

"Mother! Father! Open—we have got free, and we bring news to pale your cheeks but gladden your hearts; and we may not stay, but must fly! And—but they answer not. Mother! Father!"

I drew the king toward the other end of the hut and whispered:

"Come, now we can get to the road."

The king hesitated, was going to object; but just then we heard the door give way, and knew that those desolate men were in the presence of their dead.

"Come, my lord! in a moment they will strike a light, and then will follow that which it would break your heart to hear."

He did not hesitate this time. The moment we were in the road I ran, and after a moment he threw dignity aside and followed. I did not want to think of what was happening in the hut; I couldn't bear it; I wanted to drive it out of my mind; so I struck into the first subject that lay under that one in my mind:

"I have had the disease those people died of, and so have nothing to fear; but if you have not had it also—"

He broke in upon me to say he was in trouble, and it was his conscience that was troubling him:

"These young men have got free, they say—but how? It is not likely that their lord hath set them free."

"Oh, no, I make no doubt they escaped."

"That is my trouble; I have a fear that this is so."

"I do suspect that they escaped, but if they did, I am not sorry, certainly."

"I am not sorry, I *think*—but—"

"What is it? What is there for one to be troubled about?"

"*If* they did escape, then are we bound in duty to lay hands upon them and deliver them again to their lord; for it is not proper that one of his quality should suffer a so insolent and high-handed outrage from persons of their base degree."

There it was again. He could see only one side of it. He was born so, educated so. To imprison these men without proof and starve their families was no harm, for they were merely peasants and subject to the will and pleasure of their lord, no matter what fearful form it might take; but for these men to break out of unjust captivity was insult and outrage.

I worked more than half an hour before I got him to change the subject, and even then an outside matter did it for me. This was a something which caught our eyes as we struck the top of a small hill—a red glow, a good way off.

"That's a fire," said I.

Fires interested me considerably, because I was getting a good deal of an insurance business started, and was also training some horses and building some steam fire-engines, with an eye to a paid fire department by and by.

We stood there a while in the thick darkness and stillness, looking toward the red blur in the distance, and trying to make out the meaning of a far-away murmur that rose and fell on the night. Sometimes it swelled up and for a moment seemed less distant; but when we were hopefully expecting to learn what it was, it dulled and sank again. We started down the hill in its direction, and the winding road plunged us at once into almost solid darkness. We groped along down for half a mile, perhaps, that murmur growing more and more distinct all the time, the coming storm threatening more and more, with now and then a little shiver of wind, a faint show of lightning, and dull grumblings of distant thunder. I was in the lead. I ran against something—a soft heavy something which gave slightly to my weight; at the same moment the lightning glared out, and within a foot of my face was the face of a man who was hanging from the limb of a tree! It was a horrible sight. Straightway there was an ear-splitting explosion of thunder, and the bottom of heaven fell out; the rain poured down. No matter, we must try to cut this man down on the chance that there might be life in him yet, mustn't we? The lightning came quick and sharp now, and the place was alternately noonday and midnight. One moment the man would be hanging before me in an intense light, and the next he was blotted out again in the darkness. I told the king we must cut him down. The king at once objected.

"If he hanged himself, he was willing to; so let him be. If others hanged him, belike they had the right—let him hang."

"But—"

"But me no buts, but even leave him as he is. And for yet another reason. When the lightning cometh again—there, look abroad."

Two others hanging, within fifty yards of us!

"It is not weather fit for doing useless courtesies unto dead folk. They are past thanking you. Come, it is unprofitable to tarry here."

There was reason in what he said; so we moved on. Within the next mile we counted six more hanging forms by the blaze of the lightning, and altogether it was a ghostly excursion. That murmur was a murmur no longer; it was a roar, a roar of men's voices. A man came flying by now, dimly through the darkness, and other men chasing him. They disappeared. Presently another case of the kind occurred, and then another and another. Then a sudden turn of the road brought us in sight of that fire. It was a large manor-house, and little or nothing was left of it; and everywhere men were flying and other men raging after them in pursuit.

I warned the king that this was not a safe place for strangers. We would better get away from the light until matters should improve. We stepped back a little and hid in the edge of the wood. From this hiding-place we saw both men and women hunted by the mob.

The fearful work went on until nearly dawn. Then, the fire being out and the storm over, the voices and flying footsteps presently ceased, and it was dark and still again.

We ventured out and hurried cautiously away; and although we were worn out and sleepy, we kept on until we had put this place some miles behind us. Then we stopped at the hut of a charcoal-burner, and got what was to be had. A woman was up and about, but the man was still asleep, on straw on the clay floor. The woman seemed uneasy until I explained that I and my friend Jones, for so I called the king, were travelers and had lost our way and been wandering in the woods all night. She became talkative then, and asked if we had heard of the terrible goings-on at the manor-house of Abblasoure. Yes, we had heard of them, but what we wanted now was rest and sleep. The king broke in:

"Sell us the house and take yourselves away, for we be dangerous company, being late come from people that died of the Spotted Death."

It was good of him, but unnecessary. One of the commonest decorations of the nation was the waffle-iron face of the smallpox victim. I had early noticed that the woman and her husband were both so decorated. She made us entirely welcome, and had no fears; and plainly she was immensely impressed by the king's proposition; for, of course, it was a good deal of an event in her life to run across a person of the king's humble appearance who was ready to buy a man's house for the sake of a night's lodging. It gave her a large respect for us, and she did her best to make us comfortable.

We slept till far into the afternoon, and then got up hungry enough to make peasant food taste good to the king. There was little of it and little variety; it consisted solely of onions, salt, and the national black bread made out of horse-feed. The woman told us about the affair of the evening before. At ten or eleven at night, when everybody was in bed, the manor-house burst into flames. The country-side swarmed to the rescue, and the family were saved, with one exception —the master. He did not appear. Everybody was frantic over this loss, and two brave yeomen sacrificed their lives in ransacking the burning house seeking him. But after a while he was found—what was left of him—which was his corpse. It was in a hedge three hundred yards away, bound, gagged, stabbed in a dozen places.

Who had done this? Suspicion fell upon a humble family in the neighborhood who had been lately treated with particular harshness by the baron; and from these people the suspicion easily spread to their relatives and friends. A suspicion was enough; my lord's men-at-arms proclaimed an instant crusade against these people, and were promptly joined by the community in general. The woman's husband, Marco, had been active with the mob, and had not returned home until nearly dawn. He was gone now to find out what the general result had been. While we were still talking he came back. His report was revolting enough— eighteen persons hanged or butchered, and two yeomen and thirteen prisoners lost in the fire.

"And how many prisoners were there altogether in the vaults?"

"Thirteen."

"Then every one of them was lost?"

"Yes, all."

"But the people arrived in time to save the family; how is it they could save none of the prisoners?"

Marco looked puzzled, and said:

"Would one unlock the vaults at such a time? Some would have escaped."

"Then you mean that nobody *did* unlock them?"

"None went near them, either to lock or unlock. It stands to reason that the bolts were strong; therefore it was only needful to establish a watch, so that if any broke the bonds he might not escape, but be taken. None were taken."

"Even so, three did escape," said the king, "and ye will do well to publish it and set justice upon their track, for these murdered the baron and fired the house."

I was expecting he would come out with that. For a moment Marco and his wife showed an eager interest in this news and an impatience to go out and spread it; then a sudden something else showed in their faces, and they began to ask questions. I answered the questions myself, and narrowly watched the effects. I was soon satisfied that the knowledge of who these three prisoners were had somehow changed the atmosphere, and that our hosts' continued eagerness to go and spread the news was now only pretended and not real. The king did not notice the change, and I was glad of that. I worked the conversation around toward other details of the night's proceedings, and noted that these people were relieved to have it take that direction.

The painful thing about all this business was the quickness with which this community had turned their cruel hands against their own class. Marco and his wife seemed to feel that in a quarrel between a person of their own class and his lord, it was the natural and proper and rightful thing for that poor devil's whole class to side with the master and fight his battle for him, without ever stopping to inquire into the rights or wrongs of the matter.

The king presently showed impatience, and said:

"If you talk here all day, justice will miscarry. Think ye the criminals will abide in their father's house? They are fleeing; they are not waiting. You should look to it that horsemen be set upon their track."

The woman paled slightly, but quite noticeably, and Marco looked worried. I said:

"Come, friend, I will walk a little way with you, and explain which direction I think they would try to take."

The last remark was for the king—to quiet him. On the road Marco marched with a steady step, but there was no eagerness in it. By and by I said:

"What relation were these men to you—cousins?"

He turned as white as his layer of charcoal would let him, and stopped, trembling.

"Ah, my God, how know ye that?"

"I didn't know it; it was a chance guess."

"Poor lads, they are lost. And good lads they were, too."

"Were you actually going yonder to tell on them?"

He didn't quite know how to take that, but he said hesitatingly:

"Ye-s."

"Then I think you are a damned scoundrel!"

It made him as glad as if I had called him an angel.

"Say the good words again, brother! for surely ye mean that ye would not betray me if I failed of my duty."

"Duty? There is no duty in the matter, except the duty to keep still and let those men get away. They've done a righteous deed."

He looked pleased—pleased, and touched with fear at the same time. He looked up and down the road to see that no one was coming, and then said in a cautious voice:

"From what land come you, brother, that you speak such dangerous words and seem not to be afraid?"

"They are not dangerous words when spoken to one of my own class, I take it. You would not tell anybody I said them?"

"I? I would be drawn apart by wild horses first."

"Well, then, let me say my say. I have no fears of your repeating it. I think devil's work has been done last night upon those innocent poor people. That old baron got only what he deserved. If I had my way, all his kind should have the same luck."

Fear and depression vanished from Marco's manner, and gratefulness and a brave courage took their place:

"Even though you be a spy, and your words a trap for my undoing, yet are they such refreshment that to hear them again and others like them, I would go to the gallows happy, as having had one good feast at least in a starved life. And I will say my say now, and ye may report it if ye be so minded. I helped to hang my neighbors because it meant danger to my own life not to help in the master's cause; the others helped for no other reason. All rejoice today that he is dead, but all do go about seemingly sorrowing, for in that lies safety. I have said the words, I have said the words!—the only ones that have ever tasted good in my mouth, and the reward of that taste is sufficient. Lead on, if ye will, be it even to death, for I am ready."

There it was, you see. A man *is* a man, at bottom. Whole ages of abuse cannot crush the manhood clear out of him.

CHAPTER XXI

THE YANKEE AND THE KING ENTERTAIN

We strolled along in a lazy fashion now, and talked. We must use about the time it ought to take to go to the little village of Abblasoure and put justice on the track of those murderers and get back home again.

It was not a dull excursion for me. I managed to put in the time very well. I made various acquaintance-ships and, as a stranger, was able to ask as many questions as I wanted to. A thing which naturally interested me, as a statesman, was the matter of wages. I picked up what I could under that head during the afternoon. A man who hasn't had much experience, and doesn't think, is apt to measure a nation's prosperity or lack of prosperity by the mere size of the prevailing wages; if the wages be high, the nation is prosperous; if low, it isn't. This is an error. It isn't what sum you get, it's how much you can buy with it that's the important thing; and it's *that* that tells whether your wages are high in fact or only high in name.

I made various acquaintances in the village, and a thing that pleased me a good deal was to find our new coins in circulation—lots of cents, a good many nickels, and some silver; all this among mechanics and common folk; yes, and even some gold.

Our new money was not only handsomely circulat-
ing, but its language was already in use; that is to say,
people had dropped the names of the former moneys,
and spoke of things as being worth so many dollars or
cents. It was very pleasing. We were progressing,
that was sure.

I got to know several master mechanics, but about
the most interesting fellow among them was the blacksmith, Dowley. He was a live man and a brisk talker,
and was doing a raging business. Marco was very
proud of having such a man for a friend. Dowley and
I were friends at once. I was bound to see more of
him, so I invited him to come out to Marco's Sunday
and dine with us. Marco held his breath; and when
Dowley accepted, he was so grateful that he almost
forgot to be astonished that so great a man would dine
with us.

Then he grew thoughtful, then sad; and when he
heard me tell Dowley I should have Dickon, the boss
mason, and Smug, the boss wheelwright, out there
too, his face turned to chalk. I knew what was the
matter with him; it was the expense. He saw ruin
before him. However, on our way to invite the others,
I said:

"You must allow me to have these friends come, and
you must also allow me to pay the costs."

His face cleared, and he said with spirit:

"But not all of it, not all of it. Ye cannot well bear
a burden like this alone."

I stopped him, and said:

"Now let's understand each other on the spot, old friend. I am only a farm bailiff, it is true; but I am not poor, nevertheless. I have been very fortunate this year—you would be astonished to know how I have prospered. I tell you the honest truth when I say I could give as many as a dozen feasts like this and never care *that* for the expense!" and I snapped my fingers. I could see myself rise a foot at a time in Marco's estimation. "So you see, you must let me have my way. You can't contribute a cent to this feast; that's *settled*."

"It's grand and good of you——"

"No, it isn't. You've opened your house to Jones and me in the most generous way; Jones was remarking upon it today, just before you came back from the village; for although he wouldn't be likely to say such a thing to you—because Jones isn't a talker—he has a good heart and a grateful one and knows how to appreciate it when he is well treated; yes, you and your wife have been very hospitable toward us——"

"Ah, brother, 'tis nothing—*such* hospitality!"

"But it *is* something; the best a man has, freely given, is always something. And so we'll shop around and get up this layout now, and don't you worry about the expense."

So we went gadding along, dropping in here and there, pricing things, and gossiping with the shopkeepers about the riot.

I had noted that the clothing of Marco and his wife was patched and worn. Now I wanted to fit these people out with new suits without hurting their feelings, and I didn't know just how to get at it, until at last it struck me that as I had already been telling how grateful the king was, I should pretend he was buying the things; so I said:

"And Marco, there's another thing which you must permit—out of kindness for Jones—because you wouldn't want to offend him. He begged me to buy some little things and give them to you and your wife, Dame Phyllis, and let him pay for them without your ever knowing they came from him—you know how a delicate person feels about that sort of thing—and so I said I would, and we would keep mum. Well, his idea was a new outfit of clothes for you both—"

"Oh, it is wastefulness! It may not be, brother, it may not be. Consider the vastness of the sum—"

"Hang the vastness of the sum! We'll step in here now and price this man's stuff—and don't forget to remember not to let on to Jones that you know he had anything to do with it. He's a farmer—pretty fairly well-to-do farmer—and I'm his bailiff; *but*—the imagination of that man! You might listen to him a hundred years and never take him for a farmer, especially if he talked agriculture. Between you and me privately he doesn't know as much about farming as he does about running a kingdom; still, whatever he talks about, you want to drop your under-jaw and listen, the same as if you had never heard such wisdom in all your life before, and were afraid you might die before you got enough of it. That will please Jones."

It tickled Marco to hear about such an odd character, but it also prepared him for accidents; and in my experience when you travel with a king who is letting on to be something else and can't remember it more than about half the time, you can't take too much care.

This was the best store we had come across yet; it had everything in it, in small quantities, from anvils and dry-goods all the way down to fish and cheap jewelry. I concluded I would buy everything right here, and not go pricing around any more. So I got rid of Marco, by sending him off to invite the mason and the wheelwright, which left the field free to me. I showed money enough, in a careless way, to get the shopkeeper's respect, and then I wrote down a list of the things I wanted and handed it to him to see if he could read it. He could. He ran it through, and remarked with satisfaction that it was a pretty heavy bill. Well, and so it was, for a little concern like that. I was not only providing a swell dinner, but some odds and ends of extras. I ordered that the things be carted out and delivered at the dwelling of Marco, the son of Marco, by Saturday evening, and the bill sent me at dinner-time Sunday.

The king had hardly missed us when we got back at nightfall. He had early dropped again into his dream

of a grand invasion of Gaul with the whole strength
of his kingdom at his back, and the afternoon had
slipped away without his ever coming to himself
again.

Well, when my purchases arrived toward sunset,
Saturday afternoon, I had my hands full to keep the
Marcos from fainting. They were sure Jones and I
were ruined past help, and they blamed themselves.
You see, in addition to the dinner materials, which
called for a sufficiently round sum, I had bought a lot
of extras for the future comfort of the family: for
instance, a big lot of wheat, also a sizable dinner-
table; also two entire pounds of salt; also crockery,
stools, the clothes, a small cask of beer, and so on. I
instructed the Marcos to keep quiet about this, so as
to give me a chance to surprise the guests and show
off a little. Concerning the new clothes, the simple
couple were like children; they were up and down all
night to see if it wasn't nearly daylight, so that they
could put them on, and they were into them at last as
much as an hour before dawn.

Toward noon the guests arrived, and we assembled
under a great tree and were soon as sociable as old
acquaintances. Even the king's reserve melted a little,
though it was some little trouble to him to adjust himself to the name of Jones along at first. I had asked
him to try not to forget that he was a farmer; but I
had also considered it wise to ask him to let the thing
stand at that, and not enlarge on it any, because he

was just the kind of person you could depend on to spoil a little thing like that if you didn't warn him; his tongue was so handy and his spirit so willing, and his information so uncertain.

Dowley was in fine feather, and I early got him started, and then skilfully worked him around onto his own history for a text and himself for a hero, and then it was good to sit there and hear him hum. Self-made man, you know. They know how to talk. They do deserve more credit than any other breed of men; yes, that is true; and they are among the very first to find it out, too. He told how he had begun life an orphan lad without money and without friends able to help him; how he had lived as the slaves of the meanest master lived; how his day's work was from sixteen to eighteen hours long, and yielded him only enough black bread to keep him in a half-fed condition; how his faithful endeavors finally attracted the attention of a good blacksmith, who came near knocking him dead with kindness by suddenly offering, when he was totally unprepared, to take him as his bound apprentice for nine years and give him board and clothes and teach him the trade. That was his first great rise, his first gorgeous stroke of fortune; and you saw that he couldn't yet speak of it without a sort of wonder and delight that such a promotion should have fallen to the lot of a common human being. He got no new clothing during his apprenticeship, but on his graduation day his master tricked him out in brand-new linens and made him feel unspeakably rich and fine.

"I remember me that day!" the wheelwright sang out with enthusiasm.

"And I likewise!" cried the mason. "I would not believe they were thine own; in faith I could not."

"Nor could others!" shouted Dowley, with sparkling eyes. "I was like to lose my character, the neighbors thinking I had perhaps been stealing. It was a great day, a great day; one forgetteth not days like that."

Yes, and his master was a fine man, and prosperous, and always had a great feast of meat twice in the year, and with it white bread, true white bread; in fact, lived like a lord, so to speak. And in time Dowley succeeded to the business and married the daughter.

"And now consider what is come to pass," said he, impressively. "Two times in every month there is fresh meat upon my table." He made a pause here to let that fact sink home, and then added—"and eight times salt meat."

"It is even true," said the wheelwright.

"I know it of mine own knowledge," said the mason.

"On my table appeareth white bread every Sunday in the year," added the master smith, solemnly. "I leave it to your own consciences, friends, if this is not also true?"

"By my head, yes," cried the mason.

"I can testify it, and I do," said the wheelwright.

"And as to furniture, ye shall say yourselves what mine equipment is."

"Ye have five stools, and of the sweetest workmanship at that, although your family is but three," said the wheelwright, with deep respect.

"And six wooden goblets, and six platters of wood and two of pewter to eat and drink from withal," said the mason, impressively. "And I say it as knowing God is my judge."

"Now ye know what manner of man I am, brother Jones," said the smith, with a fine and friendly air, "and doubtless ye would look to find me a man proud and feeling superior, but trouble yourself not, as concerning that; ye well know ye shall find me a man that is willing to receive any as his equal that carrieth a right heart in his body, no matter how poor he is. And in token of it, here is my hand; and I say with my own mouth we are equals"—and he smiled around on the company with the satisfaction of a god who is doing the handsome and gracious thing and is quite well aware of it.

The king took the hand with a poorly disguised hesitation, and let go of it as willingly as a lady lets go of a fish; all of which had a good effect, for it was mistaken for an embarrassment natural to one who was being beamed upon by greatness.

Marco's wife brought out the table now, and set it under the tree. It caused a stir of surprise, it being brand new and a fine article. But the surprise rose higher still when she slowly unfolded an actual simonpure table-cloth and spread it. That was a notch above even the blacksmith's grandeurs, and it hit him hard; you could see it. But Marco was in Paradise; you could see that, too. Then she brought two fine new stools. Whew! that was a sensation; it was visible in the eyes of every guest. Then she brought two more— as calmly as she could. Sensation again—with awed murmurs. Again she brought two—walking on air, she was so proud. The guests were stunned, and the mason muttered:

"There is that about earthly display which doth ever move to admiration."

As his wife turned away, Marco couldn't help slapping on the climax while the thing was hot; so he said:

"These are enough; leave the rest."

So there were more yet! It was a fine effect. I couldn't have played the hand better myself.

From this out, the madam piled up the surprises with a rush amid the "Oh's" and "Ah's." She fetched crockery—new, and plenty of it; new wooden goblets and other table furniture; and beer, fish, chicken, a goose, eggs, roast beef, roast mutton, a ham, a small roast pig, and a wealth of genuine white wheat bread. Take it by and large, that spread laid everything far and away in the shade that ever that crowd had seen before. And while they sat there just simply stupefied with wonder and awe, I sort of waved my hand as if by accident, and the storekeeper's son came forth and said he had come to collect.

"That's all right," I said, indifferently. "What is the amount? Give us the items."

Then he read off the bill, while those three amazed men listened.

After the bill was read there was a pale and awful silence.

"Is that all?" I asked, in a voice of the most perfect calmness. "Give me the grand total, please."

The clerk leaned against the tree to steady himself, and said:

"Three dollars and ninety-one cents!"

The wheelwright fell off his stool, the others grabbed the table to save themselves, and there was a deep and general exclamation:

"God be with us in the day of disaster!"

The clerk hastened to say:

"My father chargeth me to say he cannot honorably require you to pay it all at this time, and therefore only prayeth you—"

I paid no more attention than if it were the idle breeze, but, with an air of indifference amounting almost to weariness, got out my money and tossed four dollars onto the table. Ah, you should have seen them stare!

The clerk was astonished and charmed. He asked me to keep one of the dollars as security, until he could go to town and—I interrupted:

"What, and fetch back nine cents? Nonsense! Take the whole. Keep the change."

There was an amazed murmur to this effect:

"Verily this being is *made* of money. He throweth it away even as if it were dirt."

I turned to the others and said as calmly as one would ask the time of day:

"Well, if we are all ready, I judge the dinner is. Come, fall to."

CHAPTER XXII

THE YANKEE ARGUES TOO WELL

The king ate his fill, and then, since the talk was not of battle and conquest, became drowsy and went off to take a nap. Mrs. Marco cleared the table, placed the beer-keg handy, and went away to eat her dinner of leavings in humble privacy, and the rest of us soon drifted into matters near and dear to the hearts of our sort—business and wages, of course. At a first glance, things appeared to be very prosperous in this little kingdom as compared with the state of things in my own region. They had the "protection" system in full force here, whereas we were working along down toward free trade by easy stages, and were now about half-way. Before long, Dowley and I were doing all the talking, the others hungrily listening. Dowley warmed to his work, saw an advantage, and began to put questions which he considered pretty awkward ones for me, and they did have something of that look:

"In your country, brother, what is the wage of a master bailiff, carter, shepherd, swineherd?"

"A quarter of a cent a day."

The smith's face beamed with joy. He said:

"With us they are allowed double that! And what may a mechanic get—carpenter, dauber, mason, painter, blacksmith, wheelwright, and the like?"

"On the average, half a cent a day."

"Ho-ho! With us they are allowed a cent."

His face shone upon the company like a sunburst. But I didn't scare at all. Here is the way I started in on him. I asked:

"What do you pay a pound for salt?"

"A cent."

"We pay two-fifths of a cent. What do you pay for beef and mutton—when you buy it?" That was a neat hit; it made the color come.

"It changes somewhat, but not much; one may say three-fourths of a cent the pound."

"*We* pay one-third of a cent. What do you pay for eggs?"

"One-half cent the dozen."

"We pay one-fifth cent. What do you pay for wheat?"

"At the rate of nine cents the bushel."

"We pay four cents. What do you pay for a man's linen suit?"

"Thirteen cents."

"We pay six." Then I said: "Look here, dear friend, *what's become of your high wages you were bragging so about a few minutes ago?*"—and I looked around on the company with satisfaction, for I had slipped up on him gradually and tied him hand and foot, you see, without his ever noticing that he was being tied at all. "What's become of those noble high wages of yours? I seem to have knocked the stuffing all out of them, it appears to me."

But if you will believe me, he merely looked surprised, that is all! He didn't grasp the situation at all, didn't know he had walked into a trap, didn't discover that he was *in* a trap. I could have shot him, from vexation. With cloudy eye and a struggling mind he fetched this out:

"I seem not to understand. It is *proved* that our wages be double thine; how then may it be that thou'st knocked therefrom the stuffing?"

Well, I was stunned, partly with this unlooked-for stupidity on his part, and partly because his fellows so plainly sided with him and were of his mind—if you might call it mind. My position was simple enough, plain enough; how could it ever be simplified more? However, I must try:

"Why, look here, brother Dowley, don't you see? Your wages are merely higher than ours in *name*, not in *fact*."

"Hear him! They are *double*. Ye have confessed it yourself."

"Yes, I don't deny that at all. But that's got nothing to do with it; the *amount* of wages in mere coins, with meaningless names attached to them to know them by, has got nothing to do with it. The thing is, how much can you *buy* with your wages?—that's the idea. While it is true that with you a good mechanic is allowed about three dollars and a half a year, and with us only about a dollar and seventy-five—"

"There—ye're confessing it again, ye're confessing it again!"

"Confound it, I've never denied it, I tell you! What I say is this. With us *half* a dollar buys more than a *dollar* buys with you, and *therefore* it stands to reason and the commonest kind of common sense, that our wages are *higher* than yours."

He looked dazed, and said despairingly:

"Verily, I cannot make it out. Ye've just *said* ours are higher, and with the same breath ye take it back."

I had to give it up. What those people valued was *high wages;* it didn't seem to be a matter of any consequence to them whether the high wages would buy anything or not.

I was smarting under a sense of defeat. Undeserved defeat, but what of that? That didn't soften the smart any. And to think of the circumstances! The first statesman of the age, the most capable man, the best-informed man in the entire world, sitting here apparently defeated in argument by an ignorant country blacksmith! And I could see that those others were sorry for me!—which made me blush. Put yourself in my place; feel as mean as I did, as ashamed as I felt—wouldn't *you* have struck below the belt to get even? Yes, you would; it is simply human nature. Well, that is what I did. I am not trying to justify it;

I'm only saying that I was mad, and *anybody* would have done it.

Well, when I make up my mind to hit a man, I don't plan out a love-tap. And I don't jump at him all of a sudden, and risk making a blundering half-way business of it; he never suspects that I'm going to hit him at all; and by and by, all in a flash, he's flat on his back, and he can't tell for the life of him how it all happened. That is the way I went for brother Dowley. I started to talking lazy and comfortable, as if I was just talking to pass the time.

"Boys, there's a good many curious things about law and custom and usage, and all that sort of thing, when you come to look at it; yes, and about the drift and progress of human opinion and movement, too. There are written laws—they perish; but there are also unwritten laws—*they* are eternal. Take the unwritten law of wages: it says they've got to advance, little by little, straight through the centuries. And notice how it works. We know what wages are now, here and there and yonder; we strike an average, and say that's the wages of today. We know what the wages were a hundred years ago; and what they were two hundred years ago; that's as far back as we can get, but it is enough to give us the law of progress; and so, without a document to help us, we can come pretty close to determining what the wages were three and four and five hundred years ago. Good, so far.

Do we stop there? No. We stop looking backward; we face around and apply the law to the future. My friends, I can tell you what people's wages are going to be at any date in the future you want to know, for hundreds and hundreds of years."

"What, goodman, what!"

"Yes. In seven hundred years wages will have risen to six times what they are now, here in your region, and farm-hands will be allowed three cents a day, and mechanics six."

"I would I might die now and live then!" interrupted Smug, the wheelwright, with a fine greedy glow in his eye.

"And that isn't all; they'll get their board besides —such as it is; it won't bloat them. Two hundred and fifty years later—pay attention now—a mechanic's wages will be—mind you, this is law, not guesswork— a mechanic's wages will then be *twenty* cents a day!"

There was a general gasp of awed astonishment. Dickon the mason murmured, with raised eyes and hands:

"More than three weeks' pay for one day's work!"

"Riches!—of a truth, yes, riches!" muttered Marco, his breath coming quick and short with excitement.

"Wages will keep on rising, little by little, little by little, as steadily as a tree grows, and at the end of three hundred and forty years more there'll be at least *one* country where the mechanic's average wage will be *two hundred* cents a day!"

It knocked them absolutely dumb! Not a man of them could get his breath for upward of two minutes. Then the coal-burner said, prayerfully:

"Might I but live to see it!"

"It is the income of an earl!" said Smug.

"An earl, say ye?" said Dowley; "Ye could say more than that and speak no lie; there's no earl in this realm that hath an income like to that. Income of an earl—mf! It's the income of an angel!"

"Now, then, that is what is going to happen as regards wages. In that distant day, a man will earn, with *one* week's work, that bill of goods which it takes you upward of *fifty* weeks to earn now. Some other pretty surprising things are going to happen, too. Brother Dowley, who is it that determines, every spring, what the particular wage of each kind of mechanic, laborer, and servant shall be for that year?"

"Sometimes the courts, sometimes the town council; but most of all, the magistrate."

"Doesn't ask any of those poor devils to *help* him fix their wages for them, does he?"

"Hm! That *were* an idea! The master that's to pay him the money is the one that's rightly concerned in that matter, ye will notice."

"Yes, but I thought the other man might have some little trifle at stake in it, too; and even his wife and children, poor creatures. The masters are these: nobles, rich men, the prosperous generally. These few, who do no work, determine what pay the vast number

shall have who *do* work. You see? They're a 'combine'
—a trade-union, to coin a new phrase—who band
themselves together to force their lowly brother to
take what they choose to give. Thirteen hundred years
hence—so says the unwritten law—the 'combine' will
be the other way, and then how these fine people's descendants will fume and fret and grit their teeth over
the insolent tyranny of trade-unions! Yes, indeed! the
magistrate will calmly arrange the wages from now
clear away down into the nineteenth century; and then
all of a sudden the wage-earner will consider that a
couple of thousand years or so is enough of this one-
sided sort of thing, and he will rise up and take a hand
in fixing his wages himself. Ah, he will have a long
and bitter account of wrong and humiliation to settle."

"Do ye believe—"

"That he actually will help to fix his own wages?
Yes, indeed. And he will be strong and able, then."

"Brave times, brave times, of a truth!" sneered the
prosperous smith.

"Oh, and there's another detail. In that day, a master may hire a man for only just one day, or one week,
or one month at a time, if he wants to."

"What?"

"It's true. Moreover, a magistrate won't be able to
force a man to work for a master a whole year on a
stretch whether the man wants to or not."

"Will there be *no* law or sense in that day?"

"Both of them, Dowley. In that day a man will be

his own property, not the property of magistrate and master. And he can leave town whenever he wants to, if the wages don't suit him!"

"Devil take such an age!" shouted Dowley, in strong indignation. "An age of dogs, an age barren of reverence for superiors and respect for authority!"

"Well, to change the subject—for I think I've made my point—I think some of our laws are pretty unfair. There's one thing which certainly isn't fair. The magistrate fixes a mechanic's wage at one cent a day, for instance. The law says that if any master shall venture, even under utmost press of business, to pay anything *over* that cent a day, even for a single day, he shall be fined for it; and whoever knows he did it and doesn't inform, they also shall be fined. Now it seems to me unfair, Dowley, and a deadly peril to all of us, that because you thoughtlessly confessed, a while ago, that within a week you have paid over a cent. . . ."

You ought to have seen them go to pieces, the whole gang. I saw in a moment that I had overdone the thing. I was expecting to scare them, but I wasn't expecting to scare them to death. They all began to imagine not only Dowley but themselves in danger of imprisonment. They saw themselves at the mercy of me—a stranger—and nothing in their experience led them to expect kind treatment from anyone but their own families or closest friends. It was very uncomfortable.

They were all scared stiff and it was up to me to do something to gain time and get their minds on something else. So I took a miller-gun, an invention of my own and a gift to Marco, and said I would teach them its mysteries.

I never saw such an awkward people with machinery; you see, they were totally unused to it. The miller-gun was a little double-barreled tube of toughened glass, with a neat little trick of a spring to it, which upon pressure would let a shot escape. But the shot wouldn't hurt anybody; it would only drop into your hand. In the gun were two sizes—wee mustard-seed shot, and another sort that were several times larger. They were money. So the gun was a purse; and very handy, too; you could pay out money in the dark with it with accuracy; and you could carry it in your mouth; or in your vest pocket, if you had one. I made them of several sizes—one size so large that it would carry a dollar in change. Using shot for money was a good thing for the government; the metal cost nothing, and the money couldn't be counterfeited, for I was the only person in the kingdom who knew how to make shot.

The king joined us about this time, mightily refreshed by his nap and feeling good. Anything could make me nervous now, I was so uneasy—for our lives were in danger; and so it worried me to note something in the king's eye which seemed to indicate that he had been loading himself up for a performance of some kind or other.

I was right. He began, straight off, in the most in-

nocent and awkward way, to lead up to the subject
of agriculture. The cold sweat broke out all over me.
I wanted to whisper in his ear, "Man, we are in awful
danger! Every moment is precious till we get back
these men's confidence; *don't* waste any of this golden
time." But of course I couldn't do it. Whisper to him?
It would look as if we were conspiring. So I had to sit
there and look calm and pleasant while the king stood
over that dynamite mine and mooned along about his
damned onions and things. At first my thoughts kept
up such a hurrah and confusion that I couldn't take in
a word; but presently when my plans began to form,
a sort of order and quiet followed, and I caught the
boom of the king's voice, as if out of remote distance:

—"were not the best way, methinks, although it is
not to be denied that authorities differ as concerning
this point, some contending that the onion is but an
unwholesome berry when stricken early from the
tree—"

The audience showed signs of life, and sought each
other's eyes in a surprised and troubled way.

—"while others do yet maintain, with much show
of reason, that this is not of necessity the case, in-
stancing that plums and other like cereals do be always
dug in the unripe state—"

The wild light of terror began to glow in these
men's eyes, and one of them muttered, "These be errors, every one—God hath surely smitten the mind
of this farmer."

They rose and went for him! With a fierce shout,

"The one would betray us, the other is mad! Kill them! Kill them!" they flung themselves upon us. What joy flamed up in the king's eye! He might be lame in agriculture, but this kind of thing was just in his line. He had been fasting long; he was hungry for a fight. He hit the blacksmith a crack under the jaw that lifted him clear off his feet and stretched him flat on his back. "St. George for Britain!" and he downed the wheelwright. The mason was big, but I laid him out like nothing. The three gathered themselves up and came again; went down again; came again; and kept on repeating this, with native British pluck, until they were battered to jelly, reeling with exhaustion, and so blind that they couldn't tell us from each other; and yet they kept right on, hammering away with what might was left in them; hammering each other— for we stepped aside and looked on while they rolled, and struggled, and gouged, and pounded, and bit, with the strict and wordless attention to business of so many bulldogs. We looked on without fear, for they were fast getting past ability to go for help against us, and the battlefield was far enough from the public road to be safe.

Well, while they were gradually playing out, it suddenly occurred to me to wonder what had become of Marco. I looked around; he was nowhere to be seen. Oh, but this was bad! I pulled the king's sleeve, and we glided away and rushed for the hut. No Marco there, no Phyllis there! They had gone to the road for

We worked our way along it to the body of the tree.

"He wish'd earnestly he had the feet of the fox."

help, sure. I told the king to fly, and I would explain later. We made good time across the open ground, and as we darted into the shelter of the wood I glanced back and saw a mob of excited peasants swarm into view, with Marco and his wife at their head. They were making a world of noise, but that couldn't hurt anybody; the wood was dense, and as soon as we were well into its depths we would take to a tree and let them whistle. Ah, but then came another sound— dogs! Yes, that was quite another matter. We must find running water.

We tore along at a good gait, and soon left the sounds far behind. We struck a stream and darted into it. We waded swiftly down it, in the dim forest light, for as much as three hundred yards, and then came across an oak with a great bough sticking out over the water. We climbed up on this bough, and began to work our way along it to the body of the tree; now we began to hear those sounds more plainly; so the mob had struck our trail. For a while the sounds approached pretty fast. And then for another while they didn't. No doubt the dogs had found the place where we had entered the stream, and were now waltzing up and down the shores trying to pick up the trail again.

When we were snugly lodged in the tree and curtained with leaves, the king was satisfied, but I was doubtful. I believed we could crawl along a branch and get into the next tree, and I judged it worth while to try. We tried it and made a success of it, though the king slipped at the junction and came near failing to connect. We were hidden among the leaves, and then we had nothing to do but listen to the hunt.

Presently we heard it coming—and coming on the jump, too; yes, and down both sides of the stream. Louder—louder—next minute it swelled swiftly up into a roar of shoutings, barkings, tramplings, and swept by like a cyclone.

"I was afraid that the overhanging branch would suggest something to them," said I, "but I don't mind the disappointment. Come, my lord, it were well that we make good use of our time. We've flanked them. Dark is coming on, presently. If we can cross the stream and get a good start, and borrow a couple of horses from somebody's pasture to use for a few hours, we shall be safe enough."

We started down, and got nearly to the lowest limb, when we seemed to hear the hunt returning. We stopped to listen.

"Yes," said I, "they're baffled, they've given it up, they're on their way home. We will climb back to our roost again, and let them go by."

So we climbed back. The king listened a moment and said:

"They still search—I know the sign. We did best to stay."

He was right. He knew more about hunting than I

did. The noise approached steadily, but not with a rush. The king said:

"They reason that we had no great start of them and being on foot are as yet no mighty way from where we took the water."

"Yes, sire, that is about it, I am afraid, though I was hoping for better things."

The noise drew nearer and nearer, and soon the van was drifting under us, on both sides of the water. A voice called a halt from the other bank, and said:

"If they were so minded, they could get to yon tree by this branch that overhangs, and yet not touch ground. Ye will do well to send a man up it."

"That we will do!"

I was obliged to admire my smartness in foreseeing this very thing and swapping trees to beat it. But, don't you know, there are some things that can beat smartness and foresight? Awkwardness and stupidity can. How could I, with all my gifts, make any preparation against a near-sighted, cross-eyed, pudding-headed clown who could aim himself at the wrong tree and hit the right one? And that is what he did. He went for the wrong tree, which was, of course, the right one by mistake, and up he started.

Matters were serious now. We remained still, and awaited developments. The peasant toiled his difficult way up. The king raised himself up and stood; he made a leg ready, and when the comer's head arrived in reach of it there was a dull thud, and down went the man to the ground. There was a wild outbreak of anger below, and the mob swarmed in from all around, and there we were, treed and prisoners. Another man started up; the bridging bough was detected, and a volunteer started up the tree that furnished the bridge. The king ordered me to guard the bridge. For a while the enemy came thick and fast; but no matter, the head man of each procession always got a blow that dislodged him as soon as he came in reach. The king's spirits rose; his joy was limitless. He said that if nothing occurred to spoil the prospect we should have a beautiful night, for on this line of tactics we could hold the tree against the whole country-side.

However, the mob soon came to that conclusion themselves; wherefore they called off the assault and began to debate other plans. They had no weapons, but there were plenty of stones, and stones might answer. We had no objections. A stone might possibly reach us once in a while, but it wasn't very likely; we were well protected by boughs and leaves, and were not visible from any good aiming-point. If they would but waste half an hour in stone-throwing, the dark would come to our help. We were feeling very well satisfied. We could smile—almost laugh.

But we didn't; which was just as well, for we should have been interrupted. Before the stones had been raging through the leaves and bouncing from the boughs fifteen minutes, we began to notice a smell. A couple of sniffs of it was enough of an explanation: it was smoke! Our game was up at last. We recognized that. When smoke invites you, you have to come. They raised their pile of dry brush and damp weeds higher and higher, and when they saw the thick cloud begin to roll up and smother the tree, they broke out in a storm of joy. I got enough breath to say:

"Proceed, my lord; after you is manners."

The king gasped:

"Follow me down, and then back thyself against one side of the trunk, and leave me the other. Then will we fight. Let each pile his dead according to his own fashion and taste."

Then he descended, barking and coughing, and I followed. I struck the ground an instant after him; we sprang to our appointed places, and began to give and take with all our might. The powwow and racket were great; it was a tempest of riot and confusion and thick-falling blows. Suddenly some horsemen tore into the midst of the crowd.

CHAPTER XXIII

THE YANKEE AND THE KING BECOME

SLAVES

A voice shouted: "Hold—or ye are dead men!"

How good it sounded! The owner of the voice bore all the marks of a gentleman: costly clothing, the air of command, a hard face. The mob fell humbly back, like so many dogs. The gentleman inspected us critically, then said sharply to the peasants:

"What are ye doing to these people?"

"They be madmen, worshipful sir, that have come wandering we know not whence, and—"

"Ye know not whence? Do ye pretend ye know them not?"

"Most honored sir, we speak but the truth. They are strangers and unknown to any in this region; and they be the most violent and blood-thirsty madmen that ever—"

"Peace! Ye know not what ye say. They are not mad. Who are ye? And whence are ye? Explain."

"We are but peaceful strangers, sir," I said, "and traveling upon our own concerns. We are from a far country, and unacquainted here. We have meant no harm; and yet but for your brave interference and protection these people would have killed us. As you

258

have seen sir, we are not mad; neither are we violent or bloodthirsty."

The gentleman turned to his followers and said calmly:

"Lash me these animals to their kennels!"

The mob vanished in an instant; and after them plunged the horsemen, laying about them with their whips and pitilessly riding down such as were foolish enough to keep the road instead of taking to the bush. The shrieks presently died away in the distance. and soon the horsemen began to straggle back. Meantime the gentleman had been questioning us more closely, but had dug no particulars out of us. We thanked him much, but we told nothing more than that we were friendless strangers from a far country. When his men were all returned, the gentleman said to one of his servants:

"Bring the led-horses and mount these people."

"Yes, my lord."

We were placed toward the rear, among the servants. We traveled pretty fast, and finally drew up some time after dark at a roadside inn some ten or twelve miles from the scene of our troubles. My lord went immediately to his room, after ordering his supper, and we saw no more of him. At dawn we breakfasted and made ready to start.

My lord's chief attendant wandered up at that moment and said:

"Ye have said ye should continue upon this road,

which is our direction likewise; wherefore my lord, the earl Grip, hath given commandment that ye keep the horses and ride, and that certain of us ride with ye twenty miles to a fair town that is called Cambenet, where ye shall be out of peril."

We could do nothing less than express our thanks and accept the offer. We jogged along, six in the party, at a moderate and comfortable gait, and in conversation learned that my lord Grip was a very great person in his own region, which lay a day's journey beyond Cambenet. We rode so slowly that it was near the middle of the forenoon when we entered the market-square of the town. We dismounted, and left our thanks once more for my lord, and then approached a crowd gathered in the center of the square, to see what might be the object of interest. It was part of that old band of slaves we had seen on the road! So they had been dragging their chains about, all this weary time. That poor husband was gone, and also many others; and some few purchases had been added to the gang. The king was not interested and wanted to move along, but I was full of pity. I could not take my eyes away from these worn and wasted wrecks. There they sat grouped upon the ground, silent, uncomplaining, with bowed heads—a pathetic sight. And by hideous contrast, an orator was making a speech to another gathering not thirty steps away, in praise of "our glorious British liberties!"

I was boiling. I had forgotten I was a peasant; I was remembering I was a man. Cost what it might, I would mount that platform and—

Click! the king and I were handcuffed together! Our companions, those servants, had done it; my lord Grip stood looking on. The king burst out in a fury, and said:

"What meaneth this ill-mannered joke?"

My lord merely said to his head servant, coolly:

"Put up the slaves and sell them!"

Slaves! The word had a new sound—and how unspeakably awful! The king lifted his handcuffs and brought them down with a deadly force; but my lord was out of the way when they arrived. A dozen of the rascal's servants sprang forward, and in a moment we were helpless, with our hands bound behind us. We so loudly and so earnestly claimed ourselves freemen, that we got the interested attention of the orator and his patriotic crowd; and they gathered about us and assumed a very determined attitude. The orator said:

"If, indeed, ye are freemen, ye have nothing to fear. The God-given liberties of Britain are about ye for your shield and shelter! Ye shall soon see. Bring forth your proofs."

"What proofs?"

"Proof that ye are freemen."

Ah—I remembered! I came to myself; I said nothing. But the king stormed out:

"Thou'rt insane, man. It were better, and more in reason, that this thief and scoundrel here prove that we are *not* freemen."

All shook their heads and looked disappointed; some turned away, no longer interested. The orator said— and this time in the tones of business, not of sentiment:

"If ye do not know your country's laws, it were time ye learned them. Ye are strangers to us; ye will not deny that. Ye may be freemen, we do not deny that; but also ye may be slaves. The law is clear: it doth not require us to prove ye are slaves; it requireth you to prove ye are *not*."

I said:

"Dear sir, give us only time to send to Astolat; or give us only time to send to the Valley of Holiness—"

"Peace, good man, these are extraordinary requests, and you may not hope to have them granted. It would cost much time and would inconvenience your master—"

"*Master,* idiot!" stormed the king. "I have no master, I myself am the m—"

"Silence, for God's sake!"

I got the words out in time to stop the king. We were in trouble enough already; it could not help us any to give these people the notion that we were crazy.

There is no use in stringing out the details. The earl put us up and sold us at auction. This same infernal law had existed in our own South in my time, more than thirteen hundred years later, and under it hundreds of freemen who could not prove that they were freemen had been sold into life-long slavery without this making any particular impression upon me; but the minute law and the auction block came into my personal experience, a thing which had been merely improper before became suddenly hellish. Well, that's the way we are made.

Yes, we were sold at auction, like swine. In a big town and an active market we should have brought a good price; but this place was utterly dead and so we sold at a figure which makes me ashamed, every time I think of it. The King of England brought seven dollars and his prime minister nine; whereas the king was easily worth twelve dollars and I as easily worth fifteen.

The slave-dealer bought us both and hitched us onto that long chain of his, and we made up the rear of his procession. We took up our line of march and passed out of Cambenet at noon; and it seemed to me very strange and odd that the King of England and his chief minister, marching handcuffed in a slave convoy, could move by all kinds of men and women, and yet attract no notice. Dear, dear, it only shows that there is nothing more sacred about a king than there is about a tramp, after all. But when you know who he is, it takes your very breath away to look at him. I reckon we are all fools. Born so, no doubt.

It's a world of surprises. The king was lost in

thought; this was natural. What was he thinking about? Why, about the greatness of his fall, of course —from the highest place in the world to the lowest. No, I take my oath that the thing that bothered him most, to start with, was not this, but the price he had brought. He couldn't seem to get over that seven dollars. I couldn't believe it either; it didn't seem natural.

But after I thought it over, I saw that it was natural. After all a king feels as a man, and the average man is ashamed to be valued at less than he thinks he is worth. But, confound him, he tired me with his continual arguments to show that he should have brought at least twenty-five dollars. Every subject we started led back to the same thing. And every time purchasers looked him over, it started again. To them he was a two-dollar-and-a-half chap with a thirty-dollar style. Our owner saw he had to do something to take this style out of the king if he was to find a buyer. At the end of the week there was evidence that the lash and club and fist had done their work well on the king's body. It was a sight to see and weep over, but his spirit wasn't even touched. Even that dull slave-driver could see there was such a thing as a slave who would be a man until he died, whose bones you could break, but whose manhood you couldn't. So he gave up and the king kept his style.

Well, we had a rough time for a month, tramping to and fro and suffering. And the king, who had been the most indifferent person in the kingdom about slavery, became the most interested. Once before I had asked him about doing away with slavery and had such a sharp answer, I had thought it best not to meddle with the matter further. Now he was ready to attack it. Seeing this, I was willing to take the desperate chances necessary to get us free. I set about to make a plan which would take time and patience but would be dramatic.

Now and then we had adventures. One night we were overtaken by a snow-storm so thick that we were lost and five of the feeble slaves died. It looked as though the others would follow, but our master saw his chance. A mob of people came tearing into our group following a woman they said was a witch. They were determined to burn her and the master persuaded them to do it in our midst and drove us up close to be warmed by the fire.

One day we ran into a procession in a suburb of London. All the drunken riff-raff of the kingdom seemed to be following a coffin on which sat a pretty eighteen-year-old girl with a baby squeezed to her breast. Even the priest seemed to feel sorry for her though he was ready to help hang her. He told her story. She had been a happy young wife but her husband had been snatched away from her and sent to sea without her so much as knowing what had happened. After weeks of watching and waiting for him, her money all gone, she had stolen a trifle of linen, thinking to sell it and save her child. Well, they hanged her, but the priest promised to care for the child and for this you should have seen the look of gratitude on her face as she died.

London—to a slave—was an interesting place. It was merely a great big village; and mainly mud and thatch. The streets were muddy, crooked, unpaved. The people were an ever drifting swarm of rags and splendors, of nodding plumes and shining armor. The king had a palace there; he saw the outside of it. It made him sigh; yes, and swear a little, in a poor sixth-century way. We saw knights and grandees whom we knew, but they didn't know us in our rags and dirt and raw welts and bruises, and wouldn't have recognized us if we had called to them, nor stopped to answer, either, it being unlawful to speak with slaves on a chain. Sandy passed within ten yards of me on a mule—hunting for me, I imagined. But the thing which clean broke my heart was something which happened in front of our old barrack in a square, while we were enduring the sight of a man being boiled to death in oil for counterfeiting pennies. It was the sight of a newsboy—and I couldn't get at him! Still, I had one comfort; here was proof that Clarence was still alive and banging away. I meant to be with him before long; the thought was full of cheer.

I had one little glimpse of another thing, one day, which gave me a great uplift. It was a wire stretching from housetop to housetop. Telegraph or telephone, sure. I did very much wish I had a little piece of it.

It was just what I needed in order to carry out my plan of escape. My idea was to get loose some night, along with the king, and then gag and bind our master, change clothes with him, batter him until he couldn't be recognized, hitch him to the slave-chain, take possession of the property, march to Camelot, and—

But you get my idea; you see what a stunning dramatic surprise I would wind up with at the palace. It was all possible, if I could only get hold of a slender piece of iron which I could shape into a lock-pick. I could then undo the lumbering padlocks with which our chains were fastened, whenever I might choose. But I never had any luck; no such thing ever happened to fall in my way.

However, my chance came at last. A gentleman who had come twice before to bargain for me, without result, or indeed any approach to a result, came again. I was far from expecting ever to belong to him, for the price asked for me from the time I was first enslaved was too high, and always provoked either anger or laughter; yet my master stuck stubbornly to it— twenty-two dollars. He wouldn't come down a cent. The king was greatly admired because of his grand physique, but his kingly style was against him, and he wasn't salable; nobody wanted that kind of a slave. I considered myself safe from parting from him because of my high price. No, I was not expecting ever to belong to this gentleman whom I have spoken of, but he had something which I expected would belong to me some time, if he would but visit us often enough. It was a steel thing with a long pin to it, with which his long cloth outside garment was fastened together in front. There were three of them. He had disappointed me twice, because he did not come quite close enough to me to make my plan entirely safe; but this time I succeeded; I captured the lowest clasp of the three, and when he missed it he thought he had lost it on the way.

I had a chance to be glad about a minute, then straightway a chance to be sad again. For when the purchase was about to fail, as usual, the master suddenly spoke up and said what would be worded thus, in modern English:

"I'll tell you what I'll do. I'm tired supporting these two for no good. Give me twenty-two dollars for this one, and I'll throw the other one in."

The king couldn't get his breath, he was in such a fury. He began to choke and gag, and meantime the master and the gentleman moved away discussing.

"If ye will keep the offer open—"

"'Tis open till the morrow at this hour."

"Then I will answer you at that time," said the gentleman, and disappeared, the master following him.

I had a time of it to cool the king down, but I managed it. I whispered in his ear, to this effect:

"Your grace *will* go for nothing, but after another fashion. And so shall I. Tonight we shall both be free."

"Ah! How is that?"

"With this thing which I have stolen, I will unlock

these locks and cast off these chains tonight. When he comes about nine-thirty to inspect us for the night, we will seize him, gag him, batter him, and early in the morning we will march out of this town, owners of these slaves."

That was as far as I went, but the king was charmed and satisfied. That evening we waited patiently for our fellow-slaves to get to sleep and show it by the usual sign, for you must not take many chances on those poor fellows if you can avoid it. It is best to keep your own secrets. No doubt they fidgeted only about as usual, but it didn't seem so to me. It seemed to me that they were going to be forever getting down to their regular snoring. As the time dragged on I got nervously afraid we shouldn't have enough of it left for our needs; so I made several unsuccessful attempts, and merely delayed things by it; for I couldn't seem to touch a padlock, there in the dark, without starting a rattle out of it which interrupted somebody's sleep and made him turn over and wake some more of the gang.

But finally I did get my last iron off, and was a free man once more. I took a good breath of relief, and reached for the king's irons. Too late! in comes the master with a light in one hand and his heavy walking-staff in the other. I snuggled close among the snorers to conceal as nearly as possible that I was naked of irons; and I kept a sharp lookout and prepared to spring for any man the moment he should bend over me.

But he didn't approach. He stopped, gazed absently toward us a minute, evidently thinking about something else; then he set down his light, moved toward the door, and before a body could imagine what he was going to do, he was out of the door and had closed it behind him.

"Quick!" said the king. "Fetch him back!"

Of course, it was the thing to do, and I was up and out in a moment. But, dear me, there were no lamps in those days, and it was a dark night. But I saw a dim figure a few steps away. I darted for it, threw myself upon it, and then there was a lively state of things! We fought and scuffled and struggled, and drew a crowd in no time. They took an immense interest in the fight and encouraged us all they could and, in fact, couldn't have been pleasanter if it had been their own fight. Then a tremendous row broke out behind us, and as much as half of our audience left us, with a rush to see what was happening. Lanterns began to swing in all directions; it was the watch gathering from far and near. Presently a blow fell across my back as a reminder, and I knew what it meant. I was a prisoner. So was the man I had been fighting. We were marched off toward prison, one on each side of the watchman.

Suddenly my fellow-prisoner turned his face around in my direction, and the freckled light from the watchman's tin lantern fell on it. I had supposed him to be the master, but imagine my surprise to discover he was the wrong man!

CHAPTER XXIV

AN AWFUL PREDICAMENT—AND A

RESCUE

Sleep? It was impossible. It would naturally have been impossible in that noisy jail, with its mangy crowd of drunken, quarrelsome, and song-singing rascals. But the thing that made sleep all the more a thing not to be dreamed of, was my impatience to get out of this place and find out the whole size of what might have happened yonder in the slave-quarters in consequence of that mistake of mine.

It was a long night, but the morning got around at last. I made a full and frank explanation to the court. I said I was a slave, the property of the great Earl Grip, who had arrived just after dark at the Tabard inn in the village on the other side of the water, and had stopped there overnight, he being taken deadly sick with a strange and sudden disorder. I had been ordered to cross to the city in all haste and bring the best physician; I was doing my best; naturally I was running with all my might; the night was dark; I ran against this common person here, who seized me by the throat and began to pound me, although I told him my errand, and implored him, for the sake of the great earl my master's mortal peril—

The common person interrupted and said it was a

lie and was going to explain how I rushed upon him
and attacked him without a word—

"Silence, sirrah!" from the court. "Take him hence
and give him a few stripes whereby to teach him how
to treat the servant of a nobleman after a different
fashion another time. Go!"

Then the court begged my pardon, and hoped I
would not fail to tell his lordship it was in no way the
court's fault that this high-handed thing had happened. I said I would make it all right, and so took my
leave.

I didn't wait for breakfast. No grass grew under
my feet. I was soon at the slave quarters. Empty—
everybody gone! That is, everybody except one body
—the slave-master's. It lay there all battered to pulp;
and all about were the evidences of a terrific fight.
There was a rude board coffin on a cart at the door,
and workmen, assisted by the police, were thinning
a road through the crowd in order that they might
bring it in.

I picked out a man humble enough in life to talk
with one so shabby as I, and got his account of the
matter.

"There were sixteen slaves here. They rose against
their master in the night, and thou seest how it ended."

"Yes. How did it begin?"

"There was no witness but the slaves. They said the
slave that was most valuable got free of his bonds and
escaped in some strange way—by magic arts 'twas

thought, by reason that he had no key, and the locks were neither broke nor in any wise injured. When the master discovered his loss, he was mad with despair, and threw himself upon his people with his heavy stick. They fought back and killed him."

"This is dreadful. It will go hard with the slaves, no doubt, upon the trial."

"But the trial is over."

"Over!"

"Would they be a week, think you—and the matter so simple? They were not the half of a quarter of an hour at it."

"Why, I don't see how they could determine which were the guilty ones in so short a time."

"*Which* ones? Indeed, they considered not particulars like that. They condemned them in a body. Know ye not the law?—that if one slave killeth his master all the slaves of that man must die for it."

"True. I had forgotten. And when will these die?"

"Probably within four and twenty hours; although some say perhaps they will wait a pair of days more, if they may find the missing one meantime."

The missing one! It made me feel uncomfortable.

"Is it likely they will find him?"

"Before the day is spent, yes. They seek him everywhere. They stand at the gates of the town, with certain of the slaves who will discover him to them if he cometh, and none can pass out but he will be first examined."

"Might one see the place where the rest are confined?"

"The outside of it, yes. The inside of it—but ye will not want to see that."

I took the address of that prison for future reference and then wandered off. At the first second-hand clothing shop I came to, up a back street, I got a rough rig suitable for a common seaman who might be going on a cold voyage, and bound up my face with a large bandage, saying I had a toothache. This concealed my worst bruises. I no longer resembled my former self. Then I struck out for that wire, found it and followed it to its den. It was a little room over a butcher's shop —which meant that business wasn't very brisk in the telegraphic line. The young chap in charge was drowsing at his table. I locked the door and put the vast key in my bosom.

This alarmed the young fellow, and he was going to make a noise; but I said:

"Save your wind; if you open your mouth you are dead, sure. Get to your instrument. Lively, now! Call Camelot."

"This doth amaze me! How should such as you know aught of such matters as—"

"Call Camelot! I am a desperate man. Call Camelot, or get away from the instrument and I will do it myself."

"What, you?"

"Yes, certainly. Stop gabbling. Call the palace."

He made the call.

"Now, then, call Clarence."

"Clarence *who?*"

"Never mind Clarence who. Say you want Clarence; you'll get an answer."

He did so. We waited five nerve-straining minutes —ten minutes—how long it did seem!—and then came a click that was as familiar to me as a human voice; for Clarence had been my own pupil.

"Now, my lad, get out! They would have known *my* touch, maybe, and so your call was surest; but I'm all right now."

He left the place and cocked his ear to listen, but it did him no good. I used a cipher. I didn't waste any time in sociabilities with Clarence, but squared away for business, straight-off—thus:

"The king is here and in danger. We were captured and brought here as slaves. We should not be able to prove our identity, and the fact is, I am not in a position to try. Send a telegram for the palace here which will carry conviction with it."

His answer came straight back:

"They don't know anything about the telegraph; they haven't had any experience yet, the line to London is so new. Better not try that. They might hang you. Think up something else."

Might hang us! Little he knew how closely he was

crowding the facts. I couldn't think up anything for the moment. Then an idea struck me, and I started it along:

"Send five hundred picked knights with Launcelot in the lead, and send them on the jump. Let them enter by the southwest gate, and look out for the man with a white cloth around his right arm."

The answer was prompt:

"They shall start in half an hour."

"All right, Clarence; now tell this lad here that I'm a friend of yours; and that he must be careful to say nothing about this visit of mine."

The instrument began to talk to the youth and I hurried away. I fell to figuring. In half an hour it would be nine o'clock. Knights and horses in heavy armor couldn't travel very fast. These would make the best time they could, and now that the ground was in good condition, and no snow or mud, they would probably make a seven-mile gait; they would have to change horses a couple of times; they would arrive about six, or a little after; it would still be plenty light enough; they would see the white cloth which I should tie around my right arm, and I would take command. We would surround that prison and have the king out in no time. It would be showy and picturesque enough, all things considered, though I would have preferred noonday on account of the more theatrical look the thing would have.

Now, then, I thought I would look up some of those people whom I had formerly recognized and make myself known. That would help us out of our scrape without the knights. But I must go cautiously, for it was a risky business. I must get into rich clothing, and it wouldn't do to run and jump into it. No, I must work up to it by degrees, buying suit after suit of clothes in shops wide apart, getting a little finer article with each change, until I should finally reach silk and velvet, and be ready for my project. So I started.

But the scheme fell through like scat! The first corner I turned, I came plump upon one of our slaves, snooping around with a watchman. I coughed at the moment and he gave me a sudden look that bit right into my bones. I judge he thought he had heard that cough before. I turned immediately into a shop and worked along down the counter, pricing things and watching out of the corner of my eye. Those people had stopped, and were talking together and looking in at the door. I made up my mind to get out the back way, if there was a back way, and I asked the shop-woman if I could step out there and look for the escaped slave, who was believed to be in hiding back there somewhere, and said I was an officer in disguise, and my pard was yonder at the door with one of the murderers in charge, and would she be good enough to step there and tell him he needn't wait, but had better go at once to the further end of the back alley and be ready to head him off when I rousted him out.

She was blazing with eagerness to see one of those already celebrated murderers, and she started on the errand at once. I slipped out the back way, locked the door behind me, put the key in my pocket and started off, chuckling to myself and comfortable.

Well, I had gone and spoiled it again, made another mistake. A double one, in fact. There were plenty of ways to get rid of that officer in some simple way, but no, I must pick out a dramatic one; it is the great fault of my character. And then, I had figured upon what the officer, being human, would *naturally* do; whereas when you are least expecting it, a man will now and then go and do the very thing which it's *not* natural for him to do. The natural thing for the officer to do in this case, was to follow straight on my heels; he would find a stout oak door, securely locked, between him and me; before he could break it down, I should be far away and in another disguise. But instead of doing the natural thing, the officer took me at my word and followed my instructions. And so, as I came trotting out full of satisfaction with my own cleverness, he turned the corner and I walked right into his handcuffs.

Of course, I was indignant, and swore I had just come ashore from a long voyage, and all that sort of thing—just to see, you know, if it would deceive that slave. But it didn't. He knew me. Then I reproached him for betraying me. He was more surprised than hurt. He stretched his eyes wide, and said:

"What, wouldst have me let thee, of all men, escape and not hang with us, when thou'rt the very *cause* of our hanging? Go to!"

"Go to" was their way of saying, "I should smile!" or "I like that!" Queer talkers, those people.

Well, there was a sort of justice in his view of the case, and so I dropped the matter. I only said:

"You're not going to be hanged. None of us are."

Both men laughed, and the slave said:

"Ye have not ranked as a fool, before. You might better keep your reputation, seeing you die soon."

"It will stand it, I reckon. Before tomorrow we shall be out of prison and free to go where we will, besides."

The witty officer made a rasping noise in his throat, and said:

"Out of prison, yes. Ye say true. And free likewise to go where ye will, so ye wander not out of his grace the Devil's kingdom."

I kept my temper, and said:

"Now I suppose you really think we are going to hang within a day or two."

"I thought it not many minutes ago, for so the thing was decided and proclaimed."

"Ah, then you've changed your mind; is that it?"

"Even that. I only *thought*, then; I *know*, now."

I felt sarcastic, so I said:

"Oh, wise servant of the law, condescend to tell us, then, what you *know*."

"That ye will all be hanged *today*, at mid-afternoon! Oho! that shot hit home! Lean upon me."

The fact is I did need to lean upon somebody. My

knights couldn't arrive in time. They would be as much as three hours too late. Nothing in the world could save the King of England nor me, which was more important—more important, not merely to me, but to the nation, the only nation on earth standing ready to blossom into civilization. I was sick. I said no more; there wasn't anything to say. I knew what the man meant—that, if the missing slave was found, the postponement would be recalled, and the execution take place today. Well, the missing slave was found.

As it neared four in the afternoon, a great crowd gathered just outside the walls of London. It was a cool, comfortable day, with a brilliant sun; the kind of day to make one want to live, not die. We fifteen poor devils hadn't a friend in the crowd. There was something painful in that thought, look at it how you might. There we sat on our tall scaffold, the object of the hate and mockery of all those enemies. We were being made a holiday spectacle. They had built a sort of grandstand for the nobility and gentry, and these were there in full force, with their ladies. We recognized a good many of them.

The crowd got a brief and unexpected entertainment out of the king. The moment we were freed of our bonds he sprang up, in his fantastic rags, with face bruised out of all recognition, and proclaimed himself Arthur, King of Britain, and denounced the awful penalties of treason upon every soul there present if hair of his sacred head were touched. It startled and surprised him to hear them break into a vast roar of laughter. It hurt his pride and he locked himself up in silence then, although the crowd begged him to go on and tried to provoke him to it by catcalls, jeers, and shouts of:

"Let him speak! The king! The king! His humble subjects hunger and thirst for words of wisdom out of the mouth of their master, his Serene and Sacred Raggedness!"

But it went for nothing. He put on all his majesty and sat under this contempt and insult unmoved. He certainly was great in his way. Absently, I had taken off my white bandage and wound it about my right arm. When the crowd noticed this, they began upon me. They said:

"Doubtless this sailor-man is his minister; observe his costly badge of office!"

I let them go on until they got tired, and then I said:

"Yes, I am his minister, The Boss; and tomorrow you will hear that from Camelot which—"

I got no further. They drowned me out with mocking laughter. But presently there was silence; for the sheriffs of London, in their official robes, with their staff, began to make a stir which indicated that business was about to begin. In the hush which followed, our crime was recited, the death-warrant read, and then everybody uncovered while a priest uttered a prayer.

Then a slave was blindfolded; the hangman unslung his rope. There lay the smooth road below us, we upon one side of it, the banked multitude walling its other side—a good clear road, and kept free by the police. How good it would be to see my five hundred horsemen come tearing down it! But no, it was out of the possibilities. I followed it out into the distance—not a horseman on it, or sign of one.

There was a jerk, and the slave hung dangling, dangling and hideously squirming, for his limbs were not tied.

A second rope was unslung, in a moment another slave was dangling.

In a minute a third slave was struggling in the air. It was dreadful. I turned away my head a moment, and when I turned back I missed the king! They were blindfolding him! I was paralyzed; I couldn't move; I was choking; I couldn't speak. They finished blindfolding him; they led him under the rope. I couldn't shake off that inability to move. But when I saw them put the noose around his neck, then everything let go in me and I made a spring to the rescue, and as I made it I shot one more glance down the road. By George! here they came, a-tilting!—five hundred mailed and belted knights on bicycles!

The grandest sight that ever was seen. Lord, how the plumes streamed, how the sun flamed and flashed from the endless procession of webby wheels!

I waved my right arm as Launcelot swept in; he

Here they came, a-tilting!—five hundred mailed and belted knights on bicycles!

Here they came, a thirty before hanging swayled and being banging, any wilt recognized my rag; I tore away noose and bandage, and shouted:

"On your knees, every rascal of you, and salute the king! Who fails shall sup in hell tonight!"

I always use that high style when I'm after an effect. Well, it was noble to see Launcelot and the boys swarm up onto that scaffold and throw sheriffs and such overboard. And it was fine to see that astonished multitude go down on their knees and beg their lives of the king they had just been insulting. And as he stood apart there, receiving this homage in rags, I thought to myself: well, really there *is* something peculiarly grand about the bearing of a king, after all.

I was immensely satisfied. Take the whole situation all around, it was one of the gaudiest effects I ever made.

And presently up comes Clarence, his own self! and winks, and says, very modernly:

"Good deal of a surprise, wasn't it? I knew you'd like it. I've had the boys practising this long time, privately, and just hungry for a chance to show off."

CHAPTER XXV

THE YANKEE'S FIGHT WITH THE KNIGHTS

Home again, at Camelot. A morning or two later I found the paper, damp from the press, by my plate at the breakfast-table. I turned to the advertising columns, knowing I should find something of personal interest to me there. It was this:

BY THE KING'S ORDER

Know that the great lord and illus-
trious Kni8ht, SIR SAGRAMOR LE
DESIROUS naving condescended to
meet the King's Minister, Hank Morgan, the which is surnamed The Boss,
for satisfgetion of offence anciently given,
these WilL engage in the lists by
Camelot about the fourth hour of the
morning of the sixteenth day of this
next succeeding month. The battle
will be a! outrance, since the said offence
was of a deadly sort, admitting of no
comPosition.

BY THE KING'S ORDER

Up to the day set, there was no talk in all Britain of

anything but this combat. All other topics were unimportant and passed out of men's thoughts and interest. There was abundant reason for the extraordinary interest which this coming fight was creating. It was born of the fact that all the nation knew that this was not to be a duel between mere men—Sir Sagramor and the king's minister—but a duel between two mighty magicians; a final struggle between the two master enchanters of the age. Yes, all the world knew it was going to be in reality a duel between Merlin and me, a measuring of his magic powers against mine. It was known that Merlin had been busy whole days and nights together, giving Sir Sagramor's arms and armor supernatural powers of offense and defense, and that he had secured for him from the spirits of the air a fleecy veil which would make the wearer invisible to his opponent while still visible to other men. Against Sir Sagramor, so weaponed and protected, a thousand knights could accomplish nothing; against him no known enchantments could prevail. These facts were sure; regarding them there was no doubt, no reason for doubt. There was but one question: might there be still other enchantments, *unknown* to Merlin, which could make Sir Sagramor's veil transparent to me, and make it possible for me to pierce his enchanted armor? This was the one thing to be decided in the lists. Until then the world must remain in suspense.

So the world thought there was a vast matter at stake here, and the world was right, but it was not

the one they had in their minds. No, a far greater one
was to be decided: *the life of knighthood.* I was a
champion, it was true, but not the champion of black
magic; I was the champion of hard unsentimental
common sense and reason. I was entering the lists
either to destroy knighthood or be its victim.

Vast as the show-grounds were, there were no
vacant spaces in them outside of the field of combat,
at ten o'clock on the morning of the sixteenth. The
grandstand was clothed in flags, streamers, and rich
tapestries, and packed with several acres of small-fry
kings, their followers, and the British aristocracy;
with our own royal gang in the chief place, and each
and every individual in gaudy silks and velvets—well,
I never saw anything to compare with it. The huge
camp of beflagged and gay-colored tents at one end
of the field, with a stiff-standing sentinel at every
door and a shining shield hanging by him for challenge, was another fine sight. You see, every knight
was there who had any ambition or any class feeling,
for my feeling toward their order was not much of a
secret, and so here was their chance. If I won my fight
with Sir Sagramor, others would have the right to call
me out as long as I might be willing to respond.

Down at our end there were but two tents; one for
me, and another for my servants. At the appointed
hour the king made a sign, and the heralds appeared
and made proclamation, naming the duelists and stat-
ing the cause of quarrel. There was a pause, and then

Sir Sagramor approached, and I tripped lightly up to meet him.

a ringing bugle-blast which was the signal for us to come forth. All the multitude caught their breath, and an eager curiosity flashed into every face.

Out from his tent rode great Sir Sagramor, a tower of iron, stately and rigid, his huge spear upright in its socket and grasped in his strong hand, his grand horse's face and breast cased in steel, his body clothed in rich trappings that almost dragged the ground—oh, a most noble picture. A great shout went up, of welcome and admiration.

And then out I came. But I didn't get any shout. There was a wondering and eloquent silence for a moment; then a great wave of laughter began to sweep along, but a warning bugle-blast cut it short. I was in the simplest and comfortablest of gymnast costumes—flesh-colored tights from neck to heel, with blue silk puffings about my loins, and bareheaded. My horse was not above medium size, but he was alert, slender-limbed, muscled with watch-springs, and just a greyhound to go. He was a beauty, glossy as silk, and naked as he was when he was born, except for bridle and ranger-saddle.

Sir Sagramor approached, and I tripped lightly up to meet him. We halted; he saluted; I responded; then we wheeled and rode side by side to the grandstand and faced our king and queen, to whom we bowed. The queen exclaimed:

"Alack, Sir Boss, wilt fight naked, and without lance or sword or—"

But the king checked her and made her understand, with a polite phrase or two, that this was none of her business. The bugles rang again; and we separated and rode to the ends of the field and took position. Now old Merlin stepped into view and cast a filmy veil over Sir Sagramor which turned him into Hamlet's ghost; the king made a sign, the bugles blew, Sir Sagramor laid his great lance in rest, and the next moment here he came thundering down the course with his veil flying out behind, and I went whistling through the air like an arrow to meet him —cocking my ear the while, as if noting the invisible knight's position and progress by hearing, not sight. A chorus of encouraging shouts burst out for him, and one brave voice flung out a heartening word for me:

"Go it, slim Jim!"

It was an even bet that Clarence had secured that favor for me, and furnished the language, too. When that dangerous lance-point was within a yard and a half of my breast I twitched my horse aside without an effort, and the big knight swept by, scoring a blank. I got plenty of applause that time. We turned, braced up, and down we came again. Another blank for the knight, a roar of applause for me. This same thing was repeated once more and it brought such a whirlwind of applause that Sir Sagramor lost his temper, and at once changed his tactics and set himself the task of chasing me down. Why, he hadn't any show in the world at that; it was a game of tag, with all the advantage on my side; I whirled out of his path with ease whenever I chose, and once I slapped him on the back as I went to the rear. Finally I took the chase into my own hands; and after that, turn, or twist, or do what he would, he was never able to get behind me again; he found himself always in front at the end of his ride. So he gave up that business and retired to his end of the field. His temper was clear gone now and he forgot himself and flung an insult at me. I slipped my lasso from the horn of my saddle and grasped the coil in my right hand. This time you should have seen him come—it was a business trip, sure; by his speed there was blood in his eye. I was sitting my horse at ease, and swinging the great loop of my lasso in wide circles about my head; the moment he was under way, I started for him; when the space between us had narrowed to forty feet, I sent the snaky rope through the air, and then darted aside and faced about and brought my trained animal to a halt with all his feet braced under him. The next moment the rope tightened and yanked Sir Sagramor out of the saddle! Great Scott, but there was a sensation!

Unquestionably, the popular thing in this world is novelty. These people had never seen anything of that cowboy business before, and it carried them clear off their feet with delight. From all around and everywhere, the shout went up:

"Again! Again!"

The moment my lasso was released and Sir Sagramor had been assisted to his tent, I hauled in the slack, took my station, and began to swing my loop around my head again. I was sure to have use for it as soon as they could elect someone to follow Sir Sagramor, and that couldn't take long where there were so many hungry candidates. Indeed, they elected one straight off—Sir Hervis de Revel.

Bzz! Here he came, like a house afire; I dodged; he passed like a flash, with my horse-hair coils settling around his neck; a second or so later, *fst!* his saddle was empty.

Another came; and another, and another, and still another. When I had snaked five men out, things began to look serious to the ironclads, and they stopped and consulted together. As a result, they decided that it was time to forget manners and send their greatest and best against me. To the astonishment of that little world, I lassoed Sir Lamorak de Galis, and, after him, Sir Galahad. So you see there was simply nothing to be done now but bring out the mightiest of the mighty, the great Sir Launcelot himself!

A proud moment for me? I should think so. Yonder was Arthur, King of Britain; yonder was Guenever, yes, and whole tribes of little kings and kinglets; and in the tented camp yonder, famous knights from many lands, and likewise the selectest body known to chivalry, the Knights of the Table Round, the most famous in Christendom; and the biggest fact of all, the very sun of their shining system was yonder ready to meet me, all forty thousand eyes on him; and all by myself, here was I laying for him. Across my mind flitted the dear image of a certain telephone girl of West Hartford, and I wished she could see me now. In that moment, down came Launcelot, with the rush of a whirlwind; the courtly world rose to its feet and bent forward; the fateful rope went circling through the air, and before you could wink I was towing Sir Launcelot across the field on his back and kissing my hand to the storm of waving kerchiefs and the thunder-crash of applause that greeted me!

Said I to myself, as I coiled my rope and hung it on my saddle-horn and sat there drunk with glory, "The victory is perfect; no other will venture against me; knighthood is dead." Now imagine my astonishment —and everybody else's, too—to hear the peculiar bugle-call which announces that another is about to enter the field! There was a mystery here; I couldn't account for this thing. Next, I noticed Merlin gliding away from me; and then I noticed that my lasso was gone! The old sleight-of-hand expert had stolen it, sure, and slipped it under his robe.

The bugle blew again. I looked, and down came Sagramor riding again, with his dust brushed off and his veil nicely rearranged. I trotted up to meet him, and pretended to find him by the sound of his horse's hoofs. He said:

"Thou'rt quick of ear, but it will not save thee

from this!" and he touched the hilt of his great sword.
"If ye are not able to see it, because of the influence
of the veil, know that it is no heavy lance, but a sword
—and I think ye will not be able to avoid it."

His visor was up; there was death in his smile. I
should never be able to dodge his sword, that was
plain. Somebody was going to die this time. If he got
the drop on me, I could name the corpse. We rode
forward together and saluted the royalties. This time
the king was disturbed. He said:

"Where is thy strange weapon?"

"It is stolen, sire."

"Hast another at hand?"

"No, sire, I brought only the one."

Then Merlin mixed in:

"He brought but the one because there was but the
one to bring. There exists none other but that one. It
belongeth to the king of the Demons of the Sea. This
man is a pretender, and ignorant; else he had known
that that weapon can be used in but eight bouts only,
and then it vanisheth away to its home under the sea."

"Then is he weaponless," said the king. "Sir Sagramor, ye will grant him leave to borrow."

"And I will lend!" said Sir Launcelot, limping up.
"He is as brave a knight of his hands as any that be
alive, and he shall have mine."

He put his hand on his sword to draw it, but Sir
Sagramor said:

"Stay, it may not be. He shall fight with his own
weapons; it was his privilege to choose them and

bring them. If he has made a mistake, on his head be it."

"Knight!" said the king. "Thou'rt overwrought with passion; it disorders thy mind. Wouldst kill a naked man?"

"If he do it, he shall answer to me," said Sir Launcelot.

"I will answer it to any man that desireth!" retorted Sir Sagramor hotly.

Merlin broke in, rubbing his hands and smiling his low-downest smile of mean satisfaction:

"'Tis well said, right well said! And 'tis enough of talking, let my lord the king deliver the battle signal."

The king had to yield. The bugle made proclamation and we turned apart and rode to our stations. There we stood, a hundred yards apart, facing each other, rigid and motionless like horsed statues. And so we remained, in a soundless hush, as much as a full minute, everybody gazing, nobody stirring. It seemed as if the king could not take heart to give the signal. But at last he lifted his hand, the clear note of a bugle followed, Sir Sagramor's long blade described a flashing curve in the air, and it was superb to see him come. I sat still. On he came. I did not move. People got so excited that they shouted to me:

"Fly, fly! Save thyself! This is murder!"

I never budged so much as an inch till that thundering figure had got within fifteen paces of me; then I snatched a revolver out of my holster, there was a flash and a roar, and the revolver was back in the holster before anybody could tell what had happened.

Here was a riderless horse plunging by, and yonder lay Sir Sagramor, stone dead.

The people that ran to him were stricken dumb to find that the life was actually gone out of the man and no reason for it visible, no hurt upon his body, nothing like a wound. There was a hole through the breast of his chain-mail, but they attached no importance to a little thing like that; and as a bullet-wound there produces but little blood, none came in sight because of the clothing and swaddlings under the armor. The body was dragged over to let the king and the swells look down upon it. They were stupefied with astonishment, naturally. I was requested to come and explain the miracle. But I remained in my tracks like a statue, and said:

"If it is a command, I will come; but my lord the king knows that I am where the laws of combat require me to remain while any desire to come against me."

I waited. Nobody challenged. Then I said:

"If there are any who doubt that this field is well and fairly won, I do not wait for them to challenge me, I challenge them."

"It is a gallant offer," said the king. "Whom will you name first?"

"I name none, I challenge all! Here I stand, and dare the chivalry of England to come against me— not by individuals, but in mass!"

"What!" shouted a score of knights.

"You have heard the challenge. Take it, or I proclaim you false knights and conquered every one!"

It was a "bluff" you know. At such a time it is sound judgment to put on a bold face and play your hand for a hundred times what it is worth. In just no time, five hundred knights were scrambling into their saddles, and before you could wink, a widely scattering drove were under way and clattering down upon me. I snatched both revolvers from the holsters and began to measure distances and calculate chances.

Bang! One saddle empty. Bang! Another one. Bang —bang, and I bagged two. Well, it was nip and tuck with us, and I knew it. If I spent the eleventh shot without convincing these people, the twelfth man would kill me, sure. And so I never did feel so happy as I did when my ninth downed its man and I saw the wavering in the crowd which is the signal of panic. An instant lost now could knock out my last chance. But I didn't lose it. I raised both revolvers and pointed them; the halted host stood their ground just about one good square moment, and then broke and fled.

The day was mine. Knighthood was a doomed institution. The march of civilization was begun. How did I feel? Ah, you never could imagine it.

And Brother Merlin? His stock was flat again. Somehow, every time the magic of fol-de-rol met the magic of science, the magic of fol-de-rol got left.

CHAPTER XXVI

THREE YEARS LATER—WAR

When I broke the back of knighthood that time, I no longer felt obliged to work in secret. So, the very next day I exposed my hidden schools, my mines, and my vast system of secret factories and workshops to an astonished world. That is to say, I exposed the nineteenth century to the inspection of the sixth.

Well, it is always a good plan to follow up an advantage promptly. The knights were temporarily down, but if I would keep them so I must just simply paralyze them—nothing short of that would answer.

I renewed my challenge, engraved it on brass, posted it up where any priest could read it to them, and also kept it standing in the advertising columns of the paper.

I not only renewed it, but added to it. I said, name the day, and I would take fifty assistants and stand up *against the massed knighthood of the whole earth and destroy it.*

I was not bluffing this time. I meant what I said; I could do what I promised. There wasn't any way to misunderstand the language of that challenge. Even the dullest of the knights saw that this was a plain case of "put up, or shut up." They were wise and did the latter. In all the next three years they gave me no trouble worth mentioning.

Consider the three years passed. Now look around on England. A happy and prosperous country, and strangely changed. Schools everywhere, and several colleges, a number of pretty good newspapers.

Slavery was dead and gone; all men were equal before the law; taxation had been equalized. The telegraph, the telephone, the phonograph, the typewriter, the sewing-machine, and all the thousand willing and handy servants of steam and electricity were working their way into favor. We had a steamboat or two on the Thames, we had steam warships, and the beginning of a steam commercial marine; I was getting ready to send out an expedition to discover America.

We were building several lines of railway, and our line from Camelot to London was already finished and in operation. My idea was to attract the knights and nobility, and make them useful and keep them out of mischief. The plan worked very well; the competition for the places was hot. The conductor of the 4:33 express was a duke; there wasn't a passenger conductor on the line below the degree of earl. They were good men, every one, but they had two faults which I couldn't cure, and so had to wink at: they wouldn't lay aside their armor, and they would "knock down" fare—I mean rob the company.

There was hardly a knight in all the land who wasn't

in some useful employment. They were going from
end to end of the country in all manner of useful mis-
sionary work; their love for wandering, and their
experience in it, made them altogether the best spread-
ers of civilization we had. They went clothed in steel
and equipped with sword and lance and battle-ax, and
if they couldn't persuade a person to try a sewing-
machine on the instalment plan, or a barbed-wire
fence, or prohibition journal, or any of the other
thousand and one things they canvassed for, they removed him and passed on.

I was very happy. Things were working steadily
toward a secretly longed-for point. You see, I had a
scheme in my head which was the greatest of my
projects. The project was to get a decree issued by
and by, commanding that upon Arthur's death unlimited right to vote should be introduced, and given
to men and women alike—at any rate to all men, wise
or unwise, and to all mothers who at middle age should
be found to know nearly as much as their sons at
twenty-one. Arthur was good for thirty years yet,
he being about my own age—that is to say, forty—
and I believed that in that time I could easily have the
active part of the population of that day ready and
eager for an event which should be the first of its
kind in the history of the world—a rounded and complete governmental revolution without bloodshed. The
result was to be a republic. Well, I may as well con-

fess, though I do feel ashamed when I think of it: I was beginning to have a base longing to be its first president myself. Yes, there was more or less human nature in me; I found that out.

Clarence was with me as concerned the revolution, but in a limited way. His idea was a republic, without privileged orders, but with a hereditary royal family at the head of it instead of an elective chief magistrate. He believed that no nation that had ever known the joy of worshiping a royal family could ever be robbed of it and not fade away and die of sorrow. I urged that kings were dangerous. He said, then have cats. He was sure that a royal family of cats would answer every purpose. They would be as useful as any other royal family, they would know as much, they would have the same virtues and the same treacheries, the same disposition to get up fights with other royal cats; they would be laughably vain and absurd and never know it, and they would be wholly inexpensive.

Hang him, I supposed he was in earnest and was beginning to be persuaded by him, until he exploded a cat-howl and startled me almost out of my clothes. But he never could be in earnest. He didn't know what it was. He had pictured a distinct and perfectly reasonable improvement upon constitutional monarchy, but he was too featherheaded to know it or care anything about it, either. I was going to give him a scolding, but Sandy came flying in at that moment, wild with terror, and so choked with sobs that for a minute she could not get her voice. I ran and took her in my arms, and caressed her and said, beseechingly:

"Speak, darling, speak! What is it?"

Her head fell limp upon my bosom, and she gasped, almost inaudibly:

"HELLO CENTRAL!"

You see, I had married Sandy and she had named our child Hello Central, a name she had heard me murmur time and again in my sleep as my spirit wandered in the nineteenth century. Little Hello Central was the pet of everyone including Launcelot, and Sandy was a prize as a wife. Ours was the most perfect comradeship. Well, Sandy was in terror because Hello Central had suddenly fallen sick. I diagnosed the case immediately as croup and for three days and nights Launcelot and I stood watch by her bedside until she was out of danger.

The doctors advised us to take the child to the French coast to coax her back to health; so Sandy and I left on a man-of-war with Hello Central and two hundred sixty servants. For a month the baby seemed to be doing fine and then she suddenly became worse and for two and one-half weeks both Sandy and I forgot the outside world completely as we fought for her life. We had our reward and little Hello Central began to mend; but when I turned my attention to the outside world, I found things had gone pretty completely to pieces.

Civil war had broken out with Launcelot and the king on different sides and King Arthur had been killed. The church had stepped in and with all the knights that were left was determined to defeat us and bring back the old world. It was to be a fight between science and tradition with all its old superstitions.

Clarence had been busy doing what he could, but he had been able to get only fifty-two lads to stick by us and the new ideas; all the others had sided with tradition; it was in their blood and bones. Clarence had made our headquarters an old cave of Merlin's, where we had established our first great electric plant. He had provisioned the cave for a siege and had connected it by wire with the dynamite deposits under all the vast factories, mills, workshops, magazines, etc.

I had taught that boy well. He was building a wire fence—twelve immensely strong wires, naked, not insulated—from a big dynamo in the cave—a dynamo with no brushes except a positive and a negative one. The wires were to go out from the cave and fence in a circle of level ground, one hundred yards in diameter; they would make twelve independent fences ten feet apart—that is to say, twelve circles within circles and their ends came into the cave again. The fences were fastened to heavy ash posts only three feet apart and the posts were sunk five feet in the ground. The wires had no ground connection outside the cave and only through the negative brush. The other end of every wire was to be brought back to the cave and fastened independently without any ground connection. As soon as a cavalry charge should hurl itself against the fence, it would form a connection with the negative brush through the ground and they would drop dead. In the center of the inner circle on a platform six feet high, there was a battery of thirteen Gatling guns and plenty of ammunition. Around the outer fence, there was a belt forty feet wide, equipped with dynamite torpedoes laid on the surface with a layer of sand sprinkled over them.

We were ready; we proclaimed a republic and announced where we were as an invitation to the enemy to strike. I sent an order at the same time to the factories and all our great works to stop all operations as they might be blown up any minute. It worked as planned—almost. The knights came on with a blare of trumpets, reached the belt and shot into the sky with a thunder-crash. It was a whirling tempest of rags and pieces.

It was time for the second step. I touched a button and all our noble factories went up in the air and disappeared. It was a pity, but it was necessary. We could not afford to let the enemy turn our weapons against us. I picketed the great embankments thrown up around our lines by the dynamite explosion and sent an engineer and forty boys beyond our lines to the south to turn a mountain brook that was there and bring it within our lines so that I could make use of it in an emergency. We waited a long time; then we saw a row of black dots appear along the ridge top— human heads. An armed host was taking up quarters in the ditch. I signaled to turn the current in the two inner fences.

We watched the silent lightning do its awful work; a black mass piled itself up beyond the fence. Our camp was enclosed with solid walls of dead men. I sent a current through the third fence and almost immediately through the fourth and fifth. I believed the whole army was in our trap and that the time had come for my climax. I touched a button and set fifty electric suns aflame on top of our precipice. I shot the current through all the fences and shot three revolver shots—the signal for turning on the water.

There was a sudden rush and roar and the mountain brook raged through the big ditch and made a river a hundred feet wide and twenty-five feet deep. The thirteen Gatlings opened fire; the lines broke, faced about and swept toward the ditch. One-fourth never reached the top; the others reached it but plunged to death by drowning.

The campaign was ended and we fifty-four were masters of England. But in about an hour something happened which I have no heart to write about. Let my record end here.

CHAPTER XXVII

A POSTSCRIPT BY CLARENCE

I, Clarence, must write this for The Boss. He proposed that we two go out and see if any help could be given the wounded. I was against this project. I said that if there were many, we could do but little for them; and it would not be wise for us to trust ourselves among them, anyway. But he could seldom be turned from a purpose once formed; so we shut off the electric current from the fences, took an escort along, climbed over the inclosing ramparts of dead knights, and moved out upon the field. The first wounded man who appealed for help was sitting with his back against a dead comrade. When The Boss bent over him and spoke to him, the man recognized him and stabbed him. That knight was Sir Meliagraunce, as I found out by tearing off his helmet. He will not ask for help any more.

We carried The Boss to the cave and gave his wound, which was not very serious, the best care we could. In this service we had the help of Merlin, though we did not know it. He was disguised as a woman, and appeared to be a simple old peasant goodwife. In this disguise, with brown-stained face and smooth-shaven, he had appeared a few days after The Boss was hurt, and offered to cook for us, saying her

308

people had gone off to join certain new camps which the enemy were forming, and that she was starving. The Boss had been getting along very well, and had amused himself with finishing up his record.

We were glad to have this woman, for we were short-handed. We were in a trap, you see—a trap of our own making. If we stayed where we were, the poison air from our dead would kill us; if we moved out of our defenses, we should no longer be invincible. We had conquered; in turn we were conquered. The Boss recognized this; we all recognized it. If we could go to one of those new camps and patch up some kind of terms with the enemy—yes, but The Boss could not go, and neither could I, for I was among the first that were made sick by the poisonous air bred by those dead thousands. Others were taken down, and still others. Tomorrow—

Tomorrow. It is here. And with it the end. About midnight I awoke, and saw that hag making curious passes in the air about The Boss's head and face, and wondered what it meant. Everybody but the dynamo-watch lay in sleep; there was no sound. The woman ceased from her mysterious foolery and started tip-toeing toward the door. I called out:

"Stop! What have you been doing?"

She halted, and said with an accent of evil satisfaction:

"Ye were conquerors; ye are conquered! These others are perishing—you also. Ye shall all die in this place, every one—except *him*. He sleepeth now—and shall sleep thirteen centuries. I am Merlin!"

Then such silly laughter overtook him that he reeled about like a drunken man, and presently fetched up against one of our wires. His mouth is spread open yet; apparently he is still laughing. I suppose the face will keep that laugh until the corpse turns to dust.

The Boss has never stirred—sleeps like a stone. If he does not wake today we shall understand what kind of a sleep it is, and his body will then be borne to a place deep in one of the caves where none will ever find it. As for the rest of us—well, it is agreed that if any one of us ever escapes alive from this place, he will write the fact here, and loyally hide this Manuscript with The Boss, our dear good chief, whose property it is, be he alive or dead.

CHAPTER XXVIII

FINAL NOTE BY THE AUTHOR

The dawn was come when I laid aside the stranger's Manuscript, in which I had read this strange story. The rain had almost ceased, the world was gray and sad, the exhausted storm was sighing and sobbing itself to rest. I went to the stranger's room and listened at his door, which was slightly open. I could hear his voice, and so I knocked. There was no answer, but I still heard the voice. I peeped in. The man lay on his back in bed, talking brokenly but with spirit, and thrashing about, restlessly, as sick people do in delirium. I slipped in softly and bent over him. His mutterings went on. I spoke—merely a word, to call his attention. His glassy eyes and his ashy face were alight in an instant with pleasure, gratitude, gladness, welcome:

"Oh, Sandy, you are come at last—how I have longed for you! Sit by me—do not leave me—never leave me again, Sandy, never again. Where is your hand—give it to me, dear, let me hold it—there— now all is well, all is peace, and I am happy again—*we* are happy again, isn't it so, Sandy? You are so dim, so vague; you are but a mist, a cloud, but you are *here*, and that is blessedness sufficient; and I have your hand; don't take it away—it is for only a little

311

while, I shall not require it long. . . . Was that the child? . . . Hello Central! . . . She doesn't answer. Asleep, perhaps? Bring her when she awakes, and let me touch her hands, her face, her hair, and tell her good-by. . . . Sandy! . . . Yes, you are there. I lost myself a moment, and I thought you were gone. . . . Have I been sick long? It must be so; it seems months to me. And such dreams! such strange and awful dreams, Sandy! Dreams that were as real as reality —delirium, of course, but *so* real! Why, I thought the king was dead, I thought you were in Gaul and couldn't get home, I thought there was a revolution; in the fantastic frenzy of these dreams, I thought that Clarence and I and a handful of my cadets fought and killed the whole knighthood of England! But even that was not the strangest. I seemed to be a creature out of a remote unborn age, centuries hence, and even *that* was as real as the rest! Yes, I seemed to have flown back out of that age into this of ours, and then forward to it again, and was set down, a stranger and forlorn in that strange England, with thirteen centuries yawning between me and you! between me and my home and my friends! between me and all that is dear to me, all that could make life worth living! It was awful—awfuler than you can ever imagine, Sandy. Ah, watch by me, Sandy—stay by me every moment—*don't* let me go out of my mind again; death is nothing, let it come, but not with those dreams, not with the torture of those hideous dreams —I cannot endure *that* again . . . Sandy? . . ."

He lay muttering some little time; then for a time he lay silent, and apparently sinking away toward death. Presently his fingers began to pick busily at the coverlet, and by that sign I knew that his end was at hand. With the first suggestion of the death-rattle in his throat he started up slightly and seemed to listen: then he said:

"A bugle? . . . It is the king! The drawbridge, there! Man the battlements!—turn out the—"

He was getting up his last "effect"; but he never finished it.

— THE END —

QUESTIONS FOR THE PUPIL

The pupil is to answer each question as briefly as possible and hand in the answers for all chapters completed at the end of the day's reading period. Answers must be marked with the chapter and question number.

Chapter 1

1. The stranger says "I saw it done. As a matter of fact I did it myself." To what does "it" refer?
2. What happened to the Yankee?
3. Near what place was the Yankee when he woke up?

Chapter 2

1. After following the cavalcade where did the Yankee find himself?
2. What date does the page say it is?
3. How does the Yankee plan to check on this?
4. What does the page, Clarence, tell the Yankee will happen to him?

Chapter 3

1. Did Sir Kay tell a true story of the capture?
2. Why didn't the men stop Merlin when he started to tell his story?
3. What was the sentence passed on the Yankee?
4. Why did they take his clothes?

Chapter 4

1. What was the second and most important reason Clarence gave for considering escape from the dungeon impossible?

314

2. What idea does this give the Yankee?
3. What message does he first send the king?
4. What reply does the king send?
5. What disaster does the Yankee threaten?
6. On what knowledge does he rely to make the disaster seem to happen?

Chapter 5

1. Did the people believe in the Yankee's power?
2. Who persuaded the king to change the date of execution?
3. What saved the Yankee?
4. What place of honor does the king give him?

Chapter 6

1. List ten things which the Yankee missed in his new life.
2. What was the Yankee's second miracle?
3. Why wasn't the Yankee asked for an autograph?
4. What was the title given the Yankee by the people?
5. Why did he prefer this title to the one offered by the king?

Chapter 7

1. What two reasons does The Boss give for his going to the tournaments?
2. Who challenges The Boss to a duel?
3. What is the date set for this duel?
4. Name four things The Boss had started.
5. Who was his right-hand man?
6. Why does the king feel The Boss should start out in search of adventure?

Chapter 8

1. When The Boss questions Alisande, what fact does he find out in regard to the location of the castle?

2. Who is to go with him on his journey?
3. What delayed The Boss in getting started?

Chapter 9

1. What nickname does The Boss give Alisande?
2. Why does he say he couldn't think?
3. How much were the freemen paid for working on the Bishop's road?
4. How many of them showed any interest when The Boss talked to them about the vote?

Chapter 10

1. How did The Boss overcome the knights?
2. What did the knights think he was?
3. What terms did Sandy make with the knights?
4. To whom did the castle belong which The Boss and Sandy approached?
5. Why didn't Morgan le Fay send The Boss to the dungeon?

Chapter 11

1. How does Sandy save the grandmother of the page?
2. Why hadn't the man on the rack confessed?
3. Had all the prisoners committed serious crimes?
4. How many were there whose names and crimes were not known?
5. Why hadn't these been freed?

Chapter 12

1. Why was there no outburst of anger from the people because of their cruel treatment? *Because they were use to it*
2. What did the castle look like to The Boss?

Chapter 13

1. Did Sandy leave The Boss after they had accomplished what they had set out to do?
2. Where were the pilgrims they first met going?
3. Why did the monks think the water had ceased to flow in the Valley of Holiness?
4. Why didn't this first group of pilgrims object when they saw the slaves mistreated?
5. To what one of his departments did The Boss send a message when he heard the water had again ceased to flow?

Chapter 14

1. Who does The Boss find already working to start the flow of water?
2. What methods was Merlin using on the fountain?
3. What did The Boss find that explained the well's ceasing to work?

Chapter 15

1. List eight things the experts brought to The Boss.
2. Were all these things necessary to make the water flow?
3. Why did The Boss make so much extra work for himself?

Chapter 16

1. What did The Boss find installed in the old den of the hermit?
2. What does he learn about the king's plans?
3. Did the magician prefer to tell what happened far away or close at hand? Why?

Chapter 17

1. What class always came out ahead when the king tried cases?
2. Were the nobles ashamed because they could not read, write, or figure?

3. What did the examining board consider the chief qualification for an officer?

Chapter 18

1. Who planned to go with The Boss on his tour among the common people of the country?
2. What made the people think they were healed when the king touched them?
3. How did the monks learn what was in the newspaper?
4. Was The Boss successful in making the king *look* like a peasant?
5. Was he successful in making him act like one?
6. What did The Boss have with him which saved him and the king when the king forgot himself?

Chapter 19

1. Why did The Boss drill the king?
2. What did the king lack to make him seem like a peasant?
3. What burden of The Boss did the king take?
4. What dread disease did The Boss and king find in the hut?
5. What two things does the king say would be shame for a knight?
6. Does he live up to the code or ideals of knighthood?

Chapter 20

1. Who comes into the hut as the king and The Boss leave?
2. Why does the king's conscience trouble him?
3. What two evidences of trouble do the king and The Boss see during the night?
4. What name did The Boss give the king at the hut at which they stopped?
5. Why does the king say, "Three did escape and they murdered the Baron and set fire to the house"?

Chapter 21

1. Is it what wages one gets or what one can buy with wages that determines whether or not the wages are high?
2. Who does The Boss pretend is buying the clothing for Marco and his wife?
3. What was the entire cost of the dinner and gifts?

Chapter 22

1. Does The Boss prove to his own satisfaction it is not the wage but what you can buy with it that is important?
2. Does Dowley think it will be a great age when a man can work for whomever he pleases and as long as he pleases?
3. What is the attitude or feeling toward The Boss at the end of the conversation?
4. What do the king's remarks about agriculture make the group think?

Chapter 23

1. Who rescues the king and The Boss in the fight?
2. What happens when The Boss forgets he is a peasant and shows pity for the slaves?
3. What price did each bring?
4. What bothered the king most?
5. Did beating break the spirit of the king?
6. What was The Boss's plan for escape?
7. What two things kept The Boss from appealing to some of the knights they passed whom they had known?
8. What explains The Boss's getting the wrong man?

Chapter 24

1. What had happened to the master?
2. What was the law with regard to slaves, if one killed his master?
3. What does The Boss use to reach Camelot?

4. What does Clarence promise to send?
5. How were the rescuers to recognize The Boss?
6. Was the crowd impressed when the king announced who he was?
7. How did Launcelot and his men arrive?

Chapter 25

1. What was the duel between Sir Sagramor and The Boss really to test?
2. What kind of costume did The Boss wear?
3. How did The Boss unseat Sir Sagramor and the others who followed him?
4. What is the second and last weapon which defeats the knights?

Chapter 26

1. What did The Boss wish to set up after a governmental revolution?
2. What changes have taken place in his private life during the three years that have passed?
3. What happens to take his attention away from the world?
4. Between what groups did Civil war break out?
5. How many stood by The Boss and the new ideas?
6. Name five things this small group used in waging war.

Chapter 27

1. What trap were the victors in?
2. Who comes disguised to care for the wounded Boss?
3. What does he prophesy for The Boss?
4. What happens to Merlin?

Chapter 28

1. What happens to the stranger?
2. In what century was he when we first saw him?
3. In what century does he think he is at the last?

QUESTIONS FOR DISCUSSION

These questions are designed to stimulate thinking and group discussion. Occasionally they will demand outside reading, individual reports or supplementation by the teacher.

Chapter 1

1. What was the Round Table?
2. Bring in any additional information or stories about King Arthur or any of his knights that you can find in the library.
3. Have you ever read any other stories or seen any movies that deal with souls passing from one body to another or bodies passing into other ages or times?

Chapter 2

1. What things in Camelot seemed queer to the Yankee?
2. What did the people of Camelot find queer about the Yankee?
3. Why didn't the same things seem queer to both?
4. Describe the room to which the Yankee was taken.
5. What customs were different from those you are used to?
6. What characteristics of the people does the Yankee notice?

Chapter 3

1. In what way were the knights like small boys?
2. What does the Yankee mean when he says brains were not needed in a society like that and might have made it impossible?
3. Is there anything about modern society that may indicate to later generations that we did not use our brains?
4. Sir Kay describes the Yankee in terms that did not fit at all and yet no one seemed to notice that he was not a monster

321

or a giant. Do you think that same sort of thing happens in this century? Give examples.

5. How can you explain that Sir Kay's method still works?

Chapter 4

1. What advantage does the superstition of the people give a man like the Yankee?
2. Why don't the people see that a great magician wouldn't have to depend on a boy or the king's mercy?
3. Do people today accept statements without seeing that they are contradictory? Give examples.

Chapter 5

1. What happens when there is an eclipse?
2. Where can you check on the date of past or future eclipses?

Chapter 6

1. Name some conveniences we have today that they did not have in Samuel Clemens' day.
2. How was the second miracle brought about?
3. What was the Yankee's attitude toward the social system of the sixth century?
4. How does he explain the fact that the people accept it though they have no rights?
5. What has to happen before people revolt against a system to which they are accustomed?

Chapter 7

1. What was the attitude of the ladies toward the duels?
2. What evidence do you find that medical science had not made much progress?
3. What beliefs or attitudes of the people would delay the development of medical science?

4. What was the Holy Grail?
5. What advantage does The Boss admit in the rule of a despot?
6. What disadvantages does he see in such a rule?
7. By what method does he hope to break down the system of knighthood?

Chapter 8

1. Give evidences from this chapter of the simplicity of the people.
2. Describe the armor of a knight. Do you think it was a good costume for a fight?

Chapter 9

1. What annoyances does The Boss suffer from his armor?
2. What does he think about as he travels?
3. What was the condition of the freemen?
4. Why hadn't they revolted?

Chapter 10

1. What determines the value of money?
2. How much would 15¢ in Arthur's time have been equivalent to in the 19th century?
3. How could The Boss say his advertising scheme was a part of his plan to civilize these people?

Chapter 11

1. What kind of person was Morgan le Fay?
2. The Boss's discussion of the religion of the people is an example of Clemens' satire. Why?
3. Find another example of satire in this chapter. Why do you think it is satire?
4. What evidence do you find that the upper class lived up to their "code", such as it was, in their dealings with the lower class?

5. How can you explain that the Queen could do the things she did and not realize their cruelty?

Chapter 12

1. There are good examples of Clemens' satire in this chapter. At what two 19th century institutions is he laughing?
2. What does he mean to show by his discussion of what he sees, compared to what Sandy sees?

Chapter 13

1. About what things did The Boss have to keep still for fear Sandy would think he was crazy? This illustrates a frequent attitude of the ignorant toward people when they can't understand them. Give examples from your own experience.
2. How did the ideas about holiness of the 6th century differ from the modern ideas?
3. How do the ideas of the monks about methods to make the water flow again compare with modern ideas?

Chapter 14

1. Discuss The Boss's statement "Old habit of mind is one of the toughest things in the world to get away from." Apply it to some of our modern problems. Does it keep us from solving them?
2. Why did The Boss play up the idea that making the water flow would be a difficult job? Give examples of this sort of technique from your own experience.

Chapter 15

1. Is The Boss's idea true that the people would be less impressed by the real accomplishment of turning on the water than by the spectacular show? Give examples of things we

daily take for granted which are miraculous. What would make us consider them miracles?

2. Was Merlin convinced of the truth of the stories he invented? Give proofs.

3. Is a leader justified in giving the people what they expect even though he knows better? Give arguments on both sides.

Chapter 16

1. People who are as easily fooled as the abbots and monks were by the new magician from the East are called "gullible." Do you think people of today are less gullible than those of the 6th century? If so, why?

2. Do people of our time turn as quickly from one hero to another as those of the 6th century? Give some examples.

Chapter 17

1. Why did the king find it impossible to give his decisions with complete justice, even though he tried to be fair. Try to find newspaper articles on the same subject by papers of different points of view to illustrate the same difficulty today.

2. Discuss the inability of the nobility in reading, writing, and figuring and their attitude toward it. Have you ever seen anything faintly resembling this attitude in the modern school?

Chapter 18

1. What in the tone of the newspaper does not fit 6th century attitude? Bring in some examples from newspapers showing the same style and spirit.

2. Does the court circular give you any idea why the king may be so anxious to go with The Boss on his tour?

3. Would a newspaper be of much value in the 6th century? Give the reason for your answer. If you were in The Boss's place what would your next step be?

4. Which is harder to disguise—the looks or actions of a person?

5. The king's main difficulty was his inability to understand other people's reactions. What aids, denied to the king, do you have to help you understand other people's reactions?

Chapter 19

1. What makes a man slouch and look like an underling? Show that in drilling the king, The Boss tried to work on his mental attitude.

2. Are words alone enough to make one understand other people? What else is necessary?

3. Discuss the code of knighthood as given in the king's words.

4. Did its failure lie in the failure of the knights to live up to it or in its narrowness? Do you think we live up to the ideals of democracy as completely as the knights lived up to their code? Do we still have to enlarge our ideas?

Chapter 20

1. For a time in the hut the king seemed to be a different man. Show that he has not really changed in his thinking.

2. Do the peasants turn against their own class and help the nobility only through fear or partly through believing in the system? Prove your answer from the book.

Chapter 21

1. Does the size of wages alone determine a nation's prosperity? What else must be considered?

2. Does The Boss feel sure of the king now? Prove your answer from the book.

3. It is not what we have that makes us feel rich but what we have in comparison with what we have had or with what others have. Give examples from the book to show this.

4. What do you think was giving the greatest pleasure, first to Dowley, then Marco, then The Boss?

Chapter 22

1. Were the arguments of The Boss about wages sound? Why didn't they convince Dowley? What does this show is necessary in order to get new ideas across? Discuss several human traits the author shows up in Dowley.
2. Fear and distrust started the battle between these people who had no real cause for fighting. What does this suggest is necessary for keeping the peace?

Chapter 23

1. In modern times is the law, as in King Arthur's time, supposed to judge a man guilty until proved innocent, or innocent until proved guilty? Do we live up to this rule? Justify your answer.
2. In a way it was the same trait that made the king worry over his sale price and that kept him from being broken by beatings. What was this trait?
3. Why was the king now willing to attack slavery?
4. Do modern cities have anything in common with London of the 6th century?
5. Why was such a low price put on the king? Give examples to show that qualities desirable for one job may be bad in another.

Chapter 24

1. The law in regard to slaves whose masters were killed seems unnecessarily hard. Why was it necessary? Give examples in modern times of punishment of whole groups for the acts of one or a few.

2. Discuss the attitude of the crowd toward the condemned men.
3. Sum up the qualities of the king which you admire and give examples of his behavior from the book to show he has these qualities.

Chapter 25

1. In the people's minds what was the importance of the duel between Sir Sagramor and The Boss? In The Boss's mind what was its importance?
2. Describe the costumes of Sir Sagramor and of The Boss.
3. What weapon proved fatal to knighthood?
4. Can a new weapon outmode not only a system of warfare but a way of life? Give modern examples and show why ways of life and attitudes must change with new knowledge.

Chapter 26

1. Discuss the changes that had taken place in the three years that had passed after The Boss's victory over knighthood.
2. What governmental changes does he want?
3. The fact that things went to pieces when he took his attention from them showed that mechanical changes had taken place faster than men's ideas had changed. Is this true today? Support your answer.
4. Describe the battle.

Chapter 27

1. The victors are caught in their own trap. Is this apt to be the result in modern warfare, even though not so apparent? Discuss the evil results apt to follow war which affect the victor as well as the conquered.
2. Do you think future generations might write satires on our

bungling attempts to plan for peace and find our prejudices which stand in the way as outmoded or old-fashioned as the knights' method of warfare seems to us?

3. Do the same two attitudes of mind represented by the groups in this battle still battle each other in the modern world?

Chapter 28

1. Discuss the ending. Why do you think the author shows the stranger returning in his delirium to the 6th century when he dies?